IVAN TURGENEV,

the first of the great Russian novelists to be widely read in Europe, displayed in his works a passionate concern for his country's condition and destiny. He was born in 1818 and spent much of his youth at his mother's estate, Spasskoye, where his maternal grandmother had once, in a fit of rage, smothered a young boy serf with a pillow. Later, Spasskoye became a symbol in Turgenev's writings for the oppression of an unjust social system. From 1838 to 1841, Turgenev studied at the University of Berlin, made friends with Russian liberal and radical political thinkers, and became convinced of the need for the westernization of Russia. In 1843 he became infatuated with the singer Pauline Viardot and unhappily pursued her around Europe for several years. In 1850 his story, "The Diary of a Superfluous Man," popularized the designation "superfluous man" for the idealistic but inactive hero prevalent in Russian literature. In 1852 his sympathetic depiction of the Russian peasants in *Sportsman's Sketches* helped to influence the future emperor Alexander II to free the serfs. Another story, "Mumu," further exposed the cruelties of serfdom. As a result of his views, Turgenev was arrested by the Tsar's political police in 1852 and confined at Spasskoye for eighteen months. In 1855 his most successful dramatic work, *A Month in the Country*, became a forerunner of the plays of Anton Chekhov. His first novel, *Rudin*, appeared in 1856; "First Love," one of his finest tales, in 1860; and his masterpiece *Fathers and Sons* in 1862. This brilliant novel, which applied the term "nihilist" to the radical youth of the 1860s, incensed all factions in Russia and drove Turgenev abroad for most of his remaining years. He died quietly in Paris in 1883 and was later buried in St. Petersburg, where both conservatives and radicals alike mourned the passing of one of the great masters of Russian literature.

Bantam Classics
Ask your bookseller for these other World Classics

THE COMPLETE PLAYS OF SOPHOCLES
TEN PLAYS BY EURIPIDES
THE COMPLETE PLAYS OF ARISTOPHANES
THE ORESTEIA, Aeschylus
THE AENEID, Virgil

THE INFERNO, Dante

THE PRINCE, Machiavelli

CANDIDE, Voltaire

CYRANO DE BERGERAC, Edmond Rostand
THE COUNT OF MONTE CRISTO, Alexandre Dumas
THE HUNCHBACK OF NOTRE DAME, Victor Hugo
MADAME BOVARY, Gustave Flaubert

ANNA KARENINA, Leo Tolstoy
THE DEATH OF IVAN ILYICH, Leo Tolstoy

FATHERS AND SONS, Ivan Turgenev

THE BROTHERS KARAMAZOV, Fyodor Dostoevsky
CRIME AND PUNISHMENT, Fyodor Dostoevsky
THE IDIOT, Fyodor Dostoevsky

FOUR GREAT PLAYS, Henrik Ibsen
FIVE MAJOR PLAYS, Anton Chekhov

THE·METAMORPHOSIS, Franz Kafka

Fathers and Sons
by Ivan Turgenev

Translated by Barbara Makanowitzky

With an Introduction by
Alexandra Tolstoy

BANTAM BOOKS
TORONTO · NEW YORK · LONDON · SYDNEY

FATHERS AND SONS

A Bantam Book

PRINTING HISTORY

Fathers and Sons was first published in 1862.
First Bantam edition / August 1959
Bantam Classic edition / March 1981

Library of Congress Catalog Card Number: 59–8619

ISBN 0-553-21036-X

Published simultaneously in the United States and Canada

Bantam Books are published by Bantam Books, Inc. Its trademark, con-
sisting of the words "Bantam Books" and the portrayal of a bantam, is
registered in U.S. Patent and Trademark Office and in other countries.
Marca Registrada. Bantam Books, Inc., 666 Fifth Avenue, New York, New
York 10103.

PRINTED IN THE UNITED STATES OF AMERICA

0 9 8 7 6 5 4 3 2

INTRODUCTION
by Alexandra Tolstoy

It is well known that the Russian language is a difficult one and I think I am not mistaken in saying that even very experienced writers have difficulty in translating Russian books, especially those that contain folk expressions. Therefore, it is my sincere opinion that this translation by Barbara Makanowitzky of *Fathers and Sons* is extremely good.

Fathers and Sons was first published in August 1861 in the magazine *Russian Herald*. At once, it created an enormous sensation and aroused a storm among the critics. Many of them admired the character of Bazarov, a man of the new generation, a man of steel, a scientist, an ascetic, a man who would lead the way to progress; others tried to prove that Turgenev was paying a tribute to the old generation, describing the sons as negative types, despisers of the greatest values of life: religion, love, art, family.

A report of the secret police for 1862 refers to *Fathers and Sons*: "It must be in all justice admitted that the work of the well-known writer, Ivan Turgenev, had a favorable influence. Considered as one of the leaders of Russian contemporary talents, and enjoying the sympathies of Russian cultured society, Turgenev, with this novel of his and to the surprise of the young generation who not so long ago applauded him, branded our half-educated revolutionaries with the bitter name 'nihilist' and shook the doctrine of materialism and its followers."

The young intellectuals, the contributors and the readers of the liberal magazine *Contemporary* broke with Turgenev and branded him as a conservative. On the other hand, there were rumors in St. Petersburg that Turgenev was to be summoned to the Senate to explain his relationship with exiles such as the revolutionist Michael Bakunin and others.

"I am sure," Turgenev said, "that those rumors are not true. It would have been absurd to summon me for an investigation by the Senate right now, after the publication of my *Fathers and Sons*, and after all the criticizing and unfavorable articles of the young generation." But Turgenev did appear before the Senate, and after the hearing the whole matter was dropped. As a result of this incident, Turgenev's relationships with the liberal writer Hertzen and the leaders of the *Contemporary* group were never the same.

Even now, nearly one hundred years after the novel was written, critics differ in their understanding of *Fathers and Sons*.

As a great artist, Turgenev gave a true picture of the life of his time. The characters in the novel are described so vividly that you live with them.

You feel as if you had always known the brothers Kirsanov—those typical representatives of the aristocratic class, who spoke perfect French, were well-versed in Western literature, but had no idea of sociology, political economy or science; who were liberals in theory, but who loved their way of life, their estates, and who were afraid of the new, strong, self-confident, clever man who was ready to destroy their old traditions, their religion, art, poetry—everything. You have met Arkady before— he is an average type—a youth who has no strong principles, a blind follower of Bazarov, who finally falls in love with Katya, marries her and forgets his idol and teacher; you admire the simple-hearted pretty Fenechka, who is so devoted to her benefactor, Nikolai Kirsanov, the father of her child; you suffer together with Bazarov's kind, loving old parents, who cannot understand their son, but consider him a genius. Great is their sorrow, when Bazarov dies of bloodpoisoning.

Yevgeny Bazarov is the main figure in the novel. In him Turgenev embodied all the characteristics, the ideas and moods of the young generation. A contemporary writer said, "Our generation with its aims and ideas, can recognize itself in the heroes of the novel. What is characteristic of Bazarov is scattered throughout the masses."

Bazarov was a nihilist, a man whose aims were the destruction of philosophical ideas, of spiritual values, of religion, of traditions. He was a person with neither roots nor purpose, except destruction.

"Nihilism is a struggle against landowners," the young men declared. "Art, love of nature, love for a woman— all of this romantic stuff must give way to physiology, chemistry and other useful sciences."

But even the good-natured Arkady Kirsanov, who was entirely under the influence of Bazarov, could not stand his friend's cynical attitude towards his own father and uncle and defended them. "That's all spinelessness, emptiness," Bazarov declared, after listening to Arkady's retelling of Pavel's tragic love story. "And what about the mystic relationship between a man and a woman? We physiologists know what constitutes that relationship. Study the anatomy of the eye: where does that—what you call—enigmatic look come from? That's all romanticism, humbug, rot, art."

Nikolai Kirsanov, Arkady's father, was a kind, good-natured man, but even he became bitter when he overheard a conversation between Bazarov and his son.

"Your father's a good fellow," said Bazarov, "but he's an outdated man, his day is over."

Eventually, a deep hatred arose between Pavel Kirsanov and Bazarov.

"On what basis can you act then?" Pavel asks Bazarov as the latter was renouncing everything—aristocracy, liberalism, progress, principles.

"We act on the strength of what we recognize to be useful," answers Bazarov. "At present the most useful thing of all is renunciation—we renounce!"

"Everything?"

"Everything."

How could the "little old gentlemen," as Bazarov

called them, the brothers Kirsanov, understand such an extreme point of view?

"It will be necessary to build, too," Nikolai remarks.

"That's not our concern. First we have to clear the ground."

At the end of the discussion, Pavel asks, "Just curse everything?"

"Just curse."

"And that's called nihilism?"

"And that's called nihilism," Bazarov repeated.

"You think you're progressive people . . . Force! Just remember one last thing, forceful gentlemen: that you are only four and a half men, and they—millions, who won't let you trample their sacred beliefs under foot, who will squash you!" Pavel Kirsanov says.

"If they squash us, it will serve us right," says Bazarov. "But that remains to be seen. We're not so few as you think."

And while reading this scene involuntarily your sympathies are drawn towards the "Fathers," the Kirsanovs, and not to Turgenev's "pet child," as he called Bazarov, the negligently dressed, coarse, self-confident nihilist.

The philosopher Strakhov said, "Nihilism was not a spiritual development, it was a useless jostling of ideas which cannot be formulated. And these negative ideas found their way to trodden paths—revolutionism and anarchy—which means they've gone in the wrong direction."

Once, when a group of friends were discussing *Fathers and Sons* Turgenev said: "We, the people of the forties, based our philosophy of life on moral principles but we lacked will power—these others have the will power but lack the moral principles."

Turgenev was always inspired by people he met.

"I could never invent my characters," Turgenev told his friend N. A. Ostrovsky, "I could not create an imaginary type. I had to choose a living person and combine in this person many characteristics in conformity with the type of my hero."

Turgenev would meet people, notice them, forget

about them and then suddenly they would revive in his mind and he would describe them in his novels.

"I would start making sketches of those people, as I would make sketches of mushrooms, leaves and trees. I would start my drawings until I got sick and tired of them," he wrote.

A man with whom Turgenev once happened to travel gave him the first impulse for creating Bazarov's character. They met in a train which was stopped by a snow storm. They had to spend the night in a room with only one bed, which the stranger offered to Turgenev. He could sleep anywhere, he said, it was a question of will power. And no sooner did he close his eyes—than he was asleep.

"When I created Bazarov," Turgenev wrote to Hertzen, "I did not dislike him; on the contrary, I was attracted to him."

"The character of Bazarov," he told N. A. Ostrovsky, "tormented me to such an extent, that sometimes when I sat at the dinner table, there he was sticking out in front of me. I was speaking to someone and at the same time I was asking myself: what would my Bazarov say to that?"

Turgenev even kept notes of imaginary conversations with Bazarov.

But strong as he was, with his enormous will power, Bazarov could not control the natural human feelings that were in him. Bazarov denied love, he approached women only from the point of view of physical satisfaction and yet he fell hopelessly in love with Odintsova. "This feeling tortured and maddened him, a feeling which he would have denied with contemptuous laughter and cynical abuse if anyone had even remotely hinted to him of the possibility of what was happening inside of him."

Bazarov made fun of chivalry and yet he accepted a challenge with Pavel Kirsanov and fought a duel with him. Bazarov tried to show his friend Arkady that he had no sentimental feelings towards his old parents and yet under cynical and hard words you could still feel his warmth and his love for them, which he was afraid to confess even to himself.

In his nature, Turgenev was a poet, a romantic inspired by Goethe, Schiller, Shakespeare, Byron, Lermontov, Pushkin. He worshipped Gogol, whom he called the "great" writer. He lived in the Golden Age of literature in Russia, a contemporary of Dostoevsky and Tolstoy. Turgenev was considered a Westerner in opposition to the so-called Slavophiles who stood for Russian tradition and culture, yet Turgenev once said, "Russia can live without us, but no one of us can live without Russia."

And, later still, when he was getting old, Turgenev wrote, "In days of doubt, in days of sorrowful thoughts about my mother country, you, the great, powerful and liberal Russian tongue—you are my only support and help. One cannot believe that such a language was not granted to a great country."

FATHERS AND SONS

CHARACTERS

Nikolai Petrovich Kirsanov	a small landowner
Arkady Nikolayevich Kirsanov	Nikolai's son
Pavel Petrovich Kirsanov	Nikolai's brother
Yevgeny Vassilievich Bazarov	a friend of Arkady's
Fedosya Nikolayevna Savishna (Fenechka)	Nikolai's housekeeper
Mitya	Fenechka's son
Viktor Sitnikov	a friend of Bazarov's
Avdotya Nikitishna Kukshina	a friend of Sitnikov's
Anna Sergeyevna Odintsova	a widow
Katerina Sergeyevna Lokteva (Katya)	Odintsova's sister
Vassily Ivanovich Bazarov	Bazarov's father
Arina Vlassevna Bazarov	Bazarov's mother
Princess Avdotya Stepanovna Kh——	Odintsova's aunt
Matvei Ilyich Kolyazin	a privy councillor
Porfiry Platonovich	a neighbor of Odintsova's
Father Aleksei	a village priest
Prokofich, Piotr, Dunyasha	servants of Nikolai Petrovich
Timofeich, Anfisushka, Tanyushka, Fedka	servants of Bazarov's father

Note: Russian names are composed of a first name, patronymic (father's name plus a genitive suffix such as "yevich," "ovich," or the feminine "ovna"), and last name. Thus, Arkady's middle name, Nikolayevich, means "son of Nikolai." The name and patronymic are used together in formal address, though the patronymic is frequently shortened somewhat; for example, Bazarov may be called either Yevgeny Vassil*iev* or Yevgeny Vassil*ich*.

The asterisks* in the text refer to the end notes which begin on page 205.

"Well, Piotr? Still nothing in sight?" asked a gentleman on the 20th of May, 1859, as he came out on the porch of the stage-coach inn on the road to ——. Hatless, in a dusty overcoat and checked trousers, he looked a little over forty. He was addressing his servant, a chubby fellow with small, dim eyes and whitish fuzz on his chin.

Everything about the servant—his ingratiating suavity, his pomaded, varicolored hair, even his single turquoise earring—in short, everything distinguished him as belonging to the new, emancipated generation of servants.

He looked down the road indulgently before answering, "No, sir, still nothing in sight."

"Nothing in sight?" repeated the gentleman.

"Nothing in sight," his servant answered again.

The gentleman sighed and sat down on a bench. Let us introduce the reader to him while he sits, his legs gathered up under him, pensively waiting.

His name is Nikolai Petrovich Kirsanov. He has a comfortable estate ten miles from the inn with two hundred souls—or two thousand fields (as he has put it since establishing a farm by subdividing and leasing land to the peasants).

His father, a front-line general in 1812, semiliterate, coarse, but a true Russian soul, kept his shoulder to the wheel all his life. He first commanded a brigade and then a division, always staying in the provinces, where his rank enabled him to play a fairly important role.

Like his brother Pavel—of whom more later—Nikolai

was born in southern Russia and was brought up at home
until the age of fourteen by underpaid tutors and free-
living but punctilious aides-de-camp and other regimental and staff officers.

His mother, née Kolyazin, was called Agathe as a girl,
but after her marriage to the general was always addressed by her full name: Agafokleya Kuzminishna Kirsanova. She dictated to the whole regiment, talked a great
deal in a loud voice, and wore sumptuous mobcaps and
rustling taffeta dresses. On Sundays she preceded everyone to bow to the priest's cross after mass; in the morn-
ings she let the children come kiss her hand; in the
evenings she gave them her blessing—in short, she lived
exactly as she pleased.

As the son of a general, Nikolai—although he not only
failed to distinguish himself by his courage, but even
earned the nickname "Little Coward"—was supposed to
go into military service as his brother Pavel had. However, he broke his leg the very day his appointment was
confirmed, spent two months in bed, and was left with a
slight limp the rest of his life. His father then abandoned
the idea of a military career for Nikolai and took him to
St. Petersburg to enroll him in the university as soon as
he reached eighteen.

At about the same time, his brother became an officer
in a guards regiment. The two young men moved into an
apartment under the casual supervision of their mother's
cousin, Ilya Kolyazin, an important official. Once they
were settled, their father went back to his division and
his wife. On rare occasions, the sons received large gray
sheets of stationery covered with the bold handwriting
of a public clerk and signed in flourishing script, painstakingly encircled by curlicues: "Piotr Kirsanov, Major-
General."

Nikolai graduated in 1835. In the same year, General
Kirsanov, reprimanded for failing an inspection, was
retired and went to St. Petersburg with his wife to live.
He was about to rent a house near the fashionable Tav-
richesky Gardens and had joined the English Club,
when he unexpectedly died of a stroke. Agafokleya Kuzminishna Kirsanova soon followed him. She was unable

to get used to a life of obscurity in the capital; the existence of a retired general's wife literally bored her to death.

In the meantime, while his parents were still alive, and to their not inconsiderable mortification, Nikolai managed to fall in love with the daughter of his former landlord, a bureaucrat named Prepolovensky. She was a pretty girl and, as they say, well-versed: she read serious articles in the science section of newspapers. He married her the moment his mourning period was over, and having resigned from the civil service—where he had been placed through his father's influence—he lived in bliss with his Masha. They moved first to a *dacha* near the School of Forestry, then to an attractive little apartment in town with a spotless stairway and a rather poorly heated parlor, and finally settled in the country where a son, Arkady, was soon born.

The couple lived quietly and well. They were almost never apart; they read together, played four-hands on the piano and sang duets; she grew flowers and watched over the chicken yard; he hunted from time to time and took care of the estate—and Arkady grew and grew, also quietly and well. Ten years passed like a dream.

In 1847 Kirsanov's wife died. He barely survived the shock and turned gray in a few weeks. He was on his way abroad to try to distract himself a little when the events of 1848 forced him to abandon his plans. He returned to the estate and, after a long period of inactivity, began to busy himself with its reorganization.

He entered his son in the University of St. Petersburg in 1855 and spent three winters there, trying to make friends with Arkady's young classmates and seldom going out. He was unable to accompany Arkady the last winter, and thus we see him in May, 1859, already completely gray, somewhat heavy and stooped, waiting for his son, who had just been granted the degree he once received himself.

The servant, prompted by a consideration for his master's privacy, or a desire to be out of his sight, moved off under the gateway and lit his pipe. Nikolai stared down at the worn steps of the porch. A sturdy, speckled hen strutted gravely up and down the steps, its big yellow feet extended stiffly. A mud-spattered cat, primly curled up on the porch railing, watched the fowl malevolently.

The sun was baking. From the half-darkened interior of the inn came the smell of warm rye bread. Our Nikolai became lost in daydreams. "Son . . . graduated . . . Arkady . . . Arkasha . . ." whirled aimlessly in his head. He was reminded of his dead wife . . . "She didn't live to see . . ." he whispered sadly. A plump pigeon flew into sight and hurriedly started drinking in a small puddle near the well. As Nikolai watched the bird, his ears caught the rumble of approaching carriage wheels.

"They're coming, sir," reported the servant, bobbing out of the gateway.

Nikolai jumped up and strained his eyes down the road. A coach appeared, harnessed with three post horses. Inside the coach he saw the flash of a student's cap, then the profile of a beloved face.

"Arkasha! Arkasha!" Kirsanov cried, running and waving his arms. A few moments later, his lips were clinging to the sunburned, unbearded, dusty cheek of the young graduate.

ii

"Let me shake myself off, Papasha," Arkady protested several times, his voice hoarse from the dusty road, but resonant and youthful, as he merrily returned his father's embraces. "I'll get you all dirty."

"It doesn't matter, doesn't matter," Nikolai said over and over, smiling fondly and occasionally brushing the collar of the boy's greatcoat and his own overcoat. "Let me look at you, let me look," he continued, standing back; then abruptly starting towards the inn, he called, "Over here! Fresh horses! Right away!"

Nikolai seemed much more excited than his son; he

was nervous and quite beside himself. As he started scurrying towards the inn, Arkady, stopping him, said, "Papasha, let me introduce my good friend, Bazarov, whom I wrote you about so often. He was kind enough to consent to visit us."

Nikolai whirled about, hurried up to the tall man dressed in a long shaggy peasant's overcoat who had just then gotten out of the coach, and grasped the rough red hand, which the man was slow to offer.

"I am very glad and grateful for your kindness in visiting us," Nikolai began. "I hope . . . Will you allow me to ask your name?"

"Yevgeny Vassiliev," Bazarov answered in a deep drawl and, opening the collar of his coat, unmuffled his face. Long and thin, with a high forehead, wide-bridged pointed nose, large greenish eyes and drooping sand-colored sideburns, his face was enlivened by a peaceful smile and reflected self-confidence and intelligence.

"I hope, dear Yevgeny Vassilich, that you won't get bored with us," Nikolai continued.

Bazarov's thin lips moved slightly, but he said nothing, merely raising his cap. His long, thick, dark-blond hair did not entirely hide the prominent contours of his massive head.

"So, Arkady," Nikolai said turning to his son, "shall we have the horses harnessed now? Or do you want to rest first?"

"We can rest at home, Papasha; tell them to go ahead."

"Right away, right away!" exclaimed his father. "Holla, Piotr, did you hear? Step lively there, young fellow."

Piotr, true to his role of a modern, emancipated servant, did not kiss his master's hand, but merely bowed to him from a distance and ducked back under the gateway.

"I came here in the open buggy, but there's a three-horse team for your coach," Nikolai fussed, while Arkady drank water from an iron ladle brought by the inn-keeper, and Bazarov, smoking a pipe, went over to the coachman who was unhitching the horses. "But the buggy has only two seats, so I don't know how your friend—"

"He'll go in the coach," Arkady interrupted softly. "Please don't stand on ceremony with him. He's a wonderful person—so simple. You'll see."

Nikolai's coachman led out the horses.

"Come on, hurry up, Bushy Beard!" Bazarov said to him.

"Did you hear what the master called you, Mityukha?" said another coachman, standing by with his hands thrust in his torn sheepskin coat. "Bushy Beard it is."

Mityukha just pulled at his cap and dragged the sweaty horses by the reins.

"Hurry up, hurry up, children; everyone lend a hand!" Nikolai exclaimed. "There's a tip waiting for you."

In a few minutes the horses were harnessed. Father and son got into the buggy; Piotr clambered up on the coach box; Bazarov, jumping in the coach, buried his head in the leather pillow—and both carriages rolled off.

iii

"Well, there we are. At last you've graduated and come home," Nikolai said, patting Arkady's shoulder and knee from time to time. "At last!"

"And how is Uncle Pavel? Is he well?" asked Arkady who, though filled with a sincere, almost childlike joy, wanted to switch the conversation from an emotional to a prosaic level as quickly as possible.

"He's fine. He wanted to come with me to meet you, but changed his mind for some reason."

"Did you wait for me long?" asked Arkady.

"Yes, about five hours."

"Dear Papasha!" Arkady turned vivaciously towards his father and kissed him noisily on the cheek. Nikolai laughed gently.

"I have a superb horse waiting for you," he began. "Wait till you see it. And your room is all re-papered."

"And is there a room for Bazarov?"

"Ah, we'll find him one."

"Please, Papasha, be kind to him. I can't tell you how much his friendship means to me."

"You haven't known him long, have you?"

"Not very long."

"That's what I thought. I didn't see him last winter. What does he do?"

"He's majoring in natural science. He knows absolutely everything. He wants to get his degree as a doctor next year."

"So he's in medical school," Nikolai commented, and fell silent a moment. "Piotr," he added, pointing, "could those be our peasants over there?"

Piotr turned to look where his master had pointed. Several carts pulled by work horses were rolling swiftly along a narrow side-road. In each sat one or two peasants wearing open sheepskin coats.

"You're right, sir," Piotr said.

"Where could they be going? To town?"

"To town, it's safe to say. . . . To the tavern," he added contemptuously, nodding towards the coachman as though seeking his concurrence. The coachman made no response. He was a man of the old school who disapproved of the modern generation's behavior.

"I had great difficulties with the peasants this year," Nikolai continued, turning to his son. "They won't pay their poll tax. What can one do?"

"And you're satisfied with your hired hands?"

"Yes," Nikolai muttered through clenched teeth. "The trouble is, they're stirred up by the others. And I haven't seen any really hard work done yet. They're ruining the whole system. On the other hand, they raised a fairly good crop. It'll be milled and there'll be flour. . . . Have you become interested in agriculture?"

"There isn't any shade; that's the sad thing," Arkady said, not answering the last question.

"I had a big awning put up over the balcony on the north," said Nikolai. "Now you can eat outside."

"The house will look awfully much like a summer resort—but, anyhow, that's all nonsense. What air there is here! How sweet it smells! To me there's no air so fragrant anywhere else in the world And this sky . . ."

Arkady stopped suddenly, gave a sidelong glance back, and fell silent.

"Naturally," Nikolai said, "you were born here, so everything should seem very special to you."

"But, Papasha, it doesn't make any difference where a man is born."

"Well . . ."

"No, it really doesn't make any difference."

Nikolai looked at his son, and the wheels rolled on for a quarter of a mile before the conversation was resumed.

Nikolai began: "I don't remember whether I wrote you that your old nurse Yegorovna died."

"Really? Poor old woman! And is Prokofich still alive?"

"Alive and exactly the same. Still grumbling. All in all, you won't find many changes at Marino."

"Still the same overseer, I suppose?"

"As a matter of fact, I did change him. I decided not to keep any freed serfs around any more, at least not in positions of responsibility." (Arkady gestured inquiringly towards Piotr.) *"Il est libre, en effet,"** Nikolai whispered, "but you see, he's just a valet. My new overseer is a freeman. He seems to be a capable fellow. I pay him two hundred and fifty rubles a year. By the way," Nikolai added as he rubbed his forehead, a nervous habit which betrayed an embarrassment he tried to conceal, "I just told you you wouldn't find any changes at Marino. That's not quite fair. I consider it my duty to warn you, although . . ."

He faltered a moment, then continued in French.

"A strict moralist would find my frankness amiss, but in the first place, this couldn't remain hidden, and in the second place, as you know, I have always had special convictions about what a father's relationship to his son should be. By the way, you naturally have the right to condemn me. At my age . . . In short, that—that young girl, whom you've probably already heard about . . ."

"Fenechka?" Arkady asked familiarly.

---

* For notes, see page 205.

Nikolai blushed. "Don't say her name aloud, please. Yes. She's staying with me now. In the main house—there were two little rooms. But that can all be changed. . . ."

"But Papasha, why should it?"

"Your friend will be staying with us—it's awkward—"

"Please don't worry about Bazarov. He's above all that."

"But you, after all . . ." Nikolai resumed. "The cottage was so miserable—that was the unfortunate thing."

"Please, Papasha," Arkady interrupted. "It sounds as though you were apologizing. You should be ashamed."

"Naturally I should be ashamed," answered Nikolai, blushing more and more.

"That's enough, Papasha, that's enough, please!" Arkady said, smiling fondly. "Why is he apologizing?" he thought to himself, and was filled with indulgent tenderness and, at the same time, a half-secretive feeling of superiority towards his good, soft-hearted father. "No more, please," he said again, involuntarily enjoying the awareness of his own freedom and sophistication.

Nikolai, still rubbing his forehead, glanced at his son through the fingers of his hand and felt his heart sink—but he immediately reproached himself.

After a long silence, he remarked, "Look, we're passing our own fields now.

"And those are our woods ahead, aren't they?"

"Yes, they're ours. Except that I sold the timber. The trees will be cut this year."

"Why did you sell them?"

"I needed the money. And anyway, that land will be turned over to the peasants."

"Who don't pay you their poll tax?"

"That's up to them. Besides, they'll pay me sometime."

"It's too bad about the woods," Arkady remarked and began to gaze around him.

The countryside they were passing through could not be called picturesque. Gently undulating fields stretched to the horizon; here and there patches of woods appeared; and ravines, planted with sparse, low bushes, twisted and turned, calling to mind the way they were depicted on maps of the time of Catherine the Great. There were

scattered streams with eroded banks, and tiny ponds,
overflowing their crumbling dams; villages of low hovels
under dark, disheveled thatched roofs; dilapidated threshing sheds, their walls woven out of corn shucks; wide
gates yawning into deserted granary yards; and churches,
some brick, covered with peeling plaster, some wooden,
with crosses askew and graveyards in ruins. Arkady's
heart sank. To complete the picture, the peasants they
passed were bedraggled and rode decrepit nags; the wil-
lows lining the road stood like beggars in tatters, their
bark peeling off, their branches broken; emaciated,
shaggy cows, literally consumed by hunger, tore greedily
at the grass beside the ditches. They looked as though
they had just torn themselves free from some creature's
deadly clutches. The pitiful spectacle of the enfeebled
animals on this beautiful spring day evoked the white
image of gloomy, endless winter with its blizzards, frost
and snow.

"No," Arkady thought, "this isn't rich country; it
shows no signs of either abundance or hard work; it can't
be, it mustn't be left like this; there have to be changes
—but where to begin, and how?"

Arkady was lost in these thoughts, while all around
him spring was coming into its own. Everything was
turning a golden green, moving freely and shining softly
under the gentle breath of the warm breeze, everything
—the trees, the bushes, the grass. The larks deluged it all
with endless waves of song; the lapwings screeched from
time to time, circling over low-lying meadows, then
silently running over the hillocks; crows, looking handsomely black in the delicate verdure, became lost from
sight walking through the low spring corn; only their
dark heads appeared from time to time in the smoky
waves of the already whitening grain. As Arkady continued to look, his thoughts faded and vanished. He
threw off his coat and looked at his father so merrily and
boyishly that his father hugged him again.

"We're not far away now," remarked Nikolai. "As
soon as we climb that little hill, the house will be in
sight. We'll get along together famously, Arkady. You
can help me with the estate, unless you find it boring.

We must draw close to each other now, get to know
other well, isn't that right?"

"Of course," Arkady agreed. "What a wonderful day
it is today"

"Specially for your arrival, my lamb. Yes, spring is in
full bloom. But I'm inclined to agree with Pushkin—
you remember, in 'Yevgeny Onegin':

> 'How sad to me your coming is,
> O Spring, O Spring, the time of love!
> How—' "

"Arkady," the voice of Bazarov broke in from his
coach, "send over a match. I haven't anything to light
my pipe."

Nikolai fell silent and Arkady, who had begun to
listen to his father with a little surprise, but not without
sympathy, hurriedly pulled out a small silver matchbox
which Piotr handed to Bazarov.

"Do you want a cigar?" cried Bazarov again.

"Let's have it," answered Arkady.

Piotr handed back the matchbox with a fat black cigar
which Arkady lit at once, diffusing such a strong, acrid
smell of coarse tobacco that Nikolai, a non-smoker, involuntarily averted his nose, though he did so imperceptibly to avoid hurting his son's feelings.

A quarter of an hour later, both carriages stopped in
front of the steps of a new, gray wooden house covered
with a red tin roof. This was Marino—the new, or, as the
peasants called it, The Pauper's Farm.

iv

No crowd of servants poured out on the steps to greet
the gentleman; all that appeared was one little girl of
about twelve and, following her, a young fellow strongly

resembling Piotr, dressed in a gray livery jacket whose silver buttons were stamped with a coat of arms—the servant of Pavel Petrovich Kirsanov. He silently opened the door of the buggy and unhooked the apron of the coach. Nikolai, his son and Bazarov caught sight of a young woman's face behind a door as they went through a dark, almost empty hall into a parlor decorated in the latest style.

"Here we are, home at last," Nikolai said, taking off his cap and shaking back his hair. "The main thing now is to have dinner and rest."

"Something to eat wouldn't be a bad idea," remarked Bazarov, stretching and sinking down on the couch.

"Yes, yes, let's have supper, supper right away." Nikolai stamped his feet lightly for no apparent reason. "Here comes Prokofich, just in time."

A sixty-year-old man entered, white-haired, swarthy and thin, wearing a pink scarf around his neck and a brown frockcoat with copper buttons. He simpered, kissed Arkady's hand, and bowing to the guest, retreated towards the door, where he stood, his hands clasped behind his back.

"He's here, Prokofich," Nikolai began; "he finally arrived. . . . Well? How do you find him?"

"Looking fit, sir," the old man said, simpering again; then furrowing his thick eyebrows, he suggested, "Will you want dinner served now?"

"Yes, yes, please. But don't you want to go to your room first, Yevgeny Vassilich?"

"No, thank you very much; it's not necessary. Just tell them to put my trunk there. Oh, yes, and this garb," he added, taking off his coat.

"Very good. Prokofich, take his coat." Prokofich, looking dumfounded, took Bazarov's "garb" with both hands and, holding it high above his head, went out on tiptoe. "What about you, Arkady, do you want to go to your room for a moment?"

"Yes, I should wash up," Arkady answered and turned to go, when into the parlor came a man of average height, dressed in a dark English suit, a fashionable tie and high patent-leather shoes—Pavel Petrovich Kirsanov.

He looked about forty-five; his short gray hair had a dark luster like new silver; his face, bilious but unwrinkled, was unusually clean-cut as if etched with a fine chisel, it preserved traces of remarkable beauty; the clear, dark almond-shaped eyes were particularly handsome. His whole appearance was elegant and aristocratic; he had kept his youthful carriage and that look of rising buoyantly off the ground which usually disappears after the twenties.

Pavel drew his beautiful hand with long rosy nails out of his trouser pocket and extended it towards his nephew; his hand seemed still more beautiful against the snowy-white cuff, fastened with one large opal. After a preliminary European handshake, he kissed Arkady three times in Russian fashion; that is, he brushed Arkady's cheek three times with his fragrant whiskers and said, "It's good to welcome you."

Nikolai introduced Bazarov. Pavel made a slight, supple bow and smiled faintly, but put his hand back in his pocket.

"I had already decided you weren't coming today," he said in a pleasant voice, rocking on his heels and shrugging his shoulders, his amiable smile displaying his perfect white teeth. "Did something happen to you on the way?"

"Nothing happened," Arkady answered. "We just took our time. So now we're hungry as wolves. Make Prokofich hurry up, Papasha; I'll be right back."

"Wait, I'll go with you!" cried Bazarov, suddenly tearing himself away from the sofa. Both young people left the room.

"Who's that?" asked Pavel.

"A friend of Arkady's, a very bright man, he says."

"Is he staying with us?"

"Yes."

"That hairy creature?"

"Well, yes."

Pavel drummed his nails on the table. "I find that Arkady *s'est dégourdi*,"* he remarked. "I'm glad he's come back."

At supper there was very little conversation. Bazarov

said less than anyone, but ate a great deal. Nikolai told
about various aspects of what he called his life on the
farm: about impending legislature, about the committees
and deputies, about the necessity of introducing machin-
ery, and so forth. Pavel paced slowly up and down the
dining room (he never ate supper). He occasionally took
a sip from a glass of red wine, and even more rarely
uttered a phrase or exclamation such as "Oh," "Aha"
and "Hmm." Arkady recounted a little news from St.
Petersburg, but he was conscious of a slight uneasiness
—the sort of uneasiness a young man usually feels when,
just after outgrowing childhood, he returns to a place
where he has always been considered a child. He prolonged his sentences unnecessarily, avoided the expression "papasha," and even substituted "father" once,
though he half muttered it. With exaggerated nonchal-
lance, he poured himself a much larger glass of wine
than he really wanted and drank all of it. Prokofich kept
chewing his lips, his eyes never leaving Arkady. Everyone went his own way immediately after supper.

"What an eccentric uncle you have," Bazarov remarked.
He sucked on a short pipe as he stood in his dressing
gown at the foot of Arkady's bed. "To think of finding
such foppishness in the country! Those nails, those nails
—they're good enough to hang up on the wall!"

"Well, of course you don't know, but he cut quite a
figure in his day," Arkady answered. "I'll tell you his
story sometime. He was very handsome and used to fascinate the ladies."

"That's just the point! He's living on old memories.
Unfortunately, there's no one to fascinate around here.
I took a good look at him: those wonderful collars he
has—they look carved out of stone; and his chin is so
painstakingly shaven. Arkady Nikolaich, don't you agree
it's ridiculous?"

"If you like; but he really is a good person."

"An archaic phenomenon! Your father is a pleasant
chap. He wastes his time reading poetry and probably
doesn't understand the first thing about running the
estate, but he's a good soul."

"My father has a heart of gold."

"Did you notice how timid he is?"

Arkady nodded as though he weren't timid himself.

"It's amazing," Bazarov continued. "Those little old romantics. They key themselves up to such an extent that they destroy their equilibrium. . . . Well, so long. There's a fancy English washbasin in my room, but the door won't close. All the same, that sort of thing should be encouraged—an English washbasin, that's progress!"

Bazarov left. Arkady was overwhelmed by a feeling of joy. It's sweet to go to sleep in one's own home, in a familiar bed, under a quilt worked by loving hands, perhaps nurse's hands, those kind, caressing, untiring hands. Arkady remembered Yegorovna, sighed, and wished her peace in heaven—he didn't say any prayers for himself.

Both he and Bazarov fell asleep quietly, but others in the house were awake for a long time. Nikolai was excited by the return of his son. He lay in bed, the candle still burning, his head propped on his hand, lost in thought. Pavel sat long after midnight in a big leather armchair in his study before a fireplace in which a coal fire smouldered. He hadn't undressed, merely changed his patent leather-shoes for red Chinese slippers. He held the latest issue of *Galignani* in his hand, but didn't read it; he stared fixedly at the sputtering blue flame, intermittently flaring and dying down. Heavens knows where his thoughts wandered, but they were not restricted to the past; unlike a man engrossed in memories alone, his expression was morose and tense. Meanwhile, in a small back room, on a large trunk, sat a young woman, Fenechka, alternately listening, dozing, and looking through the half-open door beyond which a crib was visible, and one could hear the even breathing of a sleeping child.

v

The next morning, Bazarov woke up before anyone else and went outside. "Ugh!" he thought, looking around, "this is a miserable little spot."

When Nikolai had subdivided the land among the peasants, he had been forced to allot to the new farmhouse four absolutely flat, bare fields. He built the house, the service quarters and farm buildings, cultivated the land for a garden, dug a pond, and sank two wells. But the young trees didn't take root well, the pond collected very little water, and the water in the wells was brackish. The only thing which flourished was one little arbor of lilacs and acacias; tea or lunch was sometimes served under it. In a few minutes, Bazarov had explored all the little paths in the garden, visited the barnyard and the stables, and sought out two young houseboys with whom he promptly made friends, and who accompanied him to a small swamp about two thirds of a mile from the farmhouse to catch frogs.

"Why do you want frogs, sir?" one of the boys asked him.

"I'll tell you why," answered Bazarov, who had a special knack of winning the confidence of inferiors, although he treated them casually and without indulgence. "I'm going to split the frog open to see what's going on inside of him; since you and I are no different from frogs, except that we walk on our hind legs, I'll find out what's happening inside of us too."

"What good will that do you?"

"Then I won't make a mistake if you fall sick and I have to cure you."

"So you're a doctor then?"

"Yes."

"Váska, listen, the master says you and I are just like frogs. That's funny."

"I'm scared of frogs," remarked Vaska, a tow-headed, barefooted boy of about seven, wearing a high-collared gray Cossack coat.

"What are you scared of? Do you think they bite?"

"Now climb in the water, you philosophers," interrupted Bazarov.

Meanwhile, Nikolai had also awakened and gone to rouse Arkady, whom he found already dressed. Father and son stepped out on the terrace under the awning; on a table near the railing, between huge bouquets of lilacs, a samovar was already bubbling.

The same little girl who had met them on their arrival the day before appeared and said in a thin voice, "Fedosya Nikolayevna is not feeling very well and can't come; she told me to ask you if you wouldn't mind pouring tea yourself or should she send Dunyasha?"

"I myself will pour," Nikolai said hastily. "How do you like your tea, Arkady? With cream or lemon?"

"With cream," Arkady answered, and after a moment's silence, said questioningly, "Papasha?"

Nikolai looked at his son quizzically. "What?" he said.

Arkady averted his eyes.

"Forgive me, Papasha, if my question strikes you as out of place," he began, "but you yourself, with your own frankness yesterday, encourage me to be frank—you won't be angry?"

"Speak up."

"You give me the courage to ask you . . . Is the reason Fen . . . Is it because I'm here that she isn't coming to pour tea?"

Nikolai turned away slightly.

"Perhaps," he said, finally, "she supposes . . . she is ashamed—"

Arkady threw a quick glance at his father.

"She has no reason to be ashamed. In the first place, you know my philosophy of life" (Arkady took pleasure in saying these words pompously), "and in the second place, I would hardly want to interfere with your life or your habits. Besides, I'm sure you couldn't have made a bad choice; if you let her live under the same roof with you, it must be because she deserves it; and in any case, a son is not his father's judge, particularly when the son is I, and the father is you, who have never in any way interfered with my freedom."

Arkady's voice trembled at first. He felt he was being magnanimous, but at the same time he realized that he was rather reading a lecture to his father; however, the sound of one's own voice is very convincing, and Arkady pronounced the last words firmly, even dramatically.

"Thank you, Arkady," Nikolai said tonelessly, and his fingers moved nervously towards his forehead again. "Your assumption is entirely correct. Naturally if this girl didn't deserve . . . It wasn't a thoughtless whim. It's awkward for me to talk to you about this; but you can understand that it would be difficult for her to come here in front of you, particularly the first day after your arrival."

"In that case I'll go to her," Arkady exclaimed with a new wave of magnanimous feelings, and he jumped up from the table. "I'll explain to her that she has nothing to be ashamed of towards me."

Nikolai also stood up.

"Arkady," he began, "I beg of you . . . how can one . . . in there . . . I didn't warn you . . ."

But Arkady, no longer listening, ran from the terrace. Nikolai watched him go and sank down on his chair in confusion. His heart was pounding. Was he at that moment imagining the inevitable strangeness of his future relations with his son? Was he admitting to himself that Arkady would have respected him more if he had never broached the matter? Was he reproaching himself for his weakness? It is hard to say: all these feelings were present, but jumbled and vague; his face remained flushed and his heart pounded.

He heard hasty steps. Arkady came onto the terrace.

"We've met, Father!" he cried with an expression of tender, benevolent triumph on his face. "Fedosya Nikolayevna really isn't feeling very well today and will come later. But why didn't you tell me I have a brother? I would have kissed him yesterday evening, as I did just now."

Nikolai wanted to say something, wanted to rise and take him in his arms. . . . Arkady fell on his neck.

"What's this? Embracing again?" Pavel's voice broke in from the garden.

Father and son were equally delighted by his appearance at that moment; there are certain touching situations which one wants to get out of as quickly as possible.

"Why so surprised?" Nikolai said merrily. "I've been waiting for Arkady for centuries—I've hardly been able to get a good look at him since yesterday."

"I'm not at all surprised," Pavel replied. "I'm not disinclined to embrace him myself."

Arkady went to his uncle and again felt the fragrant mustaches brush his cheeks. Pavel sat down at the table. He wore an elegant English-style morning suit. His head was embellished by a small fez. This fez and the carelessly knotted tie were signs of the freedom of country life, but the tight shirt collar—though it wasn't white, but colored, as it should be for correct morning attire—propped up the closely shaven chin as inflexibly as usual.

"Where's your new friend?" he asked Arkady.

"He's not in the house; he usually gets up early and goes off somewhere. The important thing is not to pay any attention to him; he doesn't like formality."

"Yes, that's obvious," Pavel began, slowly spreading butter on his bread. "Will he be staying with us long?"

"I don't know," Arkady answered casually. "He came here on the way to his father's."

"And where does his father live?"

"In the same province, about fifty miles from here. He has a small estate there. He used to be a regimental doctor."

"Tsk-tsk-tsk . . . I was just wondering: where have I heard that name Bazarov? Nikolai, do you remember—wasn't there an army doctor called Bazarov in Father's division?"

"I believe there was."

"That's it, that's it. So that doctor is his father. Hmm!"

Pavel stroked his mustaches. "And Mr. Bazarov himself, what is he?" he asked condescendingly after a pause.

"What is Bazarov?" Arkady laughed. "Do you want me to tell you what he really is, Uncle Pavel?"

"If you will be so kind, my young nephew."

"He's a nihilist."

"What?" asked Nikolai, while Pavel raised his knife with a little butter on the tip and remained motionless.

"He's a nihilist," Arkady repeated.

"A nihilist," said Nikolai. "That comes from the Latin word *nihil*, nothing, so far as I can tell; it must mean a person who—who acknowledges nothing."

"Say rather: who respects nothing," Pavel put in and began buttering his bread again.

"Who examines everything from a critical point of view," Arkady observed.

"And isn't that exactly the same thing?" asked Pavel.

"No, it isn't the same thing. A nihilist is a person who does not bow to any authorities; who doesn't accept any principle on faith, no matter how hallowed and venerated the principle is."

"And then what, is that good?" Pavel interrupted.

"That depends, Uncle Pavel. For some it's good; for others it's very bad."

"That's just it. Well, I see it's not our dish of tea. We're people of the old century; we assume that without principles" (Pavel stressed the second syllable softly in the French manner, while Arkady, on the contrary, pronounced it 'principles,' accenting the first syllable) "without accepting certain principles, as you put it, on faith, it's impossible to make a move, to breathe. *Vous avez changé tout cela.** May God grant you health and the rank of a general, and we will just feast our eyes on you, gentlemen—what was it again?"

"Nihilists," Arkady said very distinctly.

"Yes. First there were Hegelists and now nihilists. Let's see how you'll manage to exist in a void, in a vacuum; and now please ring, Nikolai, it's time for me to have my cocoa."

Nikolai rang and called: "Dunyasha!" But the person who appeared was not Dunyasha, but Fenechka. She was a young woman of about twenty-three, pale and delicate, with dark hair and eyes, childishly plump red lips and dainty hands; she wore a neat printed dress and a new blue scarf lay lightly on her rounded shoulders. After putting a large cup of cocoa in front of Pavel, she was overcome by confusion; warm blood flushed ruby-red under the thin skin of her lovely face. She averted her eyes, stopped near the table, and leaned lightly on the very tips of her fingers. It seemed as though she were ashamed of having appeared, but at the same time, rather felt she had the right to be there.

Pavel frowned severely and Nikolai looked disconcerted.

"Good morning, Fenechka," he muttered.

"Good morning, sir," she answered in a soft but clear voice, and looking sidewise at Arkady, who was smiling at her affably, she went quietly away. She had a rather swinging walk which was not unbecoming.

Silence prevailed on the terrace for several moments.

Pavel sipped his cocoa, then suddenly raising his head, said half aloud, "There comes Mr. Nihilist to favor us with a visit."

And there, walking through the garden and stepping over the flower beds, came Bazarov. His linen coat and trousers were spattered with mud; slimy swamp weeds clung to the crown of his old cap; in his right hand he held a small sack, and in the sack, something was wiggling.

Bazarov came quickly to the terrace and nodded, saying, "Good morning, gentlemen. Forgive me for being late for breakfast. I'll be right back; I just have to find a place for these prisoners."

"What do you have there, leeches?" Pavel asked.

"No, frogs."

"Do you eat them or breed them?"

"For experiments," Bazarov said indifferently as he went into the house.

"He's going to cut them open," Pavel remarked. "He doesn't believe in principles, but he believes in frogs."

Arkady looked at his uncle with chagrin and Nikolai shrugged his shoulders imperceptibly. Pavel, realizing that his witticism was not a success, began to talk about agriculture and about the new overseer, who had come to him the day before to complain that the worker Foma was "raising cain" and was out of hand: " 'He's such an Aesop,' he said among other things, 'he proclaims his own wickedness everywhere; he'll live and pass on in stupidity.' "

vi

Bazarov returned, sat down at the table, and began drinking his tea hurriedly. Both brothers looked at him in silence, while Arkady surreptitiously watched first his father, then his uncle.

"Did you walk far from here?" Nikolai finally asked.

"You have a swamp here, near the grove of aspens. I flushed five woodcocks; you could take a shot at them, Arkady."

"You're not a hunter yourself?"

"No."

"You're mainly interested in physics?" Pavel asked in turn.

"Physics, yes; and natural science in general."

"They say the Teutons have made great progress in that field recently."

"Yes, in that the Germans are our teachers," Bazarov answered nonchalantly.

Pavel had used the word "Teuton" instead of "German" with deliberate irony which, however, no one noticed.

"You have such a high opinion of the Germans?" Pavel asked with affected politeness. He had begun to feel irritated. His aristocratic sensibilities were outraged by Bazarov's complete detachment. This army doctor's son not only wasn't intimidated, but replied abruptly and grudgingly, with something rude, almost insolent, in his tone of voice.

"The scientists there are a capable lot."

"True, true. And I suppose you don't have as flattering an opinion of Russian scientists?"

"If you wish, yes, it's true."

"That's very laudable self-abnegation," said Pavel, sitting erect and throwing back his head. "But wasn't Arkady Nikolayevich just telling us that you don't acknowledge any authorities? Don't you believe in them?"

"What should I acknowledge them for? And what should I believe in? They give me the facts; I concur; and that's all."

"And do the Germans have all the facts right?" said Pavel, his face assuming an unconcerned, faraway expression as though he had removed himself to a pinnacle beyond the clouds.

"Not all Germans," Bazarov, who obviously didn't want to continue the argument, answered with a brief yawn.

Pavel glanced at Arkady as if wanting to say to him, "He's polite, your friend, I must say."

"As far as I'm concerned, sinner that I am," he began again with a certain effort, "I must confess that I don't like Germans. Russian Germans I won't even mention; everyone knows what they're like. But German Germans are also distasteful to me. There used to be a few here and there; they had—well, there was Schiller, for example, and Goethe . . . my brother likes them particularly. And now they've all turned into various kinds of chemists and materialists—"

"A passable chemist is twenty times as useful as any kind of poet," interrupted Bazarov.

"So," said Pavel, barely raising his eyebrows as though he were falling asleep. "You, therefore, don't acknowledge art?"

"Art is just a means of making money, as sure as hemorrhoids exist," Bazarov exclaimed with a contemptuous smile.

"Very well, sir, very well. That's the way you choose

to joke. So you reject all this? Let's assume you do. Does that mean you believe in science alone?"

"I've already informed you that I don't believe in anything; and what is science—science in general? There's science, as there are various trades and occupations; science in general simply doesn't even exist."

"Very well, sir. And what about the other institutions customarily accepted in human society? Do you maintain the same negative attitude towards them?"

"What is this, a cross-examination?" asked Bazarov.

Pavel blanched slightly. Nikolai felt obliged to intervene in the conversation.

"We'll discuss this subject in more detail with you another time, my dear Yevgeny Vassilich. We'll hear your views and express our own. For my part, I'm very glad you're engaged in natural science. I heard that von Liebig* made remarkable discoveries in soil improvement. You could help me with my farming—you could give me some useful advice."

"I'm at your service, Nikolai Petrovich; but Liebig is way beyond us! We have to learn the alphabet before we can start reading, and we don't know the first letter yet."

"Well, you are truly a nihilist, I see," thought Nikolai. "In any case, let me turn to you for assistance from time to time," he said aloud. "And now, Pavel, I suppose it's time for us to go talk to the overseer."

Pavel got up.

"Yes," he said, not looking at anyone, "it's a pity to live in the country for five years, far removed from great minds! Once a fool, always a fool. You try not to forget what was taught you, and then—bang! It seems that's all nonsense, and you're told that clever people aren't concerned with such trifles any more, and that you are really a backward simpleton. What can you do! It's obvious that the young are cleverer than we."

Pavel slowly turned on his heel and slowly went out; Nikolai followed immediately after him.

"Well. Is he always like that?" Bazarov asked Arkady coldly as soon as the door had closed behind the two brothers.

"Listen, Yevgeny, you were too abrupt with him just now," Arkady observed. "You offended him."

"I suppose I should baby them, these provincial aristocrats! It's all self-love, affectation, foppery! With that kind of disposition, he should have pursued his career in St. Petersburg. Anyhow, the devil with them! I found a rather rare example of a water-beetle, *Dytiscus marginatus*—you've heard of it? I'll show it to you."

"I promised I'd tell you his story . . ." Arkady began.

"The beetle's story?"

"No. Enough of that, Yevgeny. My uncle's story. You'll see he's not the sort of person you think he is. He deserves compassion more than ridicule."

"I won't argue that; but why is he so much on your mind?"

"One must be fair, Yevgeny."

"How does that follow?"

"No, listen . . ."

And Arkady told him the story of his uncle. The reader will find it in the following chapter.

vii

Pavel Petrovich Kirsanov, like his younger brother Nikolai, was educated first at home and then in the cadet corps. From childhood on, he was marked by exceptional beauty; he was furthermore self-confident, given to mockery, and had a rather biting wit—one couldn't help liking him. He began to be seen everywhere as soon as he became an officer. Everyone pampered him; he indulged himself and was capricious to the point of folly, but it was not unbecoming in him. Women lost their heads over him and men called him a fop while secretly envying him. As stated previously, he shared an apartment with his

brother, whom he loved sincerely, although they were
very unlike each other. Nikolai limped a little; he had
slight features, pleasant but somewhat melancholy, smallish dark eyes and soft thin hair; he was inclined to laziness and to reading, and was afraid of society. Pavel
never spent a single evening at home; he was renowned
for his fearlessness and skill (he was making gymnastics
fashionable among the worldly young men); the sum
total of his reading was five or six French books. At the
age of twenty-eight, he had already been made a captain;
a brilliant future awaited him. Suddenly everything
changed.

At that time, a woman who still hasn't been forgotten
made occasional appearances in St. Petersburg society—
the Princess R——. She had a well-bred and respectable
but rather stupid husband and no children. She used to
take sudden trips abroad, to return to Russia with equal
suddenness, and generally led a strange life. She was
looked upon as a light-headed coquette. She indulged in
every sort of pleasure with abandon, danced until ready
to fall with exhaustion, and laughed and joked with the
young people she received before supper in a half-darkened parlor, while at night she would cry and pray, finding no peace. Often, wringing her hands in anguish, she
paced restlessly and nervously about her room until daybreak, or sat all pale and cold over her Book of Psalms.
When morning came, she would again be transformed
into a woman of the world and would go out, laugh,
chatter, and throw herself into anything that could afford
her the slightest diversion. She was magnificently propor-
tioned. Her hair, golden and heavy as gold, fell below
her knees. No one, however, would have called her a
beauty. Her only good feature was her eyes, and they
were not really pretty, being rather small and gray—but
their glance was quick and deep, indifferent to the point
of boldness and thoughtful to the point of melancholy—
an enigmatic look. Something strange was reflected in
her eyes even when she was uttering the emptiest gib-
berish. She dressed with great care, and exquisitely.

Pavel met her at a ball, danced a mazurka with her in
the course of which she did not say one sensible word,

and fell passionately in love with her. Accustomed to conquests, here, too, he soon achieved his aim; but the ease of the victory did not cool his ardor. On the contrary, he was still more tortured, still more strongly bound to that woman in whom, even at the moments of irrevocable surrender, everything seemed to remain inviolable and unattainable, some place where no one could intrude. What that soul harbored—God knows. It was as if she were possessed by hidden forces of which she herself was ignorant, which toyed with her as they wished; her limited intellect was unable to contend with their caprices. Her entire behavior posed a series of self-contradictions. The only letters which could have aroused the righteous suspicions of her husbands, she wrote to a man who was almost a stranger to her. Her love was always tinged with sadness. She would stop laughing or joking with the man she had chosen, and would listen to and look at him with doubt. Sometimes, usually suddenly, that doubt changed into cold horror; then her face would take on an aspect of death and violence, and she would shut herself up in her bedroom. The chambermaid, pressing her ear to the keyhole, could hear her smothered sobs. More than once, coming home after a tender meeting, Pavel felt that lacerating and bitter heartbreak of final failure. "What more do I want?" he would reason with himself, but his heart still ached. He gave her a ring with a sphinx engraved on the stone.

"What's that?" she asked. "A sphinx?"

"Yes," he answered, "and that sphinx—is you."

"I?" she asked, and slowly raised her enigmatic eyes to him. "Do you know that that's very flattering?" she added with a faint smile, while her eyes continued to look at him as strangely as ever.

Pavel was oppressed by sadness even when the Princess R—— was in love with him, but when she grew cold towards him—which happened rather quickly—he almost went out of his mind. He was jealous and tormented; he gave her no peace; he ran after her everywhere. She grew tired of his importunate pursuit and went abroad. In spite of the pleas of his friends and the admonitions of his superiors, he resigned and set out after the princess.

He spent four years in foreign lands, sometimes trying to catch up with her, sometimes intentionally losing track of her; he was ashamed of himself and exasperated by his cowardice—but to no avail. Her image, that unfathomable, almost absurd, but fascinating image had become too deeply rooted in his heart. In Baden-Baden he somehow found himself in the same relationship with her as before; it seemed that she had never loved him so passionately—but in a month it was all over: the fire flared for the last time and went out forever. Foreseeing the inevitable break, he wanted at least to remain her friend—as though friendship with such a woman were possible. . . .

She left Baden-Baden quietly and avoided Pavel from then on. He returned to Russia, tried to resume his old life, but found it impossible to fall into his former routine. He wandered from place to place as though bewitched; he still went out; he preserved all the habits of a man of the world; he could boast of two or three new conquests, but he no longer expected anything of himself or of others and made no effort to accomplish anything. He grew old and turned gray. Sitting in his club in the evenings, irascibly bored, engaging apathetically in the quibbles of bachelor society—these things became a necessity for him, a bad sign, as we know. Marriage, of course, never occurred to him.

Ten years went by in this way, colorlessly, fruitlessly and quickly, terribly quickly. There is no place where time runs by as fast as in Russia; in prison, they say, it goes even faster. One evening while having dinner in his club, Pavel learned of the death of Princess R——. She had died in Paris in a condition close to insanity. He got up from the table, walked through the clubrooms for a long time, sometimes stopping as though transfixed near the cardplayers; however, he went home no earlier than usual. After some time, a messenger brought him a package containing the ring he had given the princess. She had drawn the sign of a cross on the sphinx and ordered the messenger to tell him that the cross was the key to the enigma.

This happened in the beginning of 1848, at the same time that Nikolai, having lost his wife, was visiting St.

Petersburg. Pavel had hardly seen his brother since the
latter had settled in the country (the marriage of Nikolai had taken place shortly after Pavel first met the
princess). When he returned home from abroad, Pavel
had gone to visit his brother with the intention of staying for two months or so to enjoy Nikolai's happiness,
but he stayed only one week. The contrast between their
situations was too great. In 1848 this contrast was les-
sened: Nikolai lost his wife and Pavel lost his memories;
after the death of the princess, he tried not to think
about her. But Nikolai still had the feeling of having led
a well-spent life, and the pleasure of watching his son
grow up; Pavel, on the contrary, a lonely bachelor, had
entered that uncertain, twilight time, the time of regrets
resembling hopes and hopes resembling regrets, when
youth is past and old age has not yet begun.

This time was more difficult for Pavel than for anyone
else. Having lost his past, he had lost everything.

"I'm not inviting you to Marino now," Nikolai once
said to him (he had named his estate after his wife). "You
found time heavy on your hands there when my wife was
still alive, and I think you would die of boredom now."

"I was still foolish and restless then," answered Pavel.
"I've become calmer, if not wiser since. Now, if you will
allow me, I'm ready to settle down with you for good."

Instead of answering, Nikolai embraced him; but a
year and a half went by after this conversation before
Pavel decided to carry out his intention. On the other
hand, once he had settled in the country, he never left
it, even during the three winters which Nikolai spent in
St. Petersburg with his son. Pavel started reading, more
and more in English; generally speaking, he arranged his
whole life according to English tastes. He seldom saw
his neighbors and went out only for local meetings,
where he was silent most of the time, except for rare
occasions when he annoyed and frightened the gentry of
the old school with his liberal sallies, while remaining
just as aloof from the representatives of the new generation. Both considered him a snob; both respected him
for his distinguished, aristocratic manners; for the rumors
of his conquests; for the fact that he dressed elegantly

and always stayed in the best room of the best inn; for the fact that he always ate well and had once dined with Wellington at the table of Louis Phillippe; for the fact that he always traveled with a sterling silver dressing case and a portable bath tub; for the fact that he diffused such an unusual, wonderfully "noble" scent; for the fact that he played whist masterfully and always lost; and finally, they also respected him for his irreproachable honesty. The ladies found him a fascinatingly melancholy figure, but he did not seek their company.

"So you see, Yevgeny, how unfairly you criticized my uncle," Arkady said as he finished his story. "And I haven't even mentioned how he rescued my father from calamity more than once and gave him all his money—perhaps you didn't know that the estate wasn't divided between them—anyway, he's glad to help anyone and, among other things, he always defends the peasants. It's true that when he talks to them he wrinkles his nose and sniffs eau de cologne—"

"That's understandable: it's his nerves," Bazarov interrupted.

"Perhaps, but he has a very kind heart. And he is far from stupid. He's given me such good advice—particularly—particularly about women."

"Aha! A burnt child shuns fire. We know that!"

"Well, anyway," Arkady continued, "he's profoundly unhappy, believe me; to scorn him—is sinful."

"Who's scornful?" Bazarov exclaimed. "Just the same, I maintain that a person who stakes his whole life on the card of a woman's love, then withers and sinks to the point of becoming incapable of anything when that card is trumped—a person like that isn't a man, isn't a male. You say he's unhappy; you know best. But he hasn't gotten rid of his folly. I'm sure he seriously considers himself a capable, useful person because he reads that miserable rag *Galignani* and saves a peasant from a flogging once a month."

"Yes, but remember his education, the times in which he lived," Arkady remarked.

Bazarov seized on this. "Education? Every person should educate himself—as I did, for example—and as for the times, why should I be influenced by them? Rather let them be influenced by me. No, brother, that's all spinelessness, emptiness! And what about the mystic relationship between a man and a woman? We physiologists know what constitutes that relationship. Study the anatomy of the eye: where does that—what you call—enigmatic look come from? That's all romanticism, humbug, rot, art. We'd do better to look at the beetle!"

And the two friends went off to Bazarov's room which was already pervaded by a sort of medical-surgical odor mixed with the smell of cheap tobacco.

viii

Pavel was not present long at the conversation between his brother and the overseer, a tall thin man with a soft, consumptive voice and roguish eyes, who replied to all Nikolai's remarks, "If you wish, sir, naturally," and tried to depict the peasants as drunkards and thieves. Put on a new track not long ago, the estate was creaking along like an ungreased wheel, and cracking like roughhewn furniture of raw wood. Nikolai didn't lose heart, but he often sighed and became pensive; he felt the estate would never come through without money, and his money was almost all spent.

What Arkady had said was true: more than once Pavel had helped his brother. More than once, seeing him torturing himself and racking his brains as he tried to figure out how to make ends meet, Pavel had gone slowly to the window, his hand thrust in his pockets, muttered, *"Mais je puis vous donner de l'argent,"** and given him money. That day, however, Pavel had absolutely none left and preferred to absent himself. Housekeeping wrangles distressed him; furthermore, it always seemed to him that in spite of his zeal and industry, Nikolai did not go about his work in the right way, although Pavel would not have been able to point out his errors. "My brother isn't practical enough," he used to say to himself. Nikolai, on the contrary, had a high opinion of Pavel's practicality and always asked his advice. "I am a soft, weak man; I've spent my whole life in the wilds," he would say, "while you haven't spent so much time living with people for nothing; you know them well; you have an eagle eye." In answer to these words, Pavel would just turn aside without protesting.

Leaving Nikolai in his study, he went down the corridor dividing the front part of the house from the rear and, coming to a low door, stopped, considered a moment, tugged at his mustaches, and knocked.

"Who's there? Come in," Fenechka's voice was heard.

"It is I," Pavel answered, opening the door.

Fenechka jumped up from the chair on which she had been sitting with her child, and handing him over to a little girl who immediately whisked him out of the room, hastily straightened her kerchief.

"Forgive me if I am intruding," Pavel began, not looking at her. "I only wanted to ask you . . . it seems that you're sending to town today . . . would you give orders to buy green tea for me?"

"Certainly, sir," Fenechka answered. "How much will you require?"

"About half a pound will do, I suppose. Well, there's been a change here, I see," he added, throwing a quick glance around which also skimmed over Fenechka's face. "There are curtains," he said, seeing that she didn't understand him.

"Yes, sir; there are curtains. Nikolai Petrovich kindly gave them to us. And they've been up a long time."

"And I haven't been to see you in a long time. You have a nice place now."

"Through the kindness of Nikolai Petrovich," whispered Fenechka.

"It's nicer for you here than it was in the cottage, isn't it?" asked Pavel politely but without a trace of a smile.

"Of course it's nicer, sir."

"Who's been put in your old place now?"

"The laundresses."

"Ah."

Pavel fell silent. "Now he'll leave," thought Fenechka; but he didn't leave, and she stood in front of him as if rooted to the spot, lightly twisting her fingers one by one.

"Why did you have your little one taken away?" Pavel finally broke the silence. "I love children; let me see him."

Fenechka blushed deeply with confusion and joy. She was afraid of Pavel Petrovich; he almost never spoke to her.

"Dunyasha," she cried, "would you please bring Mitya." (She addressed everyone in the house formally.) "Oh, wait a moment; he must have a dress put on."

Fenechka went towards the door.

"But it doesn't matter," Pavel said.

"I'll be right back," Fenechka answered and left the room quickly.

Pavel remained alone, and this time he looked around with great care. The smallish, low-ceilinged room in which he found himself was very clean and cosy. It smelled of a freshly painted floor and of camomile and aromatic herbs. Along the wall stood lyre-back chairs bought by the late general in Poland during the campaign; in one corner was a small bed whose high muslin canopy rose beside a round-covered traveling trunk reinforced with forged iron braces. In the opposite corner, an ikon lamp glowed in front of the large, dark image of Saint Nicholas, the miracle-worker; a tiny porcelain Easter egg suspended from his halo on a red ribbon fell to his chest. In the windows stood carefully sealed jars of last year's preserves through which the light shone green; on their paper lids, Fenechka herself had written in large letters: "GOOSEBERRIES"; this preserve was a particular favorite of Nikolai Petrovich's. A birdcage hung from the ceiling on a long cord; the short-tailed greenfinch inside it chirruped and hopped about continually, his cage swinging and shaking, while hemp seeds fell on the floor with light taps. On the wall above a diminutive commode, hung rather bad photographs of Nikolai in various postures, taken by an itinerant artist; there was also a photograph of Fenechka herself which was thoroughly unsuccessful: a sort of eyeless face smiled tensely in a dark frame—nothing more could be distinguished; and above Fenechka, General Yermolov, in a felt cloak, scowled threateningly at the distant Caucasus Mountains from under a little silk pincushion shaped like a shoe which was hung on the wall so that it fell right on his forehead.

Five minutes went by. Rustling and whispering could be heard from the next room. Pavel picked up a dog-eared stray volume of Masalsky's *Streltsy** from the commode and leafed through a few pages. . . . The door opened and in came Fenechka with Mitya in her arms. She had dressed him in a red shirt with a braided collar and had combed his hair and wiped his face; he was breathing noisily, wiggling his whole body, and waving his arms as all healthy children do; but the shirt obviously had an effect on him; an expression of pleasure was reflected in every part of his plump body. Fenechka had put her own hair in order too and arranged her kerchief better, but she could very well have remained as she was. And in truth, is there anything in the world more captivating than a beautiful young mother with a healthy baby in her arms?

"What a butterball," Pavel said indulgently, tickling Mitya's double chin with the tip of the long nail of his index finger.

The child stared at the greenfinch and began to laugh.

"That's Uncle," said Fenechka, bending her head over him and lightly bouncing him, while Dunyasha quietly put a lighted aromatic candle in the window and placed a small coin under it.

"Let's see, how many months old is he?" asked Pavel.

"Six months; soon to be seven, on the eleventh of this month."

"Isn't it eight, Fedosya Nikolayevna?" Dunyasha put in somewhat timidly.

"No, seven. What are you saying!"

The child laughed again, staring at the trunk, and

then suddenly seized his mother's nose and mouth with all five fingers.

"He looks like my brother," Pavel remarked.

"And who should he look like?" thought Fenechka.

"Yes," Pavel continued, as though to himself, "an unmistakable likeness." He looked at Fenechka intently and almost sadly.

"That's Uncle," she repeated in a whisper.

"Ah! Pavel! There you are!" the voice of Nikolai suddenly broke in.

Pavel hurriedly turned around frowning, but his brother was looking at him so joyfully, with such gratitude, that he couldn't help answering with a smile. "That's a fine youngster you have," he said and, looking at his watch, continued, "I dropped in to see about the tea . . ."

Then, assuming an expression of indifference, Pavel promptly left the room.

"Did he stop in on his own?" Nikolai asked Fenechka.

"On his own, sir; knocked and came in."

"Well, and Arkasha hasn't been to see you again?"

"No, he hasn't. Shouldn't I move back to the cottage, Nikolai Petrovich?"

"What for?"

"I think maybe it would be better for the beginning."

"N-no," Nikolai stuttered and rubbed his forehead. "It would have had to be done before. . . . Hello, little balloon," he said with sudden animation and, approaching the child, kissed him on the cheek; then he bent down slightly, putting his lips to Fenechka's hand, white as milk on Mitya's red shirt.

"Nikolai Petrovich! What are you doing?" she stammered and lowered her eyes, then slowly raised them. The expression of her eyes was charming as she looked up smiling fondly and a little foolishly.

Nikolai had met Fenechka in the following fashion. Once, three years ago, he happened to spend the night at a stage-coach inn in a remote provincial capital. He was pleasantly struck by the cleanliness of the room assigned to him, and by the freshness of the bed linen. "The woman who runs the inn must be German," was the thought which crossed his mind. However, she turned out to be Russian; a woman of about fifty, neatly dressed, with a good-looking, intelligent face and sober tongue. He chatted with her at tea and liked her very much. Nikolai had at that time just moved into his new house and, not wanting to keep serfs on his staff, was looking for hired help; the innkeeper, for her part, complained of the small number of travelers in the town and the hard times. He offered her a position as housekeeper; she agreed. Her husband had died long ago, leaving her only one daughter, Fenechka.

A fortnight later, Arina Savishna, as the new housekeeper was called, arrived at Marino with her daughter and settled in the cottage. Nikolai's choice proved to be fortunate. Arina brought order into the house. Fenechka, who was then already seventeen, was never mentioned and only rarely seen. She lived quietly and discreetly, and it was only on Sundays that Nikolai noticed the fine profile of her pale little face somewhere off to the side in the parish church. More than a year went by in this fashion.

One morning Arina appeared in his office and after bowing low as usual, asked him if he wouldn't help her daughter who had gotten a spark from the stove in her eye. Nikolai, like all homebodies, practised medical treatments, and had even ordered a medicine chest of homeopathic drugs. He immediately told Arina to bring the patient. On learning that the master had summoned her, Fenechka was very frightened, but she followed her mother. Nikolai led her to a window and took her head in both hands. After inspecting her reddened and inflamed eye carefully, he prescribed a compress, made the lotion right there himself, and tearing his handkerchief into pieces, showed her how she should bathe her eye. Fenechka listened to all he had to say, then wanted to leave. "Kiss the master's hand, silly," Arina said to her. Nikolai didn't offer her his hand, and in confusion, he himself kissed her bowed head on the hair line.

Fenechka's eye soon recovered, but the impression she had made on Nikolai did not pass quickly. The image of her pure, tender, timidly raised face was constantly before him. He felt her soft hair on the palms of his hands, and saw those innocent, slightly parted lips revealing pearly teeth which shone moistly in the sunlight. He began to watch her attentively in church. He tried to talk to her. At first she shied away from him and once, towards evening, on meeting him on a narrow footpath worn by peasants crossing the fields, she retreated into the thick tall rye, overgrown with wormwood and cornflower, in order to avoid facing him. Seeing her little head through the golden latticework of stalks from which she peered out like a small animal, he called to her affably:

"Hello, Fenechka! I don't bite."

"Good evening," she whispered without moving from her hiding place.

Little by little she began to become accustomed to him, but she was still in the habit of blushing deeply in his presence, when her mother, Arina, suddenly died of cholera. What was to become of Fenechka? She had inherited from her mother good sense, sobriety, and a love of order; but she was so young, so alone. Nikolai was himself so kind and unassuming . . . There's no need to tell the ending . . .

"So my brother just came in like that?" Nikolai asked her. "He knocked and came in?"

"Yes, sir."

"Well, that's good. Let me rock Mitya a while."

And Nikolai began to toss him almost up to the ceiling to the great delight of the little tad and the not inconsiderable concern of his mother, who stretched out her hands towards his bare legs each time he flew up in the air.

Meanwhile, Pavel returned to his elegant study with its walls covered with beautiful grayish wallpaper, with weapons hung over a multicolored Persian carpet, with walnut furniture trimmed in dark green imitation velvet, a renaissance bookcase of old black oak, bronze statuettes on the magnificent writing desk, an open fireplace. He threw himself on the couch, clasped his hands behind his head and remained motionless, looking at the ceiling with an almost desperate expression. Did he want to hide from the very walls what was revealed on his face? Whether for that or for some other reason, he got up, drew the heavy curtains over the windows, and threw himself on the couch again.

ix

That same day, Bazarov also met Fenechka. He was walking with Arkady in the garden and explaining to him why certain trees, particularly the oaks, hadn't taken root well.

"You should plant more silver poplars here . . . yes, and firs, and let's see . . . lindens, after adding some good black soil. The arbor here has done well," he added, "because of the acacias and lilacs—they're good children; they don't demand attention. Hey! There's someone there."

In the arbor sat Fenechka with Dunyasha and Mitya. Bazarov stood by, while Arkady nodded to Fenechka like an old acquaintance.

"Who's she?" Bazarov asked him as soon as they had passed by. "What a pretty girl!"

"Which one do you mean?"

"It's obvious; only one is pretty."

Arkady, with some confusion, explained briefly who Fenechka was.

"Aha!" said Bazarov. "Obviously your father's no fool. I really like your father, aye, aye. He's quite a man. But we must get to know each other," he added, turning back towards the arbor.

"Yevgeny!" Arkady cried after him with alarm. "Be careful, for God's sake!"

"Don't worry," said Bazarov. "We've lived in cities; we've been around."

Approaching Fenechka, he removed his cap.

"Allow me to introduce myself," he began with a polite bow. "I'm a friend of Arkady Nikolayevich and a peaceable man."

Fenechka rose from the bench and looked at him in silence.

"What a beautiful child!" Bazarov continued. "Don't be alarmed, I haven't put the evil eye on anyone yet. What makes his little cheeks so red? Is he cutting teeth?"

"Yes, sir," said Fenechka. "Four teeth have already come through and now his gums have swollen up again."

"Let me see—don't be afraid; I'm a doctor."

Bazarov picked up the child who, to the amazement of Fenechka and Dunyasha, did not resist and was not at all frightened.

"I see, I see. . . . It's nothing. Everything's all right. He'll have plenty of teeth. If anything happens, let me know. And are you in good health yourself?"

"I'm healthy, praise God."

"Praise God—that's the main thing. And you?" he continued, addressing Dunyasha.

Dunyasha, who was prim and proper inside the manor house and boisterous outside the gates, simply snorted in answer.

"Well, fine. Here's your hero."

Fenechka took the baby in her arms.

"How quiet he was with you," she said in a low voice.

"All children are quiet with me," Bazarov answered. "I understand this sort of thing."

"Children know who loves them," Dunyasha remarked.

"That's true," Fenechka agreed. "Take Mitya; he won't let himself be picked up by some people for anything."

"And would he let me?" asked Arkady who, after standing apart for a while, had drawn near the arbor.

He beckoned Mitya towards him, but Mitya threw back his head and squalled, to Fenechka's great embarrassment.

"Another day, when he's had time to get use to me . . ." Arkady said indulgently, and the two friends went away.

"What was her name again?" asked Bazarov.

"Fenechka—Fedosya," Arkady answered.

"And her patronymic? Have to know that too."

"Nikolayevna."

"*Bene*. I like her for not being too embarrassed. Some people might censure that in her. What nonsense! What's there to embarrass her? She's a mother—well, she's right."

"She's right," Arkady observed, "but my father—"

"And he's right too," interrupted Bazarov.

"Well, no; I don't see it that way."

"That's obvious—a superfluous heir isn't to our liking?"

"You should be ashamed to presume I have such thoughts!" Arkady objected heatedly. "I don't consider my father wrong from that point of view; I think he should marry her."

"There, there," said Bazarov calmly. "How magnanimous we are! And you still attach importance to marriage. I didn't expect that of you."

The friends walked a few steps in silence.

"I looked over your father's whole establishment," Bazarov began again. "The cattle are miserable and the horses broken-down. The construction is pretty poor and the workers look like out-and-out loafers. And the overseer is either a fool or a rascal; I haven't gotten to the bottom of it yet."

"You are severe today, Yevgeny Vassilievich!"

"And the good little peasants cheat your father every time. You know the proverb: 'The Russian peasant would gobble up God himself.'"

"I'm beginning to agree with my uncle," Arkady remarked. "You have a decidedly poor opinion of Russians."

"What's the difference! The only good thing about a Russian is that he has a very low opinion of himself. What does matter is that two and two are four—all the rest is nonsense."

"Is nature nonsense too?" Arkady asked, looking pensively at the distant multicolored fields, beautifully and softly lit by the setting sun.

"Nature is nonsense too in the way you understand it. Nature isn't a temple, but a workshop, in which man is a worker."

Just then the lingering tones of a cello floated towards

them from the house. Someone was playing Schubert's *"Die Erwartung"* with feeling, though with an unpractised hand, and the sweet melody diffused honey through the air.

"What's that?" Bazarov asked with amazement.

"That's Father."

"Your father plays the cello?"

"Yes."

"And how old is your father?"

"Forty-four."

Bazarov suddenly burst out laughing.

"Why are you laughing?"

"Good heavens! A man of forty-four, a *pater familias*, living in —— Province, playing the cello!"

Bazarov continued to laugh, but Arkady, much as he venerated his master, did not even smile this time.

x

About two weeks went by. Life at Marino flowed along its usual course: Arkady was self-indulgent, Bazarov was industrious. Everyone in the house had become used to Bazarov, to his careless manners, his rather complex, disjointed way of talking. Fenechka in particular had become so at ease with him that she had him waked at night once when Mitya had convulsions. Bazarov came, as usual half-joking, half-yawning, sat with her for two hours, and calmed her child. On the other hand, Pavel grew to hate Bazarov from the depths of his soul: he considered him an arrogant, insolent, cynical plebian; he suspected that Bazarov did not respect him; that he in fact almost despised him—Pavel Kirsanov! Nikolai was rather afraid of the young "nihilist" and doubted the usefulness of his influence over Arkady, but he

listened to him readily, and readily watched his experiments in physics and chemistry. Bazarov had brought
a microscope with him and fussed with it for hours at a
time. The servants had also become attached to him,
although he made fun of them. They felt nevertheless
that he was a brother rather than a master. Dunyasha
readily giggled with him and used to give him meaning-
ful sidelong looks as she ran past him like a little quail.
Piotr—a man who was self-satisfied and fatuous to an
extreme, his forehead perpetually wrinkled with strain
—a man whose entire merit consisted in the fact that
he had a courteous look, could spell out words, and
cleaned his frock coat with a little brush frequently—
even he smiled and brightened up when Bazarov paid
the slightest attention to him. The houseboys ran after
the "doctor" like little puppies. Old man Prokofich alone
didn't like him. He waited on Bazarov at the table with
a surly expression, called him a "shark" and a "rapscal-
lion," and declared that with his sideburns, Bazarov was
a real pig in the brush. In his own way, Prokofich was
no less an aristocrat than Pavel.

The best days of the year had begun—the first days
of June. The weather remained beautiful; it was true
that cholera was threatening again from afar, but the
inhabitants of —— Province had already become inured
to its visitations. Bazarov used to get up very early
and set out for a mile or two, not to walk—he couldn't
stand purposeless excursions—but to collect grasses and
insects. Sometimes he took Arkady with him. On the way
back an argument usually started in which Arkady was
almost always the loser, although he talked more than
his companion.

One day they dallied rather late. Nikolai went out to
meet them in the garden and, on reaching the arbor,
suddenly heard the quick footsteps and voices of the
two young people. They were passing on the other side
of the arbor where they were unable to see him.

"You don't know Father well enough," said Arkady.
Nikolai stood still.

"Your father's a good fellow," said Bazarov, "but he's
an outdated man; his day is done."

Nikolai pricked up his ears. Arkady did not say anything.

The "outdated man" stood motionless for a few minutes, then slowly trudged home.

"Day before yesterday I noticed that he's reading Pushkin," Bazarov continued in the meantime. "Explain to him, please, that that doesn't lead to anything. After all, he's not a little boy; it's time to throw out that rot. To want to be a romantic in these times! Give him something sensible to read."

"What should one give him?" asked Arkady.

"Oh, I think Büchner's *Stoff und Kraft** to begin with."

"I think so myself," Arkady agreed. "*Stoff und Kraft* is written in a popular style."

"That's the way we are, you and I," Nikolai said after supper that same day to his brother, who was sitting in his study. "We've turned into outdated people; our day is done. Well? Maybe Bazarov's right; but I confess one thing hurts me: I had hoped, particularly at this time, to become very close to Arkady, and it turns out that I've fallen behind, he's gone ahead, and we can't understand each other."

"Well, how has he gone ahead? And in what way does he differ so from us?" cried Pavel impatiently. "That *signor* rammed all that in his head, that nihilist. I loathe that little medical student; in my opinion, he's just a charlatan. I'm sure that with all his frogs he hasn't even gotten very far in physics."

"No, Pavel, you can't say that. Bazarov is intelligent and well-informed."

"And what disgusting egotism!" Pavel interrupted again.

"Yes," Nikolai said, "he's an egotist. But apparently one can't get along without that. Only here's what I can't understand. It seems to me that I do everything possible not to lag behind the times: I've set the peasants up, I've established a farm—I'm even glorified as a *red* throughout the province; I read, I study, and I try to keep up with contemporary demands in general—but they say my

day is done. And you know, brother, I myself am beginning to think that it really is done."

"Why so?"

"Here's why. Today I was sitting, reading Pushkin—I
remember, I had happened across *The Gypsies*. Suddenly
Arkady came up to me and silently, with such tender
compassion on his face, gently took away my book as he
would from a child, and replaced it with another one,
a German one. He smiled and went away, taking Pushkin
with him."

"Well! What sort of book did he give you?"

"This one."

And Nikolai took out of the back pocket of his coat
the celebrated brochure of Büchner in the ninth edition.

Pavel turned it over in his hands.

"Hmm," he muttered. "Arkady Nikolayevich is concerned about your education. So, have you tried reading
it?"

"I've tried."

"Well?"

"Either I'm stupid or it's all rubbish. I must be
stupid."

"You haven't forgotten your German?" asked Pavel.

"I understand German."

Pavel turned the book over in his hands again and
glanced up at his brother. Both were silent.

"Oh, by the way," Nikolai began, apparently wanting
to change the subject, "I received a letter from Kolyazin."

"From Matvei Ilyich?"

"Yes. He came to —— to inspect the province. He's
become a bigwig now, and wrote me that he would like
to see us, his relatives, and he invites you and me and
Arkady to the city."

"Are you going?" asked Pavel.

"No. And you?"

"I won't go either. It's hardly worth dragging one's self
thirty miles to eat pudding. *Mathieu* wants to show himself to us in his full glory; the devil with him! He'll
have the whole province burning incense to him; he'll
get along without ours. A very important personage indeed, a privy councillor. If I had stayed in the service,

remained a slave to that stupidity, I would have been an adjutant-general by now. Besides, you and I are outdated people."

"Yes, Pavel; it's clear it's time to order our coffins and cross our arms on our chests," Nikolai remarked with a sigh.

"Well, I won't give in so quickly," his brother muttered. "We'll still have a skirmish with that would-be doctor; I foresee it."

The skirmish took place that same day at afternoon tea. Pavel came into the parlor already prepared for battle, irritated and determined. He was only waiting for a pretext to fall on his enemy; but for a long time, no pretext presented itself. Bazarov generally spoke little in the presence of the "little old Kirsanovs" (as he called the brothers); that evening he felt out of sorts and drank cup after cup of tea in silence. Pavel burned with impatience; at last his wish was realized.

The conversation had turned to one of the neighboring landowners. "Trash, petty aristocrat," Bazarov, who had met him in St. Petersburg, remarked indifferently.

"Allow me to ask you," Pavel began, his lips quivering, "as you understand them, do the words 'trash' and 'aristocrat' signify one and the same thing?"

"I said: 'petty aristocrat,'" said Bazarov, lazily taking a swallow of tea.

"Exactly, sir; but I assume you have the same opinion of aristocrats as of petty aristocrats. I consider it my duty to make it clear to you that I do not share this opinion. I dare say everyone knows me as a liberal man, devoted to progress; but that's precisely why I respect aristocrats —real ones. Remember, my dear sir" (at these words Bazarov raised his eyes to Pavel) "remember, my dear sir," he repeated with exasperation, "the English aristocrats. They don't yield an iota of their rights, and therefore they respect the rights of others; they demand the fulfillment of obligations towards themselves, and therefore they fulfill their *own* obligations. The aristocracy gave England freedom and sustains it."

"We've heard that tune before," Bazarov objected, "but what do you want to prove by it?"

In his answer, Pavel intentionally mispronounced certain words as he usually did when angry, although he knew such liberties were grammatically incorrect. There was a legacy from the times of Tsar Alexander in that caprice. The bigwigs of those days, on the rare occasions when they spoke their native tongue, made similar distortions as though to say, "We are intrinsically Russian, but we're also great nobles who are permitted to break schoolbook rules."

"I wish to prove by that, my dear sir," said Pavel, "that without a feeling of one's own dignity, without respect for one's self—and these feelings are highly developed in an aristocrat—there is no durable base for the social—*bien public**—for the social structure. Character, my dear sir—that's the main thing; human character should be as firm as a rock, for everything is built on it. I know very well, for example, that you choose to find my habits, my dress, even my neatness ludicrous, but all this comes from a feeling of self-respect, from a feeling of duty, yes, sir, yes, sir, duty. I live in the country, in the wilds, but I don't let myself go; I respect the individual in myself."

"Allow me, Pavel Petrovich," said Bazarov; "you respect yourself and sit with your hands folded; what's useful for the *bien public* in that? You could *not* respect yourself and still do exactly the same thing."

Pavel blanched.

"That's an entirely different question. I'm not at all obliged to explain to you now why I sit with my hands folded, as you choose to put it. I only want to say that aristocracy is—a principle, and that only immoral or hollow people can live without principles in our time. I told Arkady this the day after his arrival, and I'm repeating it to you now. Isn't that so, Nikolai?"

Nikolai nodded.

"Aristocracy, liberalism, progress, principles," Bazarov was saying in the meantime. "Think what foreign—and useless words these are! A Russian doesn't need them for anything."

"And what, in your opinion, does he need? If we listen to you, we find ourselves outside humanity, outside its laws. Good heavens—the logic of history demands—"

"What good's that logic to us? We get along without it."

"How so?"

"Just so. I hope you don't need logic to put a piece of bread in your mouth when you're hungry. These abstractions are way beyond us!"

Pavel threw up his hands.

"I don't understand you after that. You insult the Russian people. I don't understand how it's possible not to acknowledge principles, rules. On what basis can you act then?"

"I told you before, Uncle, that we don't acknowledge authorities," Arkady put in.

"We act on the strength of what we recognize to be useful," said Bazarov. "At present the most useful thing of all is renunciation—we renounce."

"Everything?"

"Everything."

"What? Not only art, poetry—but also—it's terrible to say it . . ."

"Everything," Bazarov repeated with ineffable calm.

Pavel stared at him. He hadn't expected this; Arkady blushed with pleasure.

"But allow me to say," Nikolai put in, "you renounce everything or, to put it more precisely, you destroy everything . . . so it will be necesary to build too."

"That's not our concern. First we have to clear the ground."

"The present state of the people demands it," Arkady added importantly. "We must fulfill those demands. We don't have the right to give in to the gratification of personal egotism."

This last phrase obviously displeased Bazarov; it exuded an aura of philosophy, that is, romanticism (since Bazarov contemptuously called philosophy romanticism); but he did not consider it necessary to contradict his young disciple.

"No! No!" Pavel burst out suddenly. "I don't want to believe that you gentlemen know the Russian people so well; that you are the representatives of its needs, its aspirations! No, the Russian people are not what you imagine. They honor tradition as sacred, they . . . are patriarchal, they can't live without faith . . ."

"I'm not about to argue that," Bazarov interrupted. "I'm even ready to agree that *in this case* you're right."

"Then if I'm right . . ."

"All the same, it doesn't prove anything."

"It just doesn't prove anything," Arkady repeated with the assurance of an experienced chess player who has anticipated a dangerous move on the part of his opponent, and is therefore not at all disconcerted by it.

"What do you mean, it doesn't prove anything?" muttered Pavel, bewildered. "Then you're going against your own people?"

"And what if I am?" exclaimed Bazarov. "The people believe that when thunder crashes, it's the Prophet Elijah riding across the sky in his chariot. Well? Should I agree with them? And moreover—they're Russian; am I not Russian myself?"

"No, you're not a Russian after all you've just said! I can't accept you as a Russian."

"My grandfather plowed the land," Bazarov answered with haughty pride. "Ask any of your peasants which one of us—you or me—he would sooner accept as a compatriot. You don't even know how to talk to him."

"And you talk to him and despise him at the same time."

"What's the difference, if he deserves to be despised! You condemn my point of view, but how do you know it came to me by chance, that it wasn't evoked by that same national spirit whose name you're defending so vigorously?"

"Well now! Nihilists are certainly badly needed."

"Whether they're needed or not isn't for us to decide. You consider yourself not unuseful too."

"Gentlemen, gentlemen, please, no personalities!" Nikolai cried, standing up.

Pavel smiled, and putting his hand on his brother's shoulder, made him sit down again.

"Don't worry," he said. "I won't forget myself, mainly

because of that feeling of dignity which the gentleman—the gentleman doctor makes fun of so mercilessly. Allow me," he continued, turning towards Bazarov again, "perhaps you think your teaching is a novelty? You're deceiving yourself. The materialism you preach has gotten started more than once and has always proved insolvent—"

"Another foreign word!" interrupted Bazarov. He had begun to feel furious and his face took on a sort of harsh copper color. "In the first place, we aren't preaching anything; that's not one of our habits . . ."

"Then what exactly are you doing?"

"I'll tell you what we're doing. Formerly—not very long ago—we used to say that our officials took bribes, that we had no roads, no commerce, no just courts . . ."

"Well, yes, yes, you are denunciators—it seems that's the term for it. I agree with many of your denunciations, but . . ."

"And then it dawned on us that just to talk on and on about our ulcers wasn't worth the trouble and would only lead to mediocrity and doctrinairism. We observed that our wise men, such as the so-called progressive people and denunciators, are good for nothing, that we spend our time on rot, debating so-called art, meaningless creations, parliamentarianism, jurisprudence, and the devil knows what, when it's a question of our daily bread, when we're being choked by the crudest superstitions, when all our businesses are disintegrating apparently only because of a lack of honest people, when the very freedom the government is fussing about would hardly benefit us because our peasant is glad to rob himself solely in order to drink himself into a stupor in the tavern."

"So," interrupted Pavel, "so: you became convinced of all this and decided not to undertake anything seriously yourselves."

"And decided not to undertake anything," Bazarov repeated gruffly. He had become suddenly annoyed with himself; why had he talked so unrestrainedly in front of that squire?

"Just curse everything?"

"And just curse."

"And that's called nihilism?"

"And that's called nihilism," Bazarov repeated again, this time with marked insolence.

Pavel blinked.

"So that's how it is," he said in a strangely calm voice. "Nihilism is supposed to cure all ills, and you are our liberators and heroes. All right. But why do you abuse the others, including even the denunciators? Aren't you merely talking like everyone else?"

"We've other sins, but not that one," Bazarov muttered through his teeth.

"So, then. You do act, is that it? You're preparing to take action?"

Bazarov didn't answer. Pavel shuddered, but immediately got hold of himself.

"Hmmm! . . . To act, to destroy . . ." he continued. "But how can you destroy without even knowing why?"

"We destroy because we are a force," Arkady remarked.

Pavel looked at his nephew and smiled at him.

"Yes, a force—and therefore not accountable," Arkady said, squaring his shoulders.

"Unfortunate creature!" Pavel groaned; he was decidedly no longer able to restrain himself. "As though you've given a thought to *what* you stand for in Russia with your vulgar ideas. No, this would try the patience of an angel! Force! The savage Kalmuck and the Mongol have force—but what good is it to us? Civilization is dear to us, yes, yes, my dear sir; its fruits are dear to us. And don't tell me these fruits are of no consequence. The meanest scribbler, *un barbouilleur*,* a piano player who gets five kopecks an evening—they're more useful than you, because they represent civilization, not a crude Mongol force! You think you're progressive people, but you're only fit for riding in a Kalmuck's cart! Force! Just remember one last thing, forceful gentlemen: that you are only four and a half men, and they—millions, who won't let you trample their sacred beliefs under foot, who will squash you!"

"If they squash us, it will serve us right," Bazarov said.

"But that remains to be seen. We're not so few as you think."

"What? You're seriously thinking of conquering the whole population?"

"A penny candle burned down Moscow, you know," Bazarov answered.

"Yes, yes. An almost satanic arrogance to begin with, then ridicule. There—there's what captivates youth, what subjugates the inexperienced hearts of youngsters. There —look—one of them is sitting next to you; see how he almost worships you; you should be pleased." (Arkady turned away frowning.) "And this plague is already far-spread. I've been told that our artists in Rome never set foot in the Vatican. They almost consider Raphael a fool, just because he's an authority, of course, while they themselves are disgustingly impotent and unsuccessful and their imagination doesn't grasp anything beyond "The Girl at the Fountain," no matter how they try. And that girl is wretchedly painted. In your opinion, they're fine fellows, isn't that true?"

"In my opinion," Bazarov countered, "Raphael's not worth a cent and they're no better than he."

"Bravo! Bravo! Listen, Arkady—that's how young people today should express themselves! When you think of it, how could they fail to follow you! Young people used to have to study. If they didn't want to be considered ignoramuses, they were forced to exert themselves, like it or not. And now all they have to do is say: Everything in the world is rubbish!—and it's in the bag. Young people are delighted. In reality, while they used to be simply blockheads, now they've suddenly become nihilists."

"And your boasted feeling of personal dignity has failed you," Bazarov remarked phlegmatically, while Arkady boiled with anger, his eyes flashing. "Our argument has gone too far. I believe it would be better to break it off. And I'll be ready to agree with you," he added, standing up, "when you give me just one institution in our contemporary existence, in private or public life, which doesn't deserve complete and merciless annihilation."

"I'll give you a million such institutions," cried Pavel, "a million! There's the commune, for example."

Bazarov's lips twisted in a cold smile. "Well, so far as the commune is concerned," he said, "you had better talk to your brother. He seems to have learned through experience what sort of thing a commune is, its sense of mutual responsibility, temperance, and little things like that."

"The family, after all, the family as it is among our peasants!" cried Pavel.

"That question, also, I think you had better not examine too closely. I suppose you've heard a few things about arranged marriages? Listen to me, Pavel Petrovich; give yourself a day or two's time; you could hardly find anything immediately. Think over all our classes of society and consider each one carefully. Meanwhile Arkady and I will—"

"Ridicule everything," Pavel broke in.

"No; cut up frogs. Let's go, Arkady; good-by, gentlemen!"

The two friends left. The brothers remained alone and at first just looked at each other.

"There you are," Pavel finally began; "there's today's youth for you! There they are—our heirs!"

"Our heirs," repeated Nikolai with a dejected sigh. He had sat on tenterhooks throughout the argument and confined himself to surreptitious, hurt glances at Arkady. "You know what I kept thinking of, Pavel? I quarreled with Mother once. She shouted, didn't want to listen to me. I finally told her, 'You really can't understand me; we really belong to two different generations.' She was terribly offended, but I thought: what can one do? It's a bitter pill—but it has to be swallowed. So now our turn has come, and our heirs can say to us: 'You really aren't of our generation—swallow the pill.'"

"You are excessively kind-hearted and modest," Pavel exclaimed. "I, on the contrary, am sure we are much more in the right than those lordlings, although we may express ourselves in a somewhat obsolete language—*vieilli*,* and we don't have such insolent self-confidence. How bombastic young people are today! Ask one of them what kind of wine he would like, red or white. 'I have the habit of preferring red!' he'll answer in a bass voice with as solemn an expression as if the whole world were watching him at that moment."

"Wouldn't you like more tea?" said Fenechka, thrusting her head through the door. She had been undecided about entering the parlor while it resounded with quarreling voices.

"No, you can tell them to take the samovar," Nikolai answered, rising to meet her. Pavel abruptly said *"Bon soir"* to him and went to his study.

xi

A half hour later, Nikolai went into the garden, to his beloved arbor. Sad thoughts had overtaken him. For the first time he was fully conscious of his isolation from his son; he foresaw that it would become greater day by day. So it was in vain that he had spent the winters in St. Petersburg pouring over the latest works for days on end; in vain that he had listened to young people's talk attentively; in vain that he had rejoiced when he succeeded in interjecting his own words in their heated discussions. "My brother says we're right," he thought, "and, all vanity aside, it seems to me too that they're further from the truth than we, but at the same time I feel they have something in back of them we don't have, some kind of advantage over us. . . . Youth? No: it's not just youth alone. Is their advantage the fact that they have fewer traces of feudalism than we?"

Nikolai bowed his head and passed his hand over his face.

"But to repudiate poetry," he thought again, "to have no feeling for art or nature? . . ."

And he looked around as if trying to understand how
anyone could fail to have a feeling for nature. The day
was already turning into evening; the sun was hidden
behind a small grove of aspen lying a quarter of a mile
from the garden; its shadow stretched endlessly through
the motionless fields. A peasant on a little white horse
jogged along a dark, narrow path beside the grove; all
of him was clearly visible, all, to the very patches on his
clothes, although he was passing through the shade; the
legs of the horse twinkled with pleasing precision. The
sun's rays, penetrating the grove from the other side of
the thicket, drenched the trunks of the aspens with such
a warm light that they looked like trunks of fir trees,
and their foliage turned almost azure, while above them
rose a pale blue sky, barely reddened by the sunset.
Swallows flew high overhead; the wind had died completely; a few straggling bees droned lazily and drowsily
in the lilac blossoms; tiny gnats jostled each other in a
column above a single, far-reaching branch. "My God,
how wonderful!" thought Nikolai, and beloved verses
were on the tip of his tongue; he remembered Arkady's
Stoff und Kraft—and fell silent, though he continued to
sit, continued to indulge in the bitter and consoling game
of solitary thoughts. He loved to meditate; country living
had developed this faculty in him. It couldn't be long
ago that he had meditated in this way, watching for his
son at the stage-coach inn, but there had already been
such changes; their relations, then still unclear, had
already become defined—with such consequences! His
late wife appeared to him again, but not the one he had
known over the course of many years, not the kind,
thrifty housewife, but the young girl with the slender
body, innocent searching look, and hair twisted in a
tight braid on her childish neck. He remembered how he
had seen her for the first time. He met her on the stairs
of the apartment building in which he lived, brushed
against her accidentally, turned, wanting to apologize,
and was only able to mutter, "Pardon Monsieur"; and
she bowed her head, smiled, then suddenly, as if she had
been frightened, ran up the stairs; halfway up, she

glanced at him quickly, assumed a serious expression, and blushed. And then came the first shy exchanges, a half-word, a half-smile, and doubt, and sadness, and outbursts, and finally that breathless joy. . . . Where had it all gone so quickly? She had become his wife; he had been happy as few are on earth. . . . "But," he thought, "those first sweet moments—why couldn't one live them for an eternal, immortal life?"

He made no effort to clarify his own thought, but he felt a desire to hold that blissful time with something stronger than memory; he wanted to feel the closeness of his Maria anew, to sense her warmth and breathing; it already seemed to him as if above him . . .

"Nikolai Petrovich," the voice of Fenechka rang out from near by. "Where are you?"

He started. He was neither pained nor ashamed. He didn't even admit the possibility of comparing his wife with Fenechka, but he was sorry she had thought of looking for him. Her voice reminded him at once of his gray hairs, his age, his present . . . The magic world he had just entered, which still arose from the nebulous waves of the past, quivered—and disappeared.

"I'm here," he answered; "I'm coming. Get along!" "There they are, those traces of feudalism," flashed through his head. Fenechka peered silently in the arbor at him and withdrew out of sight.

Meanwhile he noticed with astonishment that night had fallen during his revery. Everything had grown dark and silent, and Fenechka's face had glided in front of him so small and white. He got up to go back to the house, but his heart, stirred by tender thoughts, could not be pacified, and he began to walk slowly around the garden, now looking pensively at his feet, now raising his eyes to the heavens where stars already swarmed and winked at each other. He walked a long time, until he was almost worn out, but his restlessness, a kind of searching, undefined, sorrowful restlessness, still did not subside. Oh, how Bazarov would have laughed at him if he had known what was going on inside him then! Even Arkady would have censured him. He, a forty-four-year-old man, a farmer and a landowner, had tears starting in his eyes, groundless tears; this was a hundred times worse than the cello!

Nikolai continued walking, unable to make up his mind to go into the house, into that peaceful, agreeable nest which looked at him invitingly with all its lighted windows; he did not have the strength to leave the darkness, the garden, the feeling of the fresh breeze on his face, and that sadness, that restlessness. . . .

Pavel met him at a turn in the path.

"What's wrong with you?" he asked Nikolai. "You're pale as a ghost; you're not well; why don't you lie down?"

Nikolai explained his state of mind in a few words and moved away. Pavel walked to the edge of the garden where he, too, fell into thought and also raised his eyes to the heavens. But his beautiful dark eyes reflected nothing but the light of the stars. He was not born a romantic and his elegantly dry and ardent nature with its French misanthropy was incapable of daydreaming.

"You know what?" Bazarov said to Arkady that same night. "A superb idea just occurred to me. Your father said today he'd received an invitation from your illustrious relative. Your father's not going; let's you and me hop over to ———; after all, the gentleman invited you too. You see what fine weather we're having here; we can set off, look over the town, hang around five or six days and that'll be that!"

"But you'll come back here from there?"

"No, I have to go to Father's. He lives twenty miles beyond ———, you know. I haven't seen him in a long time, or Mother either; I have to comfort the old folk. They're good people, particularly Father; he's very amusing. I'm their only child, after all."

"Will you stay with them long?"

"I don't think so. It'll probably be boring."

"But you'll visit us on the way back?"

"I don't know—I'll see. Well, what do you say? Let's go!"

"If you wish," Arkady remarked lazily. He was inwardly delighted with his friend's suggestion, but he considered himself obliged to hide his feeling. He was not a nihilist for nothing.

The following day he left for —— with Bazarov. The young people at Marino were sorry to see them go; Dunyasha even shed a few tears—but the elders breathed more easily.

xii

The town of ——, to which our two friends were headed, was under the jurisdiction of a governor belonging to the younger generation, who was simultaneously a progressive and a despot, as is frequently the case in Russia. During the first year of his administration, he managed to quarrel not only with the leading man in the province—a retired captain of the horse guards, breeder of the best horses and a generous host—but also with his own officials. The disputes which ensued finally acquired such dimensions that the ministry in St. Petersburg found it necessary to dispatch a trusted person with orders to investigate everything on the spot. The higher authorities' choice fell on Matvei Ilyich Kolyazin, the son of that Kolyazin who was once guardian to the Kirsanov brothers. He also belonged to the "younger generation," that is, he had recently turned forty, but he had already set his sights on becoming a high statesman, and wore decorations on either side of his chest. (One, it's true, was foreign and rather insignificant.) Like the governor he had come to pass judgment on, he was considered a progressive and, although already a bigwig, was not like the majority of bigwigs. He had the highest opinion of himself; his vanity knew no bounds, but he behaved simply, listened indulgently, looked approvingly, and laughed so good-naturedly, that at first glance he could almost pass for a good fellow. On important occasions, however, he knew how to, as the saying goes, "make the dust fly." "Energy is vital," he would say then; *"L'énergie est la première qualité d'un homme d'état";** in spite of all this, he was frequently duped and any somewhat experienced official could lead him by the nose. Kolyazin used to speak of Guizot* with great admiration and tried to show everyone in every possible way that he was not one of the routine, outdated bureaucrats, and that there wasn't a single aspect of public life which he failed to pay attention to. All the useful phrases were very familiar to him. He even followed the development of contemporary literature, though with the offhanded haughtiness with which a grown man might join in a procession of small boys met by chance on the street. In essence, Kolyazin was little different from those statesmen of the time of Alexander who used to read a page of Condillac* in the morning in preparation for a reception that evening at Madame Swetchine's* in St. Petersburg; the only difference was that Kolyazin's methods were different, more contemporary. He was an agile courtier, very crafty, and very little else. He was not a good judge of business. He had no intellect, but was capable of managing his own affairs; there, no one could unsaddle him, and that, of course, is the essential thing.

Kolyazin received Arkady with the good nature characteristic of an enlightened dignitary, one might even say with jocularity. However, he was astonished to learn that relatives invited by him had chosen to remain in the country. "Your papa always was a little odd," he remarked, fingering the tassels of his magnificent velvet dressing gown one by one. Then suddenly turning to a young official buttoned up in an exceptionally well-fitting dress uniform, exclaimed with a preoccupied expression, "What?" The young man, whose lips were glued from prolonged silence, arose and looked at his superior with bewilderment—however, having succeeded in disconcerting his subordinate, Kolyazin had already stopped paying attention to him.

Our dignitaries customarily love disconcerting their subordinates; the methods they resort to for the achievement of this aim are rather varied. The following method, among others, is in great vogue, "is quite a favorite," as the English say. The dignitary suddenly stops understanding the simplest words; he has an attack of deafness. For example, he asks:

"What day is today?"

They announce with great deference, "It's Friday today, your Exc-c-c-cellency."

"Eh? What? What's that? What did you say?" the dignitary repeats with great effort.

"Today is Friday, your Exc-c-cellency."

"Which? What? What's Friday? Which Friday?"

"Friday, your Exc-ccc-ccc-cellency, a day of the week."

"Well, well. Are you trying to teach me something?"

Kolyazin was a true dignitary, even though he considered himself a liberal.

"I advise you to go pay a visit to the governor, my friend," he said to Arkady. "You understand that I'm not advising you to do this because I cling to old-fashioned views about the necessity of making a bow to the authorities, but simply because the governor is a fine person; besides, you probably want to meet the local society—you're not a bear, I hope? He's holding a big ball day after tomorrow."

"Will you be at the ball?" asked Arkady.

"He's giving it for me," said Kolyazin, almost regretfully. "Do you dance?"

"I dance, but badly."

"That's a waste. There are some pretty girls here, and it's a shame for a young man not to dance. Again, I'm not saying this on the basis of old-fashioned views; I certainly don't think a man's mind is in his feet, but Byronism is ridiculous—*il a fait son temps*."*

"But, Uncle, it's certainly not because of Byronism that I—"

"I'll introduce you to the ladies here; I'll take you under my wing," Kolyazin interrupted with a complacent laugh. "It'll be cosy for you, eh?"

A servant entered to announce the arrival of the head of the provincial bureau of revenue, a sweet-eyed old man with puckered lips, who had an overweening love for nature, particularly on a summer day when, in his own words, "every little bee takes his little bribe from every little flower." Arkady withdrew.

He found Bazarov in the inn where they were staying, and spent a long time persuading him to call on the governor. "There's no way out!" Bazarov said at last. "We've committed ourselves; we have to go through with it. We came to look at the gentry; let's have a look at them!"

The governor received the young men politely, but neither sat down nor asked them to sit. He was constantly bustling and hurrying; from morning on he wore a close-fitting dress uniform and an extremely tight necktie; he never finished a meal or a drink, and issued orders constantly. Throughout the province he was known by the nickname "Burdal," not after the well-known French preacher Bourdaloue, but after the word *"burda"* (slop). He invited Kirsanov and Bazarov to his ball, then repeated his invitation two minutes later, taking them for brothers and calling them the Kaiserovs.

They were on their way home from the governor's when suddenly, a rather short man wearing a Hungarian hussars' jacket (the mark of a Slavophile)* jumped out of one of the passing cabs. Crying, "Yevgeny Vassilievich!" he threw himself at Bazarov.

"Ah! It's you, Herr Sitnikov," said Bazarov, continuing to walk along the sidewalk. "What brings you here?"

"Just imagine, it's entirely by chance," he answered and, turning back to the cab, waved his hand five or six times, crying: "Follow us, follow us!"

"My father has some business here," he continued, hopping over a gutter, "well, so he asked me . . . I heard about your arrival today and already went to see you . . ." (And in fact, when the friends returned home they found a card with corners turned down with the name Sitnikov in French on one side and Slavonic letters on the other.) "I hope you're not coming from the governor's."

"Don't hope; we just left him."

"Ah! In that case I'll call on him too. Yevgeny Vassilievich, introduce me to your—to—"

"Sitnikov, Kirsanov," Bazarov grunted without slowing down.

"I'm very flattered—" Sitnikov began, walking side-wise, simpering, and hurriedly pulling off his much too elegant gloves. "I've heard a great deal . . . I'm an old acquaintance of Yevgeny Vassilievich, and I might add —a disciple of his. I'm indebted to him for my regeneration."

Arkady looked at Bazarov's disciple. The small but pleasant features of his clean-scrubbed face had a restless and dull-witted expression; smallish deep-set eyes stared fixedly and uneasily, and he laughed uneasily—a sort of short, wooden laugh.

"Would you believe it," he continued, "when Yevgeny Vassilievich first said in front of me that one shouldn't acknowledge authorities, I felt such excitement—it literally opened my eyes! 'There,' I thought, 'finally I've found a man!' By the way, Yevgeny Vassilievich, you absolutely must meet a certain lady here who is completely capable of understanding you and for whom your visit will be a real feast. You've heard of her, I suppose?"

"Who's that?" Bazarov asked reluctantly.

"Kukshina, Eudoxie—Yevdoksiya Kukshina. She is a remarkable nature, *émancipée* in the true sense of the word—a progressive woman. You know what? Let's go see her together now. She lives two steps from here. . . . We'll have lunch there. Look here, you haven't had lunch yet, have you?"

"Not yet."

"Well, that's splendid. You understand, she's separated from her husband. She doesn't depend on anyone."

"Is she pretty?" interrupted Bazarov.

"N—no, you couldn't say that."

"Then why the devil are you asking us to see her?"

"Come, come, silly man—she'll open a bottle of champagne for us."

"So that's it! Now we can see the practical man. By the way, does your father still have the same monopoly?"

"Still the same," Sitnikov said hastily, then laughed. "Well? Shall we go?"

"I don't know, really."

"You wanted to see people; go," Arkady remarked in an undertone.

"And what about you, Mr. Kirsanov?" added Sitnikov. "Please come too; we can't go without you."

"But how can we drop in like that all at once?"

"It doesn't matter; Kukshina's marvelous."

"There'll be a bottle of champagne?" asked Bazarov.

"Three!" cried Sitnikov. "I'll vouch for it!"

"With what?"

"With my own head."

"Your father's purse would be better—but anyway, let's go."

xiii

The rather small town house built in the Moscow manner in which Yevdoksiya Nikitishna Kukshina lived was located on one of the recently burned-out streets of ——; it's common knowledge that our provincial towns burn down every five years. On the door, the handle of a little bell was visible above a crookedly tacked visiting card, and in the entrance hall, the arriving guests were met by a woman in a mobcap who looked like neither servant nor companion—unmistakable signs of the progressive inclinations of the hostess. Sitnikov asked if Yevdoksiya Nikitishna was at home.

"Is that you, Viktor?" a shrill voice rang out from the adjoining room. "Come in."

The woman in the mobcap disappeared immediately.

"I'm not alone," said Sitnikov, adroitly pulling off his Hungarian jacket (under which appeared something on the order of a smock or sack coat), and throwing a sidelong glance at Arkady and Bazarov.

"It doesn't matter," answered the voice. *"Entrez."*

The young people went in. The room in which they

found themselves looked more like a work study than a parlor. Papers, letters, thick issues of Russian magazines, most of them uncut, were scattered on dusty tables; there were discarded cigarette butts littered everywhere. On a leather couch, a woman was half reclining, blond, still young, somewhat disheveled, wearing a rather untidy silk dress, with massive bracelets on her short arms and a lace kerchief on her head. She got up from the couch and, carelessly drawing a velvet cloak with yellowed ermine over her shoulders, said lazily, "Hello, Viktor"—and extended her hand to Sitnikov.

"Bazarov, Kirsanov," he said curtly, in imitation of Bazarov.

"Welcome," answered Kukshina and, fixing Bazarov with her round eyes, between which her tiny, reddened, snub nose glowed forlornly, added, "I know you," then gave him her hand also.

Bazarov frowned. There was nothing unsightly about the small, plain form of this emancipated woman, but her expression had an unpleasant effect on the beholder. One involuntarily wanted to ask her, "What's wrong, are you hungry? Or bored? Or timid? Why are you all bottled up?" As with Sitnikov, something grated on her mind constantly; she spoke and moved very freely and at the same time awkwardly; she evidently considered herself a good-hearted, simple creature, but no matter what she did, it always seemed to be the very thing she particularly didn't want to do; all her actions were done—as children say—on purpose, that is, neither simply nor naturally.

"Yes, yes, I know you, Bazarov," she repeated. (She was given to the habit, peculiar to many provincial and Moscow ladies, of calling a man by his last name immediately after being introduced.) "Would you like a cigar?"

"Cigar or no cigar," put in Sitnikov, who was already sprawling in an armchair with his feet dangling in midair, "but give us some lunch; we're terribly hungry. And tell them to set up a little bottle of champagne for us."

"Sybarite," Yevdoksiya commented and laughed. (When she laughed, her upper gum was bared above her teeth.) "Isn't it true he's a sybarite, Bazarov?"

"I love the comforts of life," Sitnikov pronounced importantly. "That doesn't interfere with my being a liberal."

"No, it interferes, it interferes!" Yevdoksiya exclaimed, but she ordered her maid to see to both lunch and champagne. "What do you think about it?" she added, turning to Bazarov. "I'm sure you share my opinion."

"Well, no," Bazarov demurred. "A piece of meat's better than a piece of bread, even from a chemical standpoint."

"Are you interested in chemistry? It's my passion. I've even invented a putty myself."

"Putty? You?"

"Yes, I. And do you know why? To make dolls, dolls' heads, that won't break. I'm also practical, you see. But all that's not ready yet. I still have to read Liebig. By the way, did you read Kislyakov's article about female labor in the *Moscow News*? Read it, please. Of course you're interested in the feminist question? And schools too? What does your friend do? What's his name?"

Madame Kukshina dropped one question after another with womanish carelessness, not waiting for answers; spoiled children talk that way with their nurses.

"My name is Arkady Nikolayevich Kirsanov," said Arkady, "and I don't do anything."

Yevdoksiya burst out laughing.

"Now that's sweet! What, don't you smoke? Viktor, you know I'm angry with you."

"What for?"

"They say you began praising George Sand again. She's nothing more than an outdated woman! How can she be compared to Emerson! She has no idea of any kind about education, or physiology, or anything. I'm sure she hasn't even heard of embryology, and in our time—how can you do without it?" Yevdoksiya even gesticulated with her hands. "Ah, what a remarkable article Yelisevich wrote on that subject! There's a talented gentleman." (Yevdoksiya always used the word "gentleman" instead of "man.") "Bazarov, sit next to me on the couch. You probably don't realize it, but I'm terribly afraid of you."

"Why so? If I may be curious."

"You're a dangerous gentleman; you're such a critic. Oh, my Lord! It's funny, I'm talking like a sort of back-country landowner. However, I really am a landowner. I manage my estate myself, and just imagine, I have a village elder, Yerofei—a remarkable type, exactly like Cooper's Pathfinder: there's something so undissimulating about him! I've settled here permanently. It's an unbearable town, isn't it? But what can one do?"

"A town's a town," Bazarov remarked coldly.

"Those petty interests all the time, that's what's awful! I used to spend the winters in Moscow—but now my spouse, M'sieu Kukshin, resides there. Well, and Moscow today—I really don't know—really isn't quite the same. I'm thinking of going abroad; last year I was all ready to go."

"To Paris, I suppose?" Bazarov asked.

"To Paris and to Heidelberg."

"Why Heidelberg?"

"Why, Bunsen* lives there, of course."

Bazarov found nothing to say to this.

"Pierre Sapozhnikov . . . You know him?"

"No, I don't."

"Of course you do: Pierre Sapozhnikov—he's still at Lidya Khostatova's all the time."

"I don't know her either."

"Well, he took it on himself to be my escort. Thank God I'm free, I haven't any children . . . What did I say, 'Thank God'? Anyway, it doesn't matter."

Yevdoksiya rolled a cigarette with tobacco-stained fingers, ran her tongue over it, sucked the tip, and began smoking. A maid came in with a tray.

"Ah, here's lunch. Will you have something to eat? Viktor, uncork the bottle; that's your department."

"It's mine, it's mine," Sitnikov muttered, and broke into a squealing laugh again.

"Are there any pretty women here?" asked Bazarov, emptying his third glass.

"There are," Yevdoksiya answered, "but all of them are so empty-headed. For example, *mon amie* Odintsova is not bad. It's a pity her reputation is such a . . . How-

ever, that wouldn't matter, except that she has no freedom of mind at all, no breadth, nothing of that sort. The
whole system of education must be changed. I've already
given that some thought; our women are very poorly
educated."

"You can't do anything with them," Sitnikov put in.
"They deserve contempt. I have contempt for them, completely and utterly!" (The opportunity of having and
expressing contempt was the most pleasurable sensation
possible for Sitnikov; he attacked women in particular,
not suspecting that a few monthe later he would be
cringing before his wife just because she was born Princess Durdolesova.) "Not one of them would be capable of
understanding our conversation; not one of them is
worth being talked about by serious men like us."

"But it's entirely unnecessary for them to understand
our conversation," said Bazarov.

"Whom are you talking about?" interrupted Yevdoksiya.

"About pretty women."

"What? So you share Proudhon's opinion?"

Bazarov drew himself up arrogantly.

"I don't share anyone's opinions; I have my own."

"Down with authorities!" shouted Sitnikov, delighting
in an occasion to express himself sharply in the presence
of the person he fawned on.

"But Macaulay himself—" Kukshina began.

"Down with Macaulay!" thundered Sitnikov. "Are you
defending those sissies?"

"Not the sissies, but women's rights, which I swore to
defend to my last drop of blood."

"Down with them!" But there Sitnikov stopped. "Well,
I'm not denying them," he said.

"No, I see you're a Slavophile!"

"No, I'm not a Slavophile! However, of course—"

"No, no, no! You're a Slavophile. You're a follower of
Domostroi!* You want to have a whip in your hand!"

"A whip is a good thing," Bazarov remarked, "but
we've used up the last drop—"

"Of what?" interrupted Yevdoksiya.

"Of champagne, most respected Avdotya Nikitishna, of champagne—not of your blood."

"I can't listen indifferently when women are attacked," Yevdoksiya continued. "It's awful, awful. Instead of that, instead of attacking them, you'd do better to read Michelet's book, *De l'Amour.** It's a miracle! Gentleman, let's talk about love," Yevdoksiya added, languidly letting her hand drop on the rumpled couch cushion.

A sudden silence fell.

"No, why talk about love?" said Bazarov. "You just mentioned Odintsova—that's her name, I believe? Who is she?"

"An enchantment! An enchantment!" squeaked Sitnikov. "I'll introduce you. Clever, rich, widowed. Unfortunately, she's not sufficiently enlightened; she should get to know our Yevdoksiya better. I drink to your health, Eudoxie! Let's clink glasses! *'Et toc, et toc, et tin-tin-tin! Et toc, et toc, et tin-tin-tin!'* "

"Viktor, you're a rascal."

Lunch lasted a long time. The first bottle of champagne was followed by a second, a third, and even a fourth. Yevdoksiya chattered without stopping; Sitnikov seconded her. They had a long discussion about what marriage is—a prejudice or a crime; and what people are at birth—are they identical or not?—and what constitutes individuality? All this finally led to Yevdoksiya, very flushed from drinking wine, tapping her blunt nails on the keys of the untuned piano, and undertaking a harsh-voiced rendition of gypsy songs, followed by Seymour Schiff's song, "Granada Lies Slumbering," while Sitnikov tied a scarf around his head and acted the swooning lover during the words:

> "And thy lips to mine
> In burning kiss entwine."

Arkady finally couldn't stand it. "Gentlemen, it's begun to sound like bedlam," he remarked aloud.

Bazarov, whose participation in the conversation had been limited to an occasional caustic remark—he was more interested in the champagne—yawned loudly, got up and, without saying good-by to the hostess, went straight out the door with Arkady. Sitnikov bounded after them.

"Well, what did you think? What did you think?" he asked, cringing and running from side to side. "You see, I told you: a remarkable personality! Our women should be more like that. In her way, she's a highly moral phenomenon."

"And that establishment of *thy* father's, is it also a highly moral phenomenon?" said Bazarov, pointing his finger at the tavern they were just then passing.

Sitnikov laughed whiningly again. He was very ashamed of his origin, and didn't know if he should feel flattered or insulted by Bazarov's unexpected use of the familiar "thy."

xiv

Several days later, the ball took place at the governor's residence. Kolyazin was the real hero of the occasion; the provincial leader announced to all and sundry that he had come solely out of admiration for him, while the governor, even at the ball, even while standing motionless, continued to "issue orders." The suavity of Kolyazin's behavior was only equaled by his majesty. He was amiable to everyone—to some with a shade of hypercriticism, to others with a shade of deference; he spread himself before the ladies *"en vrai chevalier français"** and and continually laughed a strong, sonorous and unvarying laugh, appropriate to a dignitary. He patted Arkady on the back and loudly called him his "little nephew," honored Bazarov, clothed in a rather old dress coat, with an absent-minded but indulgent sidelong glance and an unintelligible but affable bellowing, in which the only things which could be deciphered were "I . . ." and "quite, quite"; he extended a finger to Sitnikov and smiled at him while already turning away; even to Kukshina—who appeared at the ball without any crinolines and in dirty gloves, but with a bird of paradise in her hair—even to Kukshina he said: *"Enchanté."* There was an endless swarm of people and no shortage of dancing partners; the civilians, for the most part, crowded along the wall, but the military danced zealously, particularly one of them who had spent six weeks in Paris, where he had learned various bold and daring expressions on the order of *"Zut," "Ah fichtrrre," "Pst, pst, mon bibi,"* etc. He pronounced them to perfection, with a real Parisian chic, but at the same time he said, *"si j'aurais"* instead of *"si j'avais,"** *"absolument"* in the sense of by all means—in brief, he expressed himself in that Great Russian-French dialect which the French make fun of so when not obliged to assure us that we speak their language like angels, *"comme des anges."*

Arkady danced badly, as we already know, while Bazarov didn't dance at all; they both placed themselves in a corner; Sitnikov attached himself to them. Assuming a contemptuous smile and dropping venomous remarks, he looked around impertinently and seemed to be really enjoying himself. Suddenly his face changed, and turning to Arkady, he said as if embarrassed: "Odintsova has arrived."

Arkady looked around and saw a tall woman in a black dress pausing by the entrance to the hall. He was struck by the dignity of her carriage. Her bare arms followed her elegant form gracefully; light sprays of fuschia fell gracefully from her shining hair to her shapely shoulders; calmly and intelligently—calmly and not pensively—her luminous eyes looked out below a somewhat prominent white forehead, and her lips smiled in a barely perceptible smile. Her face radiated a kind, tender strength.

"Do you know her?" Arkady asked Sitnikov.

"Intimately. Do you want me to introduce you?"

"Please do—after this quadrille."

Bazarov also noticed Odintsova.

"What's that?" he said. "It's not like the other hags."

After waiting for the quadrille to end, Sitnikov led Arkady to Odintsova; however, he hardly knew her intimately; he stumbled over his own words, and she looked at him with some astonishment. On the other hand, her expression changed into one of delight when she heard Arkady's last name. She asked him if he were not the son of Nikolai Petrovich.

"Exactly."

"I saw your papa twice and heard a great deal about him," she continued. "I'm very glad to meet you."

At this moment one of the adjutants flew up to her and asked her for a quadrille. She agreed.

"You dance, then?" Arkady asked respectfully.

"I dance. And why did you think I didn't? Or do I seem too old to you?"

"Forgive me, how could you think . . . But in that case, allow me to ask you for a mazurka."

Odintsova smiled at him indulgently.

"If you wish," she said, and looked at Arkady in a way which was not superior, but rather the way a married sister looks at her very young brothers.

Odintsova was not much older than Arkady—she had just turned twenty-eight—but in her presence he felt like a schoolboy, a student, so that the difference in years between them seemed much more significant. Kolyazin approached her with stately bearing and humble speech. Arkady went off to the side, but continued to watch her; he didn't take his eyes off her throughout the quadrille. She chatted with her dancing partner just as freely as she had with the dignitary; her head and eyes moved softly, and she laughed gently a few times. Her nose was a little too broad, like almost all Russian noses, and her complexion was not entirely clear; but despite this, Arkady decided he had never met such an enchanting woman before. The sound of her voice never left his ears; even the folds of her dress seemed to fall differently on her than on others, more gracefully and grandly, and her movements were exceptionally fluid and natural at the same time.

Arkady felt a certain timidity when, at the first strains of the mazurka, he sat down near his partner with the intention of starting a conversation, then just sat running his hand over his hair, unable to find a single word.

But he was not troubled and shy long; Odintsova's calmness communicated itself to him. Before a quarter of an hour had passed, he was talking freely about his father, his uncle, and life in St. Petersburg and the country. Lightly opening and closing her fan, Odintsova listened to him with polite interest. His chatter was interrupted when she was asked to dance; Sitnikov, incidentally, asked her twice. She would return, sit down again, and take up her fan with barely a quickening of her breath, while Arkady would begin to chatter again, filled with happiness to be near her, to talk to her, to look at her eyes, her magnificent forehead, and her whole charming, serious, intelligent face. She herself said little, but her words showed a knowledge of life; through some of her observations, Arkady came to the conclusion that this young woman had already had occasion to experience and reflect a great deal.

"Who was it you were standing with," she asked him, "when Mr. Sitnikov brought you over to me?"

"Did you notice him?" Arkady asked in turn. "Doesn't he have a pleasant face? He's a man called Bazarov—my friend."

Arkady undertook to tell her about "his friend."

He spoke of him in such detail and with such enthusiasm, that Odintsova turned towards him and watched him attentively. In the meantime, the mazurka was nearing its end.

Arkady regretted leaving his lady; he had spent almost an hour with her so delightfully! It's true that he had felt throughout this time as if she were indulging him, but such feelings don't weigh heavily on young hearts.

The music stopped.

"*Merci*," said Odintsova rising. "You promised to visit me—bring your friend with you, too. I shall be most curious to see a person who has the audacity not to believe in anything."

The governor came up to Odintsova, announced that supper was served, and offered her his arm with a preoccupied expression. As she left, she turned to smile and nod to Arkady a last time. He bowed low and followed her with his eyes (How graceful her form, revealed by

the grayish luster of her black dress, seemed to him!).
Thinking, "At this moment she has already forgotten my
existence," he felt a sort of exquisite resignation.

"Well?" Bazarov asked Arkady as soon as the latter had
rejoined him in the corner. "Did you enjoy it? A gentleman was just telling me that that lady—oi-oi-oi! But the
gentleman looks like a fool. Anyway, in your opinion is
she really—oi-oi-oi?"

"I don't quite understand that description," Arkady
answered.

"That's the end! What an innocent!"

"In that case, I don't understand your gentleman.
Odintsova is very nice—indisputably, but she behaves so
severely and coldly that—"

"Still waters—you know!" Bazarov interjected. "You
say she's cold. That's what makes the flavor. You like
ices, don't you?"

"Perhaps," Arkady muttered. "I can't judge that. She
wants to meet you and asked me to bring you to visit
her."

"I can imagine how you described me. However, you
did well. Take me along. Whatever she is, simply the
provincial lioness or an *"émancipée"* on the order of
Kukshina, she still has shoulders the like of which I
haven't seen in a long time."

Bazarov's cynicism jarred Arkady, but—as often happens—he reproached his friend for something unrelated
to the thing which had offended him.

"Why don't you want to let women have freedom of
thought?" he said in a low voice.

"Because, brother, according to what I've observed,
the only women who are free-thinkers are hags."

The conversation broke off at this point. The two
young men left immediately after supper. As they left,
Kukshina laughed after them nervously and maliciously,
though not without timidity. Her vanity was deeply
wounded by the fact that neither had paid any attention
to her. She stayed later at the ball than anyone, and at
four o'clock in the morning, danced a polka-mazurka
with Sitnikov in the Parisian manner. This edifying spectacle brought the gubernatorial festivities to a close.

xv

"Let's see what category of mammals this one belongs to," Bazarov said to Arkady the following day as they climbed the stairs of the hotel in which Odintsova was staying. "My nose tells me that something's not quite right."

"I'm surprised at you!" Arkady exclaimed. "What? You, you, Bazarov, clinging to narrow-minded morals which—"

"What an odd one you are!" Bazarov interrupted carelessly. "Don't you know that in our dialect, between us, 'not all right' means 'all right'? That means it's an advantage. Didn't you yourself say today that she married strangely? While in my opinion, marrying a rich old man is not strange at all, but, on the contrary, very wise. I don't believe the town gossips, but I like to think, as our cultured governor says, that they're justified."

Arkady knocked on the door of the hotel suite without answering. A young servant in livery led the friends into a large room, badly furnished like all rooms in Russian hotels, but decorated with flowers. Odintsova herself soon appeared in a simple morning dress. She seemed even younger in the spring sunlight. Arkady presented Bazarov to her and noticed with hidden amazement that his friend seemed disconcerted, whereas Odintsova remained completely calm, as on the previous day. Bazarov was conscious of being disconcerted and became annoyed with himself. "A fine thing! Scared by a female!" he thought, and sprawling in his armchair in Sitnikov's style, he talked with exaggerated ease, while Odintsova's clear eyes never left him.

Anna Sergeyevna Odintsova was the daughter of Sergei Nikolayevich Loktev, a well-known Adonis, adventurer

and gambler who, after scraping by while making quite
an uproar in Moscow and St. Petersburg for fifteen
years, ended by losing his last cent gambling and being
forced to settle in the country, where he soon died, leaving his tiny estate to his two daughters, Anna—twenty,
and Katerina—twelve. Their mother, of the impover-
ished family of Prince Kh——, had died in St. Petersburg while her husband was still in his prime. The death
of Anna's father left her in a difficult position. The
brilliant education she had received in St. Petersburg
had not prepared her to bear the difficulties of managing
an estate and a household—of living an obscure country
life. She knew absolutely nobody in the entire district
and had no one she could consult. (Her father had tried
to avoid contact with his neighbors; he despised them
and they despised him, each in his own way.) She did
not lose her head, however, and promptly sent for her
mother's spinster sister, Princess Avdotiya Stepanovna
Kh——, a malicious, conceited old woman who, once
settled in her niece's house, took over all the best rooms
for herself, growled and grumbled from morning to night,
and wouldn't even walk in the garden except in the company of her only serf, a surly lackey in a three-cornered
hat and threadbare pea-green livery trimmed in sky-blue.
Anna endured all her aunt's whims with patience, took
care of her sister's education little by little, and seemed
to have become reconciled to the thought of withering
away in the wilds—but fate treated her differently. She
was seen by chance by a certain Odintsov, a very rich
man of forty-six, an eccentric and a hypochondriac,
bloated, ponderous and spiritless, but neither stupid nor
evil; he fell in love with her and proposed; she agreed
to marry him. He lived with her six years and died, leaving her his whole fortune. Anna remained in the country
for about a year after his death; she then set off on a
trip abroad with her sister, but went no farther than Germany, where she became bored and returned to settle
permanently in her pleasant estate, Nikolskoye, about
twenty-five miles from the town of ——. There she
had a magnificent, handsomely appointed house and a
beautiful garden with a greenhouse; the late Odintsov

had denied himself nothing. Anna was very seldom seen in town, usually only on business, and then not for long. She was not liked in the province; there was a terrible outcry at her marriage to Odintsov; every imaginable falsehood was told about her; it was commonly alleged that she had helped her father in his card swindles; it was said that she had not gone abroad for nothing, but because she had to hide certain unfortunate consequences . . . "You understand what I mean?" the indignant gossips would add. "She's been through hell and high water," they said of her; and a well-known provincial wag usually added, "And hot water, too." All these rumors reached her, but she turned a deaf ear; her character was independent and quite resolute.

Odintsova sat leaning back in her chair with her hands clasped, and listened to Bazarov. Contrary to his usual custom, he talked quite a lot and made an obvious effort to interest his listener, to Arkady's renewed astonishment. He couldn't decide whether or not Bazarov was achieving his aim. It was difficult to guess Odintsova's impressions from her face, which retained the same expression throughout—courteous and astute; her magnificent eyes shone with interest, but a passive interest. During the first minutes of his visit, Bazarov's awkwardness affected her unpleasantly, like a bad smell or a sharp sound, but she soon realized that he felt ill at ease, and this even flattered her. Only the banal repelled her, and no one could accuse Bazarov of banality. Arkady constantly had occasion to be surprised that day. He had expected Bazarov to talk to Odintsova as he would to an intelligent woman—about his convictions and opinions; she herself had expressed a desire to listen to a man "who has the audacity not to believe in anything"; but instead of that, Bazarov spoke of medicine, homeopathy and botany. It was apparent that Odintsova had not wasted her time in isolation; she had read some good books and expressed herself in correct Russian. She directed the conversation to music but, on noticing that Bazarov didn't believe in art, tactfully returned to botany, even though Arkady was just starting to talk about the significance of folk melodies. Odintsova continued to treat

Arkady like a younger brother: she seemed to value his goodness and youthful ingenuousness—and only that. The conversation lasted three hours and more, unhurried, varied and lively.

The friends finally got up and started to say good-by. Odintsova looked·at them affably, extended her beautiful white hand to both and, after thinking a moment, said with an indecisive but pleasant smile:

"If you're not afraid of boredom, gentlemen, come visit me in Nikolskoye."

"Heavens, Anna Sergeyevna!" exclaimed Arkady. "I would consider it a great happiness to—"

"And you, M'sieu Bazarov?"

Bazarov merely bowed—and, for the last time, Arkady gave way to astonishment as he noticed his friend was blushing.

"Well?" he said to Bazarov on the street, "do you still think she's—oi-oi-oi?"

"Who can tell! You saw how frozen she is!" Bazarov answered and, after a short silence, added: "She's a duchess, a sovereign individual. All she needs is a train in back and a crown on her head."

"Our duchesses don't speak Russian like that," Arkady observed.

"She's had her ups and downs, brother, and a taste of hard times."

"All the same, she's an enchantment," said Arkady.

"What a generous body!" Bazarov continued. "If it were only in the dissecting room right now."

"Stop that, for the love of God, Yevgeny! That's unspeakable!"

"Well, don't get angry, mollycoddle. That means it's first rate. We must go visit her."

"When?"

"Why not day after tomorrow? What do we have to do here? Drink champagne with Kukshina? Listen to your relative, the liberal dignitary? . . . Let's be off day after tomorrow. By the way, my father's little place is not far from there. Isn't this Nikolskoye on —— Road?"

"Yes."

"*Optime.** There's nothing to wait around for; only

fools wait around—and weaklings. I repeat: a generous body!"

Three days later the two friends were rolling along the road to Nikolskoye. The day was bright and not too hot, and the well-fed stage-coach horses trotted briskly, lightly swinging their twisted, braided tails. Arkady looked at the road and smiled without knowing why himself.

"Congratulate me," Bazarov suddenly exclaimed. "Today is the twenty-second of June, my guardian angel's day. Let's see how he'll take care of me. They're awaiting me at home today," he added, lowering his voice. "Well, they can wait—what does it matter!"

xvi

The estate on which Odintsova lived was located on the open slope of a hill, not far from a yellow stone church with a green roof, white columns and a fresco over the main entrance representing "The Resurrection of Christ" in the "Italian" style. With his rotund contours, the swarthy, helmeted soldier sprawled in the foreground of the fresco was particularly remarkable. Behind the church, a long village stretched in two rows, with chimneys glistening here and there above the thatched roofs. The manor house was built in the same style as the church, the style we call Alexandrian; the house was also painted yellow, and also had a green roof and white columns, over which there was a pediment with a coat of arms. The provincial architect had erected both buildings with the approval of the late Odintsov, who didn't tolerate what he called empty and arbitrary innovations. The dark trees of an old-fashioned garden flanked the house on either side, and an alley of clipped firs led to the entrance.

Our friends were received in the antechamber by two tall footmen in livery, one of whom immediately ran to fetch the major-domo. The major-domo, a fat man in a black dress coat, appeared instantly, and conducted the guests up a carpeted staircase to a guest room where two beds had been prepared and all the necessary toiletries laid out. Order clearly reigned in the house; everything was clean; everywhere there was a respectable smell like that found in ministerial reception rooms.

"Anna Sergeyevna requests you come to her in half an hour," the major-domo announced. "Will you have any instructions in the meantime?"

"No instructions, most venerable one," Bazarov answered, "unless you will have the kindness to bring a little glass of vodka."

"Certainly, sir," the major-domo said, not without bewilderment, and went away with squeaking boots.

"What *granzhanr!*"* Bazarov remarked. "Isn't that what you people call it? She's a duchess, and fully one."

"A fine duchess," exclaimed Arkady, "inviting such great aristocrats as you and I to visit her at first sight."

"Particularly me, a future country doctor and an army doctor's son, and a deacon's grandson. You know, don't you, that I'm the grandson of a deacon? Like Speransky," Bazarov added, twisting his lips, after a brief silence. "But just the same, she's been pampering herself; she's really been pampering herself, this noblewoman! Maybe this even calls for dress coats?"

Arkady simply shrugged his shoulders—but he also felt slightly disconcerted.

Half an hour later, Bazarov and Arkady went down into the parlor. It was a spacious, high-ceilinged room, furnished luxuriously enough, but with no particular taste. Heavy, expensive furniture stood in the usual stiff order along walls covered with brown, gold-patterned wallpaper; the late Odintsov had ordered it from Moscow through his friend and purchasing agent, a wine merchant. Over the main couch hung a portrait of a flabby blond man who seemed to look at the guests in an unfriendly way. "That must be *he*," whispered Bazarov to Arkady and, wrinkling his nose, added, "Shall we bolt?"

But at that moment the hostess entered. She wore a light soft wool dress; her hair, combed smoothly behind her ears, gave her clear fresh face a girlish look.

"I'm grateful to you for keeping your promise," she began. "You must stay a while with me. It's really not bad here. I'll introduce you to my sister; she plays the piano very well. It doesn't matter to you, M'sieu Bazarov, but I believe you, M'sieu Kirsanov, are fond of music. Besides my sister, I have an old aunt living with me; there is one neighbor who sometimes comes to play cards: that's our whole society. And now let's sit down."

Odintsova delivered this little speech with marked precision as if she had memorized it; then she turned to Arkady. It appeared that Odintsova's mother had known Arkady's mother and had even been her confidante in her love for Nikolai Petrovich. Arkady started talking about his mother with great warmth, while Bazarov began leafing through albums. "What a milksop I've become," Bazarov thought to himself.

A handsome greyhound with a sky-blue collar ran into the parlor, nails tapping on the floor. Right behind came a girl of eighteen, black-haired and dark, with a rather round but pleasant face and small dark eyes. She held a basket full of flowers in her arms.

"Here's my Katya," said Odintsova, nodding in her direction. Katya made a little curtsey, placed herself next to her sister, and started to sort the flowers. Wagging its tail, the greyhound, whose name was Fifi, went up to the guests and thrust her cold nose into the hands of each in turn.

"Did you pick all those yourself?" Odintsova asked.

"Yes," Katya answered.

"And is Auntie coming to tea?"

"Yes."

When Katya spoke, she smiled very charmingly, timidly and candidly, and looked up and down in a rather amusingly stern way. Everything about her was still young and green: her voice, the down on her face, her rosy hands with white-circled palms, her slightly pinched shoulders. She blushed continually and breathed quickly.

Odintsova turned to Bazarov.

"You're looking at pictures out of politeness, Yevgeny Vassilich," she began. "That can't interest you. Move closer to us instead, and let's argue about something."

Bazarov came closer.

"What subject do you command?" he asked.

"Whatever you like. I warn you I'm a dreadfrul arguer."

"You?"

"I. That seems to surprise you. Why?"

"Because, as far as I can judge, you have a calm, cool disposition, and arguments require enthusiasm."

"How could you possibly get to know me so quickly? In the first place, I'm impatient and stubborn—just ask Katya. And in the second place, I am very easily aroused."

Bazarov looked at Odintsova.

"Perhaps—you know best. So, you want to argue—as you wish. I was looking at views of Saxon Switzerland in your album when you remarked that that couldn't interest me. You said that because you assume I don't have any artistic appreciation—and I actually don't have any; but those pictures could interest me from the standpoint of geology, the standpoint of the formation of the mountains, for example."

"Excuse me; as a geologist you would be more likely to turn to a book or a specialized work than a sketch."

"A sketch tells me as much in a glance as a dozen pages of print."

Odintsova was silent a moment.

"And so you haven't a single drop of artistic appreciation?" she said, leaning her elbows on the table and in the same movement bringing her face closer to Bazarov. "How do you get along without it?"

"And what's it needed for, if I may ask?"

"Well, to at least be able to study and understand people."

Bazarov laughed.

"In the first place, that's what life experience is for; and in the second place, if I may say so, studying individual personalities isn't worth the trouble. All people resemble each other in mind as in body; each of us has a brain, a spleen, a heart, lungs—identical in form; and the so-called moral qualities are one and the same for all: slight modifications are of no consequence. One human specimen is sufficient for judging all the rest. People are trees in a forest; no botanist would study every individual birch tree."

Katya, who was leisurely sorting her flowers one by one, looked up at Bazarov with bewilderment; on meeting his quick, careless glance, she flamed red to the tips of her ears. Odintsova shook her head.

"Trees in a forest," she repeated. "Then in your opinion, there's no difference between stupid and intelligent people, between good and evil?"

"No, there is; just as there is between the sick and the healthy. The consumptive's lungs are not in the same condition as yours and mine, although identical in form. We know approximately what produces bodily diseases, while moral sicknesses are produced by bad education, by all the nonsense with which people's heads are crammed from infancy on—by the outrageous state of society, in brief. Reform society and there will be no sicknesses."

While Bazarov said all this, he looked as if he were simultaneously saying to himself: "Believe me or not; it's all the same to me!" He stroked his sideburns leisurely with his long fingers, and his eyes flicked from corner to corner.

"Then you assume," said Odintsova, "that when society is reformed, there will be no stupid or evil people?"

"At least, in a correctly organized society, it will be of absolutely no importance whether a man is stupid or intelligent, good or evil."

"Yes, I understand; everyone will have one and the same spleen."

"Exactly, Madame."

Odintsova turned to Arkady.

"And what is your opinion, Arkady Nikolayevich?"

"I agree with Yevgeny," he answered.

Katya glanced up at him without raising her head.

"You amaze me, gentlemen," said Odintsova, "but we'll talk about it further. However, just now I hear Auntie coming to tea; we must spare her ears."

In came Odintsova's aunt, Princess Kh——, a thin little woman with a face squeezed into a fist and malevolent eyes, immobile under a gray wig. Barely bowing to the guests, she lowered herself into a wide velvet armchair in which no one but her had the right to sit. Katya put a footstool under her feet; the old woman neither looked at her nor thanked her, just fluttered her hands under the yellow shawl covering almost all of her emaciated body. The princess loved yellow; her mobcap also had bright yellow ribbons.

"How was your nap, Auntie?" asked Odintsova, raising her voice.

"That dog in here again," the old woman grumbled in answer, and, noticing that Fifi had taken two uncertain steps in her direction, cried, "Scat, scat"

Katya called Fifi and opened the door for her.

Fifi rushed out joyfully in expectation of being taken for a walk; but, on being left alone outside the door, began to scratch and whine. The princess frowned; Katya wanted to go out . . .

"Tea's ready, I believe," said Odintsova. "Come, gentlemen; Auntie, please come to tea."

The princess silently got up from her chair and preceded everyone out of the parlor. They all followed her into the dining room. A young page in livery noisily drew back from the table another equally inviolable armchair, covered with cushions, into which the princess lowered herself; Katya, pouring tea, served her first in a cup embellished with a coat of arms. The old woman put honey in her cup (she found drinking tea with sugar both sinful and expensive, although she didn't spend a kopeck for anything herself), then suddenly asked in a croaking voice:

"And what does Prince Ivan write?"

No one answered her. Bazarov and Arkady soon gathered that no one paid any attention to her although everyone treated her with respect.

"For the sake of her prestige, because she's of princely birth," thought Bazarov. After tea, Odintsova suggested going for a walk, but it had begun to drizzle, and the whole company, with the exception of the princess, returned to the parlor. The neighbor arrived, an enthusiastic cardplayer named Porfiry Platonich, a rotund, gray little man with short spindlelegs, very polite and jocular. Odintsova, who was conversing with Bazarov more and more, asked him if he would not like to pit himself against them in an old-fashioned game of preference. Bazarov agreed, saying he ought to prepare himself in advance for his duties as a country doctor.

"Be on your guard," Odintsova remarked; "Porfiry Platonich and I will beat you. And you, Katya," she added, "play something for Arkady Nikolayevich; he loves music; we'll listen too."

Katya went to the piano unwillingly; and although he did love music, Arkady followed her unwillingly: he felt Odintsova was dismissing him. As in every young man of his age, a rather uneasy, oppressive feeling, which resembled a foreshadowing of love, churned inside his heart. Katya raised the piano lid. Without looking at Arkady, she whispered:

"What should I play you?"

"Whatever you want," Arkady answered indifferently.

"What music do you like best?" Katya repeated, not moving.

"Classical," Arkady answered in the same voice.

"You like Mozart?"

"I like Mozart."

Katya took out the C-Minor Fantasy Sonata of Mozart. She played well, although a little severely and drily. Not lifting her eyes from the notes, and firmly compressing her lips, she sat motionless and upright, and it was only at the end of the sonata that her face flushed and a small lock of hair which had become loosened fell on her dark forehead.

Arkady was particularly struck by the last part of the sonata, that part in which the captivating gaiety of a carefree melody is suddenly pierced by outbursts of sad, almost tragic sorrow. But the thoughts evoked in him by the sounds of Mozart were not related to Katya. Looking at her, he merely thought: "Well, this young lady doesn't play badly, and she's not bad-looking either."

On finishing the sonata, before even lifting her hands

from the keyboard, Katya said, "Enough?" Arkady declared he could not impose on her further and started talking to her about Mozart. He asked her, had she chosen that sonata herself or had someone recommended it to her? But Katya answered him in monosyllables. She hid, withdrew inside herself. Whenever this happened to her, she was slow to come out again, and an obstinate, almost dull-witted expression came over her face. She was not so much timid as distrustful, and a little frightened of the sister who had brought her up and who, naturally, never suspected this. In order to appear at ease, Arkady was reduced to calling over Fifi (who had come back in), and stroking her head with a benevolent smile. Katya busied herself with her flowers again.

Meanwhile Bazarov lost round after round. Odintsova played cards masterfully, and Porfiry Platonich was also able to hold his own. Bazarov sustained a loss which, although insignificant, was still not altogether pleasurable for him. At supper Odintsova again directed the conversation to botany.

"Let's take a walk tomorrow morning," she said to him. "I want you to teach me the Latin names of field plants and their properties."

"What do you need Latin names for?" asked Bazarov.

"One must have order in everything."

"What a marvelous woman Anna Sergeyevna is!" Arkady exclaimed when he was alone with his friend in their allotted room.

"Yes," Bazarov answered, "a female with a brain. Well, she's seen some sights."

"How do you mean that, Yevgeny Vassilich?"

"The good way, the good one, Arkady Nikolaich, old man! I'm sure she runs her estate very well, too. But the marvel—is not she, but her sister."

"What? That little dark thing?"

"Yes, that little dark thing. That one's fresh, and untouched, and skittish, and silent, and anything you want. There's someone worthy of interest. You could make whatever you wanted out of her, but the other one—is an old crust of bread."

Arkady did not answer Bazarov, and each went to bed with his private thoughts in his head.

Odintsova was thinking about her guests that night too. She liked Bazarov—liked his lack of affectation and the very sharpness of his opinions. She saw in him something new which she had not happened to meet before, and she was curious.

Odintsova was a rather strange being. Not having any prejudices whatsoever, and not even having any strong convictions, she neither shrank from anything nor sought anything. She had seen many things clearly, many things had interested her, and nothing had satisfied her fully; she even hardly desired full satisfaction. Her mind was inquisitive and indifferent at the same time; her doubts never dwindled, and never grew into anxiety. Had she not been rich and independent, perhaps she would have thrown herself into the fray, would have known passion. But living was easy for her, though she was bored at times, and she continued to go along from day to day, unhurried and only rarely disturbed. She sometimes saw the shimmer of rainbows before her eyes, but she felt relieved when they faded, and did not regret them. Her imagination was at times carried beyond the limits of what is considered permissible by common moral standards, but even then her blood continued to flow as calmly as ever in her poised, tranquil body. Sometimes, coming out of a scented bath, all warm and relaxed, she would become lost in daydreams about the nothingness of life, about its grief, toil and evil. . . . Her soul would fill with sudden daring and boil with noble aspirations; then a little draft would blow through the half-open window, and she would shrink back, complaining, almost angry, and feeling only one immediate need: for that nasty breeze not to blow on her.

Like all women who fail to fall in love, she wanted something without knowing exactly what herself. Essentially she did not long for anything, but it seemed to her that she longed for everything. She had been barely able to stand the late Odintsov (she had married him calculatingly, although she probably would not have agreed to become his wife if she had not considered him a kind person), and she had acquired an inner aversion towards all men, whom she never thought of other than as slovenly, heavy and slothful, impotently tiresome beings. Once, somewhere abroad, she had met a handsome young Swede with a noble expression and honest blue eyes under a high forehead; he had made a strong impression on her, but it hadn't prevented her from returning to Russia.

"A strange man, that medical student!" she thought, lying in her magnificent bed on lace pillows under a light silk cover. Odintsova had inherited a bit of her father's taste for luxury. She had loved her sinful but kind father deeply, and he had idolized her, joked affably with her as with an equal, trusted her fully, and sought her advice. Her mother she barely remembered.

"Strange, that medic!" she repeated to herself. She stretched, smiled, threw her hands behind her head, ran her eyes over a few pages of a foolish French novel, dropped the book—and fell asleep, all clean and cold in clean, fragrant linens.

Immediately after breakfast the following morning, Odintsova went botanizing with Bazarov and returned just before dinner; Arkady went nowhere and spent about an hour with Katya. He was not bored with her; she offered to repeat the sonata of yesterday evening for him herself, but when Odintsova returned at last, when he caught sight of her—his heart turned over. She was walking through the garden with a somewhat tired gait; her cheeks were rosy and her eyes sparkled more brightly than usual under her straw picture hat. She was twisting the thin stem of a field flower in her fingers; her light mantilla had slipped down to her elbows, and the wide gray ribbons of her hat clung to her bosom. Bazarov followed her, self-confident and careless as always, but his expression, although gay and even tender, displeased Arkady. Muttering "Good morning!" Bazarov went off towards his room, while Odintsova shook Arkady's hand absent-mindedly and also went on past him.

"Good morning . . ." thought Arkady. "As if we hadn't seen each other today."

xvii

Time, as is well known, flies at times like a bird, at times crawls like a worm; but a man is particularly blessed when he doesn't even notice whether its passing is quick or slow. Arkady and Bazarov spent two weeks at Odintsova's in exactly that state. The order she had established in her house and her life contributed to that, in part. She adhered to it strictly and compelled others to submit to it. Everything in the course of the day happened at a certain time. In the morning, punctually at eight o'clock, the whole company gathered for breakfast; between breakfast and dinner, each did as he pleased; the hostess was busy with the housekeeper, the major-domo and the overseer (the estate was on the tenant system). Before supper, the whole company reassembled for conversation or reading; the evening was devoted to walking, cards and music; at half-past ten, Odintsova went to her room, gave orders for the following day and went to bed. Bazarov did not like this measured, somewhat solemn precision in daily life; "running on rails," he called it. Liveried footmen and punctilious major-domos offended his democratic feelings. He felt that carried this far, it was logical to dine in the English style in tails and white ties. He once explained his views on this to Odintsova.

Her behavior was such that anyone could speak his mind before her without fear of reproach. She heard him through, then said: "From your point of view, you're right, and perhaps, in this case I'm—an aristocrat; but one can't live in the country without order; boredom would win out";—and she continued to do things her own way. Bazarov grumbled, but both he and Arkady found living effortless at Odintsova's because of the fact that everything in her house "ran on rails." With all this, a change took place in both young people from the very first days of their stay at Nikolskoye. Bazarov, whom Odintsova obviously favored, although she rarely agreed with him, began to show a hitherto unprecedented anxiety. He was easily irritated, spoke unwillingly, looked angry, and was as unable to sit in one place, as though he were literally being swept away in a tide.

Meanwhile Arkady, who had finally decided within himself that he was in love with Odintsova, began to give way to a gentle melancholy. This melancholy, however, did not prevent him from becoming better acquainted with Katya; it even helped him to enter into a tender, friendly relationship with her. "*She* doesn't appreciate me! So be it! . . . But at least this kind creature doesn't reject me," he thought, and his heart again savored the sweetness of elevated sentiments. Katya vaguely understood that he was seeking a kind of consolation in her company, and denied neither him nor herself the innocent pleasure of a half-timid, half-trusting friendship. In the presence of Odintsova, they did not talk to each other; Katya always shrank under the keen eye of her sister, while Arkady, as becomes a man in love, was unable to pay attention to anything else when near the object of his affections; on the other hand, he found it pleasant alone with Katya. He felt he lacked the power to interest Odintsova; he was timid and at a loss when left alone with her, and she did not know what to say to him—he was too young for her. But with Katya, Arkady was at home. He treated her condescendingly and did not inhibit her in expressing the impressions aroused in her by music, reading stories, verses and other nonsense—without noticing or confessing to himself that such nonsense interested him too.

For her part, Katya did not intrude on his melancholy. Arkady found it pleasant with Katya, Odintsova with Bazarov, and therefore it usually happened, particularly during their walks, that the two couples went their separate ways after being together for a short while. Katya *adored* nature, and Arkady loved it, but was afraid to admit it; Odintsova was fairly indifferent to it, as was

Bazarov. The almost continual separation of our friends was not without consequences; the relations between them began to change. Bazarov stopped talking to Arkady about Odintsova, and even stopped criticizing her for her "aristocratic ways"; it is true that he praised Katya as before and that his only advice was to keep her sentimental tendencies in check, but his praise was hasty, his advice unfeeling, and in general he talked to Arkady much less than before—he seemed to avoid him, as if ashamed of him.

Arkady observed all this, but kept his observations to himself.

The true cause of all these changes was the feeling inspired in Bazarov by Odintsova, a feeling which tortured and maddened him, and which he would have immediately denied with contemptuous laughter and cynical abuse if anyone had even remotely hinted to him of the possibility of what was happening inside him. Bazarov was a great connoisseur of women and of feminine beauty, but love in the ideal or, as he put it, the romantic sense, he called tomfoolery and inexcusable idiocy; he considered chivalry a sort of deformity or disease, and more than once expressed his astonishment that Toggenburg and all the minnesingers and troubadors had not been put in the nut house. "If a woman pleases you," he used to say, "try to get to the point; if that's impossible, well—too bad; turn your back—you're not at the end of your rope." Odintsova pleased him. The wide-spread rumors about her, her freedom and independence of mind, her definite inclination towards him —everything, it seemed, spoke in his favor; but he soon understood that he would not "get to the point" with her, and to his amazement, he lacked the strength to turn his back on her. His blood caught fire at just the thought of her; he could have easily subdued his blood, but there was something else taking root inside him—something he did not tolerate at all, which he had always jeered at, and which aroused all his pride. In conversations with Odintsova, he expressed his cool contempt for all romanticism more strongly than ever; but when alone, he recognized the romantic in himself with indignation.

Then he would head for the woods and walk through
them with long strides, breaking fallen branches and
softly cursing her and himself; or else he would climb in
the hayloft in the barn and, obstinately shutting his
eyes, make an effort to sleep in which, of course, he
was not always successful. He would suddenly imagine
those chaste hands twining around his neck one day,
those proud lips responding to his kiss, those intelligent
eyes tenderly—yes, tenderly dwelling on his, and his
head would swim and he would forget himself for an
instant before boiling with indignation again. He caught
himself in all sorts of "shameful" thoughts, as if a devil
were mocking him. It sometimes seemed to him that
there was a change in Odintsova too, that something
special appeared in her face, that perhaps . . . But at
this point he usually stamped his feet or ground his
teeth and shook his fist at himself.

Bazarov was not entirely mistaken. He had struck
Odintsova's imagination; he interested her; she thought
about him a great deal. In his absence, she was neither
bored nor expectant, but his appearance immediately
enlivened her; she enjoyed being alone with him and
enjoyed talking to him, even when he angered her or
offended her taste, her exquisite ways. She seemed to
want to try him and test herself.

Once, walking with her in the garden, he suddenly
said in a gruff voice that he intended to leave soon for
his father's village. She blanched as though something
had stung her heart; stung so hard that she was amazed
and wondered for a long time what it could mean.
Bazarov had not announced his departure to her with
the thought of testing her to see what came of it; he never
"fabricated." That morning he had seen his father's
overseer, Timofeich, who had taken care of him when
he was a child. This Timofeich, a seasoned, lively old
man with faded yellow hair, weathered red face and tiny
teardrops in shriveled eyes, unexpectedly appeared before Bazarov in his tarred boots, and short jacket of
thick gray-blue broadcloth, belted with a leather thong.

"Ah! Good morning, old man!" exclaimed Bazarov.

"Good morning, young master, Yevgeny Vassilich," began the old man with a joyful smile which suddenly covered his whole face with wrinkles.

"What brings you here? They sent you after me, eh?"

"Please, young master, how can you say that!" stammered Timofeich (he remembered the strict orders he had received from his master on leaving). "We were going to town on estate business and heard about your grace, and so we looked in on our way, that is—to see your grace—and naturally we wouldn't dare bother you."

"Come, don't lie," Bazarov interrupted him. "Is this the road you take to town?"

Timofeich faltered and didn't answer.

"Is Father well?"

"Thank God, sir."

"Mother too?"

"Arina Vlassevna too, praise the Lord."

"They're awaiting me, I suppose?"

The old man tilted his tiny head sidewise. "As God is my witness, it breaks my heart just looking at your parents."

"Well, all right, all right! Don't describe it. Tell them I'll be along soon."

"Certainly, sir," Timofeich answered with a sigh.

Leaving the house, he pulled his cap over his eyes with both hands, clambered up into the battered droshky he had left at the gates, and went off at a slow trot, but not in the direction of town.

The evening of that same day, Odintsova sat in her study with Bazarov while Arkady strolled up and down the drawing-room and listened to Katya play. The princess had gone upstairs to her own room; she could not stand guests in general, and these "new poppycocks," as she called them, she found particularly unbearable. She was merely sulky in the front rooms, while in her own, in the presence of her chambermaid, she sometimes broke into such abuse that her mobcap bobbed on her head, wig and all. Odintsova was aware of all this.

"How can you be about to leave?" Odintsova began. "What about your promise?"

Bazarov gave a start. "What promise, Madame?"

"You've forgotten? You were going to give me a few lessons in chemistry."

"What can I do? Father's waiting for me; I can't dawdle any longer. However, you can read Pélouse et Frémy's *Notions Générales de Chimie*; a good book and clearly written. You'll find everything you need in it."

"But remember, you told me a book can never replace . . . I've forgotten how you put it, but you know what I mean—remember?"

"What can I do!" repeated Bazarov.

"Why go?" said Odintsova, lowering her voice.

He glanced at her. She leaned her head on the back of the armchair and crossed her arms, bare to the elbows. She looked pale in the light of the solitary lamp covered with a perforated paper shade. A full white dress enveloped her in its soft folds; the tips of her feet, also crossed, were barely visible.

"And why stay?" answered Bazarov.

Odintsova turned her head slightly.

"What do you mean, why? Aren't you enjoying yourself at my house? Or do you think that you won't be missed here?"

"I'm convinced of that."

Odintsova was silent a moment.

"You're wrong to think so. However, I don't believe you. You couldn't have said that seriously." Bazarov continued to sit motionless. "Yevgeny Vassilievich, why are you so silent?"

"Well, what should I say to you? People are generally not worth missing, to say nothing of me."

"Why is that?"

"I'm a staid man, uninteresting. I can't talk."

"You're fishing for compliments, Yevgeny Vassilievich."

"That's not one of my habits. You know, don't you, that the gracious side of life is out of reach for me, the side you value so much?"

Odintsova bit a corner of her handkerchief.

"Think what you like, but I'll be bored when you leave."

"Arkady will remain," Bazarov remarked.

Odintsova shrugged her shoulder slightly.

"I'll be bored," she repeated.

"Truly? In any case, you won't be bored long."

"Why do you think so?"

"Because you yourself told me that you're only bored when your routine is broken. You've arranged your life with such infallible precision that there can't be any room in it for boredom, or longing—or any gloomy feelings."

"And you conclude that I'm infallible—that is, that I've arranged my life so precisely?"

"Definitely! Here's an example: in a few minutes it will strike ten, and I know in advance that you'll turn me out."

"No, I won't turn you out, Yevgeny Vassilievich. You may stay. Open the window—I am stifling."

Bazarov stood up and gave the window a shove. It flew open at once with a crash. He hadn't expected it to open so easily; furthermore, his hands were shaking. The dark, soft night looked into the room with its almost black sky, gently rustling trees and fresh smell of pure open air.

"Lower the blind and sit down," said Odintsova. "I want to chat with you before you leave. Tell me something about yourself; you never speak of yourself."

"I try to talk about useful things to you, Anna Sergeyevna."

"You're very modest. But I'd like to know something about you, about your family, about your father, for whom you're abandoning us."

"Why does she use those words?" Bazarov wondered.

"None of that's the least bit interesting," he said aloud, "particularly for you; we're obscure people . . ."

"And I, in your opinion, am an aristocrat?"

Bazarov raised his eyes to Odintsova.

"Yes," he said with exaggerated sharpness.

She smiled at him.

"I see you know me very little, although you maintain that all people are alike and not worth the trouble of studying. I'll tell you my life story sometime—but you first tell me yours."

"I know you very little," Bazarov repeated. "Perhaps you're right; perhaps, in fact, every person is an enigma. Take you, for example: you avoid company, you're depressed by it, yet you invited two students to stay with you. Why do you, with your intelligence and your beauty, live in the country?"

"What? How did you put that?" Odintsova interrupted vivaciously. "With my—beauty?"

Bazarov frowned.

"That's unimportant," he muttered; "I just meant I don't exactly understand why you settled in the country."

"You don't understand it. . . . But you have some sort of explanation for it?"

"Yes—I suppose you always stay in one place because you pamper yourself, because you love comfort, ease, and are quite indifferent to anything else."

Odintsova smiled again.

"You definitely refuse to believe that I'm capable of being carried away by my feelings?"

Bazarov looked up at her.

"By curiosity—perhaps. Nothing else."

"Truly? Well, now I understand why we were drawn to each other; you see, you're like me."

"Drawn to each other . . ." Bazarov said dully.

"Yes! . . . I'd forgotten you want to go away."

Bazarov got up. The lamp burned dimly in the middle of the darkened, fragrant, isolated room; through the occasionally fluttering blind poured the provocative freshness of the night, and its mysterious whispering was audible; Odintsova didn't move a finger, but a covert restlessness gradually enveloped her. It communicated itself to Bazarov. He suddenly became conscious of being alone with a beautiful young woman. . . .

"Where are you going?" she said slowly.

Not answering, he let himself down in a chair.

"So, you consider me a calm, weak, coddled creature," she continued in the same voice without taking her eyes from the window. "But I know this much about myself: I am very unhappy."

"You unhappy! Why? You don't attach any importance to vile gossip, do you?"

Odintsova frowned. It annoyed her that he had understood her in that way.

"That gossip doesn't even amuse me, Yevgeny Vassilievich, and I'm too proud to allow it to bother me. I'm unhappy because—because I have no desire, no will to live. You look at me suspiciously; you're thinking: there speaks an 'aristocrat' all in lace and sitting on a velvet chair. I won't hide it: I love what you call comfort, but at the same time I have little desire to live. Reconcile that contradiction as best you can. But that's all romanticism in your eyes."

Bazarov shook his head.

"You're healthy, independent, rich; what else is there? What do you want?"

"What do I want?" Odintsova repeated and sighed. "I'm very tired, I'm old; it seems to me I've lived a very long time. Yes, I'm old," she added, gently pulling the edges of the lace dress over her bare arms. Her eyes met Bazarov's and she blushed imperceptibly. "I already have so many memories behind me; life in St. Petersburg, wealth, then poverty, then the death of my father, marriage, the usual trip abroad . . . many memories, and nothing to remember, and in the future before me—a long, long road and no goal—and I've no desire to go on."

"Are you so disenchanted?" asked Bazarov.

"No," Odintsova replied with deliberation, "but I'm not satisfied. I believe if I could attach myself to something strongly—"

"You want to fall in love," Bazarov interrupted her, "and you can't fall in love: there lies your unhappiness."

Odintsova began to examine the sleeve of her dress.

"Can't I fall in love?" she said.

"Hardly! Only I was wrong to call that unhappiness. On the contrary, the victim of that joke is more deserving of pity."

"Victim of what?"

"Falling in love."

"And how do you know that?"

"By hearsay," Bazarov answered angrily. "You're playing the coquette," he thought; "you're bored and teasing me for lack of anything to do, while I . . ." His heart felt torn.

"In addition, you're perhaps too demanding," he added, leaning his whole body forward and playing with the fringe of the armchair.

"Perhaps. For me it's all or nothing. A life for a life. Take mine, give up yours, and without regret or turning back. Otherwise it's better to have nothing."

"Well?" Bazarov observed. "Those are fair terms, and I'm surprised that you haven't yet—found what you wanted."

"But do you think it's easy to surrender yourself completely to anything whatsoever?"

"Not easy if you start to deliberate and be on your guard, and put a price on yourself, value yourself, that is; but if you don't deliberate, it's very easy to surrender."

"How can one not value one's self? If I have no price, who needs my devotion?"

"It's not up to me; it's up to someone else to determine my price. The main thing is to be able to surrender."

Odintsova raised herself from the back of the armchair.

"You talk," she began, "as though you had experienced all that."

"It came out by chance, Anna Sergeyevna; all that, you know, isn't my specialty."

"But you would be able to surrender?"

"I don't know; I don't want to brag."

Odintsova said nothing; Bazarov fell silent too. The sounds of a piano floated in to them from the parlor.

"How late Katya is playing," Odintsova remarked.

Bazarov stood up.

"Yes, it really is late now; it's time for you to rest."

"Wait a moment; where are you going so fast? I have something to say to you."

"What?"

"Wait a moment," whispered Odintsova.

Her eyes were fixed on Bazarov; she appeared to be observing him intently.

He walked up and down the room, then suddenly approaching her, hurriedly said, "Good-by," squeezed her hand so that she almost cried out, and left the room abruptly. She lifted her crushed fingers to her lips, blew on them, and suddenly rising impetuously from her chair, went to the door with quick steps as if she wanted to call Bazarov back. . . . A chambermaid came into the room with a decanter on a silver tray. Odintsova stopped, ordered her to leave, sat down again, and again lost herself in thought. Her hair unwound and fell like a dark snake on her shoulder. The lamp remained burning a long time in Odintsova's room, and she was motionless a long time, except for occasionally running her fingers over her arms, which ached a little from the cold of the night.

And Bazarov returned to his room two hours later, disheveled and morose, his boots wet with dew. He found Arkady at the desk with a book in his hands, his frock coat buttoned up to his neck.

"You haven't gone to bed yet?" he asked as if displeased.

"You sat with Anna Sergeyevna a long time today," said Arkady, ignoring his question.

"Yes, I sat with her the whole time you were playing the piano with Katerina Sergeyevna."

"I wasn't playing . . ." Arkady began, then fell silent. He felt tears starting in his eyes, but he did not want to cry in front of his sardonic friend.

xviii

When Odintsova appeared for breakfast the following day, Bazarov sat bent over his cup for a long time, then suddenly glanced at her. She turned towards him as if he had bumped against her, and it seemed to him that her face had become slightly paler overnight. She soon went off to her room and reappeared only at dinner. The weather had been rainy since morning, and there was no possibility of taking a walk. The whole company gathered in the parlor. Arkady got the latest issue of a review and began reading. The princess, in her usual way, first looked amazed, as though he had devised something indecent, then stared at him malevolently, but he paid no attention to her.

"Yevgeny Vassilievich," Odintsova said, "let's go to my study. I want to ask you . . . You mentioned a certain textbook yesterday . . ."

She got up and went towards the door. The princess looked around with an expression which seemed to say: "Look, look, how astonished I am!"—and stared at Arkady again, but he raised his eyes, exchanged glances with Katya, who was sitting beside him, and continued reading.

Odintsova went to her study with quick steps. Bazarov promptly followed her without raising his eyes and only catching with his ears the thin swish and rustle of the silk dress gliding in front of him. Odintsova sank down in the very same armchair she had sat in the night before; Bazarov also resumed his position of yesterday.

"What was that book called?" she began after a brief silence.

"Pélouse et Frémy, *Notions Générales*," Bazarov answered. "However, may I also recommend to you Ganot's *Traité Elémentaire de Physique Expérimentale?* The illustrations in that book are more precise, and on the whole it . . ."

Odintsova stretched out her hand.

"Yevgeny Vassilich, forgive me, but I didn't ask you here to discuss textbooks. I wanted to renew our conversation of yesterday. You left so suddenly . . . You won't be bored?"

"I am at your service, Anna Sergeyevna. But what was it we were chatting about yesterday?"

Odintsova threw a sidelong glance at Bazarov.

"We were discussing happiness, I believe. I talked to you about myself. By the way, I mentioned the word

'happiness.' Tell me why, even when we're enjoying
something like, for example, music, a pleasant evening,
a conversation with congenial people, why does all that
seem more like a hint of some immeasurable happiness
somewhere rather than actual happiness, that is, the
kind we're experiencing ourselves? Why is that? Or perhaps you never feel anything similar?"

"You know the proverb: The grass is greener on the
other side of the fence," Bazarov replied. "Furthermore,
it was you who said yesterday that you weren't contented.
Such thoughts simply never enter my head."

"Perhaps you find them ridiculous?"

"No, but they don't enter my head."

"Really? You know, I should very much like to know
what *you* think about?"

"What? I don't understand you."

"Listen, I have wanted to speak plainly with you for
a long time. You don't have to be told—you know this
yourself—that you're not an ordinary person; you're still
young—your whole life lies before you. What are you
preparing yourself for? What future awaits you? I mean
—what aims do you want to reach, where are you going,
what's in your heart? In a word, who are you, what are
you?"

"You surprise me, Anna Sergeyevna. You know I'm
engaged in natural science, while who I am . . ."

"Yes, who are you?"

"I've already told you that I'm a future country doctor."

Anna Sergeyevna gestured impatiently.

"Why do you say that? You don't believe it yourself.
Arkady could answer me that way, but not you."

"And how would Arkady—"

"Stop it! Is it possible you'd be satisfied with such a
humble occupation, and aren't you always protesting
yourself that so far as you're concerned, medicine doesn't
even exist? You—with your ambition—a country doctor!
You're giving me that kind of answer to brush me off
because you don't have any confidence in me. But,
Yevgeny Vassilich, you should know that I'm capable of
understanding you: I myself was poor and ambitious

like you; perhaps I went through the very same trials as you."

"That's all very fine, Anna Sergeyevna, but you must excuse me. I'm not generally accustomed to expressing my feelings, and there is such a distance between us. . . ."

"What distance? Are you telling me I'm an aristocrat again? Enough, Yevgeny Vassilich; I thought I had proved to you—"

"But besides that," Bazarov broke in, "what urge is there to think and talk about the future, which for the most part doesn't depend on us? Should an opportunity come along to do something—fine; if not—at least one has the satisfaction of not having jabbered for nothing beforehand."

"You call a friendly conversation jabbering. . . . Or, perhaps, you don't consider me, being a woman, worthy of your confidence? Of course, you despise us all!"

"You I don't despise, Anna Sergeyevna, and you know it."

"No, I know nothing—but let's assume it; I understand your unwillingness to talk about your future occupation; but what's happening inside you now . . ."

"Happening!" repeated Bazarov. "As if I were a kind of state or society! In any case, it's not at all interesting; and besides, can a person always say out loud everything that's 'happening' inside him?"

"I don't see why one can't say everything one has on one's mind."

"Can *you?*" asked Bazarov.

"I can," answered Anna Sergeyevna after a brief hesitation.

Bazarov bowed his head.

"You're happier than I."

Anna Sergeyevna looked at him questioningly.

"As you wish," she continued, "but something tells me all the same that we weren't drawn together for nothing, that we shall be good friends. I'm certain your, how can I say it, your tenseness, reserve, will disappear in the end."

"So you've noticed reserve in me—and as you also said —tenseness?"

"Yes."

Bazarov rose and went to the window.

"And you would like to know the reason for this reserve, you would like to know what's happening inside me?"

"Yes," repeated Odintsova with a kind of fear she was not yet able to understand.

"And you won't get angry?"

"No."

"No?" Bazarov was standing with his back towards her. "Then know that I love you, foolishly, madly. . . . There's what you elicited!"

Odintsova stretched out both hands, but Bazarov leaned his forehead against the windowpane. He was gasping; his whole body was visibly trembling. But it was not the trembling of youthful timidity, not the sweet dismay of the first confession of love which had overcome him; it was passion struggling inside him, strong and tragic—a passion resembling hatred, and perhaps related to it. Odintsova felt both fear and pity for him.

"Yevgeny Vassilich . . ." she said, and an involuntary strain of tenderness came into her voice.

He turned around quickly, threw a rapacious glance at her—and seizing both her hands, suddenly drew her to his chest.

She did not free herself from his embrace immediately; but in an instant she was standing, looking at Bazarov from a remote corner. He rushed towards her. . . .

"You misunderstood me," she whispered with sudden fear. It seemed as though if he took another step she would scream. Bazarov bit his lips and left.

Half an hour later, a maid gave Odintsova a note from Bazarov; it consisted of only one line: "Should I leave today—or may I stay till tomorrow?" "Why go? I didn't understand you—you misunderstood me," Odintsova answered, thinking: I didn't understand myself either.

She did not appear until supper, and walked back and forth in her room incessantly, her hands behind her back, stopping from time to time, first in front of the window, then in front of the mirror, and slowly bringing her handkerchief to her neck where she still seemed to feel a warm spot. She asked herself what had made her "elicit"

—to use Bazarov's expression—his frankness: whether
she had suspected something . . . "I'm guilty," she said
aloud, "but I couldn't have foreseen this." She reflected
and blushed, remembering the almost savage face of
Bazarov when he threw himself at her. "Or?" she suddenly said, stopping and shaking back her curls. . . . She
caught sight of herself in the mirror; her head thrown
back with a mysterious smile on half-closed, half-opened
eyes and lips seemed in that second to tell her something
which disconcerted her. . . .

"No," she decided at last, "God knows where that
would lead; one mustn't trifle with that; peace is still the
best thing in the world."

Her peace was not shaken; however, she remained depressed and even began crying once, not knowing why
herself, but not from having suffered an insult. She did
not feel insulted; she was closer to feeling guilty. Under
the influence of various confused sensations, the consciousness of life passing by, the desire for novelty—she
made herself go up to a certain limit, made herself look
beyond it, and saw there not an abyss, but emptiness—or
ugliness.

xix

No matter how self-controlled she was, and how much
above conventionality, Odintsova felt awkward when she
appeared in the dining room for dinner. Nevertheless, it
went off fairly satisfactorily. Porfiry Platonich came and
told a number of anecdotes; he had just been to town.
Among other things, he reported that the governor,
Burdal, had ordered his officials to wear spurs on special
assignments in case he had to dispatch them on horseback
for greater speed. Arkady talked with Katya in a low

voice and attended to the princess diplomatically. Bazarov maintained a stubborn, surly silence. Twice Odintsova looked—not furtively, but directly at his face, stern, bilious, with lowered eyes and the imprint of disdainful determination in every trait—and she thought to herself: No . . . No . . . No . . .

After dinner she accompanied the whole group into the garden, then seeing that Bazarov wanted to talk to her, took a few steps to one side and stopped. He came near her but did not raise his eyes as he said dully, "I have to apologize to you, Anna Sergeyevna. You must be furious with me."

"No, I'm not angry with you, Yevgeny Vassilievich," Odintsova answered, "but I'm saddened."

"So much the worse. In any case, I'm sufficiently punished. My position, as you probably agree, is most stupid. You wrote me: Why go? But I couldn't and wouldn't want to stay. Tomorrow I'll be gone."

"Yevgeny Vassilich, why are you . . ."

"Why am I going?"

"No, that's not what I meant to say."

"You can't change the past, Anna Sergeyevna—and sooner or later it was bound to happen. Consequently, I must leave. I can conceive of only one condition under which I could stay, but this condition will never be. It's true, isn't it—forgive my impertinence—you don't love me and you won't ever love me?"

Bazarov's eyes flared briefly under his dark eyebrows. Odintsova didn't answer him. "I'm afraid of this man," flashed through her head.

"Farewell, Madame," Bazarov said as if guessing her thought, and went towards the house.

Slowly following him, Odintsova called Katya and took her arm. She did not leave Katya's side until evening. She played cards without stopping and laughed more and more often, which seemed incongruous with her pale agitated face. Puzzled, Arkady watched her as young people do, that is, constantly asking himself: what could it possibly mean? Bazarov shut himself up in his room; he returned, however, for tea. Odintsova felt like saying a kind word to him, but didn't know how to approach him. An unexpected event took her out of her quandry: the major-domo announced the arrival of Sitnikov.

It is hard to put into words the young progressive's quail-like flight into the room. Having decided with his characteristic effrontery to go to the country to visit a woman he hardly knew, who had never invited him, but at whose house, he had gathered, such clever and close friends of his were staying, he was nevertheless completely overcome by timidity. As a result, instead of giving the apologies and greetings he had prepared in advance, he muttered some idiocy: Yevdoksiya, said he, Kukshina, had sent him to inquire about Anna Sergeyevna's health, and Arkady Nikolayevich also always spoke to him with the highest possible praise . . . At this word he stammered and became so confused that he sat on his own hat. However, as no one turned him out, and as Odintsova went so far as to introduce him to her aunt and her sister, he soon recovered and began chatting for all he was worth. The appearance of mediocrity is often salutary in life; it relaxes excessively high-pitched strings and sobers overly self-confident or self-forgetful feelings by a reminder of its close affinity with them. With the arrival of Sitnikov, everything became duller, emptier—and simpler; everyone even ate more heartily at supper and went off to bed a half hour earlier than usual.

Lying down on his bed, Arkady told Bazarov, who was undressing, "Now I can repeat to you what you once said to me: 'Why are you so sad? Verily, have you just performed some holy obligation?'"

The two young people had fallen some time ago into a kind of falsely smooth banter which is always a sign of hidden discontent or unspoken suspicions.

"I'm off to see the old man tomorrow," said Bazarov.

Arkady raised himself and leaned on his elbow. He was both surprised and, for some reason, delighted.

"Ah!" he commented. "And is that why you're sad?"

Bazarov yawned. "If you know too much you'll grow old."

"And what about Anna Sergeyevna?" Arkady continued.

"What about Anna Sergeyevna?"

"I mean, will she let you go?"

"I'm not in her employ."

Arkady sank into thought; Bazarov lay down, turning his face to the wall. Several minutes went by in silence.

"Yevgeny!" Arkady exclaimed suddenly.

"Well?"

"I'm leaving with you tomorrow, too."

Bazarov didn't answer.

"Only I'll go home," Arkady continued. "We'll go to Khokhlovsky village together, and you can take horses from Fedot there. I'd be very happy to meet your family, but I'm afraid of getting in their way and yours. You'll come back to us again afterwards, won't you?"

"I left all my things at your place," Bazarov answered without turning over.

"Why doesn't he ask me why I'm going? And just as suddenly as he?" thought Arkady. "In fact, why am I going and why is he going?" he continued his reflections. He was unable to answer his own question satisfactorily; something bitter swelled up in his heart. He felt it would be hard to part with this life to which he had become so accustomed, but to stay on alone was somehow strange. "Something happened between them," he decided to himself. "Why should I hang around here after his departure? I'll end by boring her to death; I'll lose what little remains." He began to picture Odintsova to himself; then another face gradually overshadowed the beautiful countenance of the young widow. "I'm sorry about Katya too," Arkady whispered in his pillow, onto which a tear had already fallen. He suddenly tossed his hair and said aloud, "Why the devil did that fool Sitnikov show up?"

Bazarov at first just stirred in bed, then made the following pronouncement:

"Brother, you're still stupid, I see. Sitnikovs are essential to us. I—understand this—I need half-wits like that. After all, it's not for God to scorch the kettle."

"Aha!" Arkady thought to himself, and just then the bottomless pit of Bazarov's egotism suddenly opened before him. "I suppose you and I are gods? That is—you're a god and the half-wit is me, eh?"

"Yes," Bazarov repeated gruffly. "You're still stupid."

Odintsova showed no particular surprise when Arkady told her the next day that he was leaving with Bazarov; she seemed absent-minded and tired. Katya looked at him silently and seriously; the princess crossed herself under her shawl in such a way that he could not avoid noticing it; on the other hand, Sitnikov was utterly alarmed. He had just come down to breakfast in new finery, this time not in Slavophile attire; the night before, he had amazed the servant assigned him with the quantity of linen he had brought—and suddenly his comrades were deserting him! He shuffled his feet slightly, cast about like a hunted rabbit on the edge of a forest—then suddenly, almost fearfully, almost shouting, he announced that he also intended to leave. Odintsova did not try to detain him.

"I have a very smooth-riding buggy," the unhappy young man added, turning to Arkady. "I can take you, and Yevgeny Vassilich can ride in your coach; it will be more convenient that way."

"But really, it's not on your road at all, and it's a long way to my place."

"That's nothing, nothing; I have lots of time; besides I have business over there."

"Your father's monopoly?" asked Arkady a bit too contemptuously.

But Sitnikov was in such despair that he didn't even laugh as usual.

"I assure you, the buggy is exceptionally smooth," he muttered, "and there'll be room for everyone."

"Don't hurt M'sieu Sitnikov's feelings by refusing," Odintsova said.

Arkady glanced at her and nodded significantly.

The guests left after breakfast. Saying good-by to Bazarov, Odintsova held out her hand to him and said, "We'll see each other again, won't we?"

"As you command," Bazarov answered.

"In that case, we'll see each other."

Arkady went out on the steps first. He climbed up into Sitnikov's buggy. The major-domo settled him in the buggy deferentially; Arkady could have struck him with pleasure or burst into tears with equal ease. Bazarov took his place in the coach.

On reaching Khokhlovsky village, Arkady waited while Fedot, the hostler, changed the horses; then going up to the coach, said to Bazarov with his old smile, "Yevgeny, take me along; I want to go with you."

"Sit down," Bazarov muttered through his teeth.

Sitnikov, who was whistling vivaciously, strolling around the wheels of his carriage, simply gaped on hearing these words, while Arkady coolly took his things out of Sitnikov's buggy, sat down next to Bazarov—and bowing politely to his former traveling companion, cried, "Move on!" The coach rolled off and was quickly lost from sight. Sitnikov, completely discomfited, glanced at his coachman, who was unconcernedly flicking his whip over the off horse. Then Sitnikov leaped into the buggy— and thundering at two passing peasants, "Put on your caps, you fools!" drove slowly into town, where he arrived very late and where, the following day at Kukshina's the two "repulsive snobs and boors" came in for strong abuse.

On sitting down beside Bazarov, Arkady squeezed his hand firmly and said nothing for a long time. Bazarov seemed to understand and appreciate this gesture and silence. He had not slept at all the night before, had not smoked, and had eaten practically nothing for several days. His emaciated profile, gloomy and harsh, jutted out under the cap pulled over his eyes.

"Well, brother," he said at last, "let's have a cigar. . . . Look, is my tongue yellow?"

"It's yellow," Arkady answered.

"I thought so—besides that, the cigar doesn't taste. The machine has fallen apart."

"You really have changed lately," Arkady remarked.

"It doesn't matter! We'll straighten out. There's one annoying thing—my mother's so soft-hearted: if you don't grow a fat belly and eat ten times a day, she has a fit. Father's all right, he's been around himself, he's been through the mill. No, smoking's no good," he added, flinging the cigar in the dust of the road.

"Is it fifteen miles to your estate?" asked Arkady.

"Yes, fifteen. Here, ask that wise man." Bazarov pointed to Fedot's groom, who was sitting on the coach box. But the wise man answered that "for all one could tell, miles weren't measured thereabouts," and continued to abuse the shaft horse in an undertone for "kicking her top," that is, "tossing her head."

"Yes, yes," said Bazarov, "there's a lesson for you, my young friend, an instructive example. It's a fine kettle of fish! Every man hangs by a thread, the abyss can open up under him any minute, but he still devises all sorts of unpleasantness for himself and ruins his own life."

"What are you hinting at?" asked Arkady.

"I'm not hinting at anything. I'm saying outright that you and I both behaved foolishly. What's the point of talking about it! Although I've noticed in the wards that the man who gets angry at his pain always overcomes it."

"I don't quite understand you," Arkady said; "it didn't look as though you had anything to complain about."

"If you don't quite understand me, let me tell you this: in my opinion, it's better to split rocks on the road than to allow a woman to take possession of so much as the tip of your finger. It's all," Bazarov was about to use his favorite word, "romanticism," but restrained himself and said, "rubbish. You won't believe me now, but let me tell you, you and I fell into feminine society and found it pleasant, but brushing such society aside is just like dousing yourself with cold water on a hot day. Men don't have time for such nonsense; a man should be fierce, as the excellent Spanish proverb says. Look here, you," he added, turning to the peasant on the coach box, "you, smart fellow, do you have a wife?"

The peasant turned his dull, mole-eyed face towards the friends.

"A wife, eh? Sure. How else?"

"Do you beat her?"

"The wife, eh? Anything can happen. But not without reason."

"Fine. And does she beat you?"

The peasant yanked on the reins. "That's a good one, sir. You're all for jokes." He was obviously offended.

"Do you hear that, Arkady Nikolayevich? And you and I just took a beating. That's what it means to be educated people."

Arkady gave a forced laugh, while Bazarov turned away and did not open his mouth throughout the remainder of the trip.

Fifteen miles seemed like thirty to Arkady. But finally, on the other side of a gentle hill, appeared the small hamlet in which Bazarov's parents lived. Near by, in a young grove of birches, the little manor house could be seen under its thatched roof. In front of the first hut, two peasants wearing caps stood yelling at each other. "You're a big swine," one said to the other, "and worse than a suckling pig." "And your wife's a witch," the latter retorted.

"By their unrestrained manners," Bazarov said to Arkady, "and their playfulness of expression, you can tell that my father's peasants aren't too oppressed. There he is himself, coming out on the steps of his home. He must have heard the harness bell. It's he, it's he—I recognize his face. Ah! But how gray he's gotten, poor soul!"

xx

While Bazarov leaned out of the coach, Arkady, craning his neck behind his companion's back, caught sight of a tall, lean man with disheveled hair and a thin, aquiline nose on the steps of the little manor house. Wearing an unbuttoned old military frock coat, he stood, legs wide apart, smoking a long pipe and squinting from the sun.

The horses stopped.

"You finally decided to come," said Bazarov's father, continuing to smoke, although the pipestem seemed to dance between his fingers. "Well, climb down, climb down, let's greet each other."

He began to embrace his son. . . . "Yenusha, Yenusha," echoed a quavering feminine voice. The door flew open and on the threshold appeared a plump, short, little old woman in a white mobcap and colored blouse. She gasped, reeled, and would certainly have fallen if Bazarov hadn't held her. Her fat little hands were instantly clasped around his neck, her head pressed against his chest, and there was a hush. The only sound was her broken sobbing.

The elder Bazarov breathed deeply and squinted more than ever.

"Now, that's enough, that's enough, Arisha! Stop," he said, exchanging glances with Arkady, who stood motionless by the coach, while the peasant on the coach box turned his face away. "That's not at all necessary! Please stop."

"Ah, Vassily Ivanich," stammered the old woman, "what ages it's been since my beloved, my own darling Yenushenka . . ." and without unclasping her hands, she lifted her face, crumpled, agitated, wet with tears, looked at Bazarov with rather comically blissful eyes, then fell on his neck again.

"Now, now, of course it's all in the nature of things," Vassily Ivanich said, "only it would be better to go into the house. There's a guest here with Yevgeny. Sorry," he added, turning to Arkady and clicking his heels lightly. "You understand, a woman's weakness—and, of course, a mother's heart . . ."

His own lips and eyebrows twitched, and his chin was quivering—but he obviously was trying to control himself and to appear almost indifferent. Arkady bowed.

"Come along, little Mother, really," Bazarov put in, and led the enfeebled old woman into the house. Settling her in a comfortable armchair, he embraced his father quickly once more and introduced Arkady to him.

"I'm so very glad to meet you," Vassily Ivanovich said, "but I hope you don't expect too much; everything here in my house is simple, on a military footing. Arina Vlassevna, calm yourself, I beg you; what is this faintheartedness? Our honored guest will think ill of you."

"My dear sir," the old woman said through her tears, "I don't have the honor of knowing your name and patronymic . . ."

"Arkady Nikolaich," Vassily Ivanovich prompted gravely in a low voice.

"Forgive me, I'm being foolish." The old woman blew her nose and, bending her head right and left, painstakingly wiped one eye after the other. "Forgive me. But, I thought I would die without seeing my da-a-ar-ling."

"And here we lived to see him, Madame," Vassily Ivanovich added quickly. "Tanyushka," he said, turning to a barefooted girl of about thirteen in a bright-red cotton dress, who was peering apprehensively from behind the door, "bring the mistress a glass of water—on a tray, do you hear?—and you, gentlemen," he added with rather old-fashioned waggishness, "allow me to invite you to the study of a retired veteran."

"Let me embrace you just once more, Yenushechka," Arina Vlassevna whimpered. Bazarov leaned over her. "My, how handsome you've grown!"

"Well, handsome or not," remarked Vassily Ivanovich, "but a man, as they say: *omfay.** And now I hope, Arina Vlassevna, that having sated your maternal heart, you'll worry about satiating your dear guests because, as you well know, you can't feed nightingales on fairy tales."

The old woman got up from the armchair.

"This very minute, Vassily Ivanich, the table will be set, I myself will run to the kitchen and order the samovar put on, everything will be done, everything. After all, for three years I haven't seen him, haven't given him food or drink, is that easy?"

"Come now, little housewife, get busy, don't disgrace yourself; and you, gentlemen, I invite you to follow me. Here's Timofeich come to greet you, Yevgeny. I guess he's glad too, the old watchdog. Well? You are glad, aren't you, old dog? Follow me, if you please."

And Bazarov's father bustled ahead, scraping and shuffling his worn slippers.

His whole house consisted of six tiny rooms. One of them, the one to which he led our friends, was called the study. A thick-legged table, covered with papers so blackened with old dust that they looked like ashes, took up the entire space between two windows; on the walls hung Turkish rifles, whips, a saber, two maps, some sort of anatomical sketches, a portrait of Hufeland,* a monogram made of hair in a black frame, and a diploma under glass; a leather couch, sunken and torn in places, stood between two enormous cupboards of speckled birch; crowded in disorder on the shelves were books, little boxes, stuffed birds, bottles and phials; in one corner stood a broken electrical gadget.

"I warned you, my dear visitor," Vassily Ivanovich began, "that we live here, so to speak, in bivouacs—"

"Now stop it, what are you apologizing for?" Bazarov interrupted. "Kirsanov knows very well that you and I aren't Croesuses, and that you don't have a palace. Where'll we put him, that's the question."

"Please, Yevgeny; I have an excellent room there in the cottage: he'll be very comfortable there."

"So you've acquired a cottage?"

"Indeed, sir; where the bath is, sir," Timofeich put in.

"That is, next to the bath," Vassily Ivanovich supplemented hastily. "It's summer now . . . I'll run over there right away, make the necessary arrangements; and you, Timofeich, can bring their things meanwhile. As for you, Yevgeny, I'll leave you my study, of course. *Suum cuique.*"*

"Well, there you are! A funny old chap and very kind," Bazarov commented as soon as his father had left. "A joker like yours, but in another way. He does talk an awful lot."

"And your mother seems to be a fine woman too," Arkady remarked.

"Yes, she's without malice. Wait and see what a dinner she'll set before us."

"You weren't expected today, young master; they didn't get meat," said Timofeich, who had just dragged in Bazarov's trunk.

"Then we'll get along without meat; one can't cry for he moon. Poverty's no crime, they say."

"How many souls does your father have?" Arkady suddenly asked.

"The estate isn't his, it's Mother's. Fifteen souls, I think."

"And twenty-two in all," Timofeich remarked with displeasure.

A shuffling of slippers was heard, and Vassily Ivanovich appeared again.

"Your room will be ready to receive you in a few minutes," he announced triumphantly, "Arkady . . . Nikolaich? That, I believe, is your patronymic? And here's your servant," he added, indicating a close-cropped young boy who entered with him in a dark-blue caftan, torn at the elbows, and borrowed boots. "He's called Fedka. Once more I repeat, even though my son forbade it, don't expect too much. However, filling a pipe is something he can do. You smoke, I suppose?"

"I smoke cigars mostly," Arkady answered.

"And it's well you do so. I myself have a preference for cigars, but in our out-of-the-way districts it's exceedingly difficult to obtain them."

"You've been playing Lazarus long enough," Bazarov interrupted again. "Sit down here on the couch instead, and let us have a look at you."

Vassily Ivanovich laughed and sat down. His face greatly resembled his son's, except that his forehead was lower and narrower, his mouth somewhat wider, and he was constantly in motion—moving his shoulders as if his clothing chafed him under the arms, blinking, coughing, and drumming his fingers—while his son was distinguished by a rather casual immobility.

"Playing Lazarus!" repeated Vassily Ivanovich. "Yevgeny, you don't believe I want to, so to speak, move the guests to pity by saying: look what a desert we live in. On the contrary, I'm of the opinion that there is no desert for a thinking man. At least I try, in so far as possible, not to be, so to speak, overgrown with moss; not to fall behind the times."

Bazarov's father drew out of his pocket a new yellow silk scarf which he had managed to grab while running to Arkady's room, and continued, waving it in the air:

"I won't even talk about how, for example, I put the peasants on a tenant system, not without considerable sacrifices on my part, and gave them my own land for half the produce. I considered that my duty; prudence itself enjoined it, although other landowners aren't even considering the idea. But I'm talking about science, about culture."

"Yes; I see you have here *The Friend of Health* for the year 1855," Bazarov remarked.

"An old comrade sends me that out of friendship," Vassily Ivanovich said hastily. "But we have, for example, an understanding of phrenology," he added, although addressing Arkady more than Bazarov as he pointed to a rather small plaster head divided into numbered squares standing in the cupboard, "and Schönlein isn't unknown to us either—and Rademacher."*

"You mean they still believe in Rademacher in —— Province?" Bazarov asked.

Vassily Ivanovich cleared his throat. "In the province . . . Of course, you gentlemen know best; how could we keep up with you? You have come to replace us. In my time, a certain humoralist named Hoffmann, and a certain Brown, with his vitalism, seemed quite ridiculous, but they had their day of glory once too. For you, Rademacher has been replaced by someone else, to whom you pay homage, and in twenty years he'll be laughed at too."

"To console you, I'll tell you that we now laugh at medicine in general and don't pay homage to anyone," Bazarov rejoined.

"How is that possible? But you want to be a doctor, don't you?"

"I do, but one doesn't cancel the other."

The old man poked at the still smoldering embers in his pipe with his middle finger. "Well, maybe, maybe—I won't argue. What am I, after all?—a retired army medic, *volla too*;* now turned farmer. . . . I served in your grandfather's brigade," he added, turning towards

Arkady again. "Yes, sir, yes, sir; I've seen some sights in my day. And the societies I've been in, the people I've seen. I, this same I whom you see before you now, I've felt the pulse of Prince Wittgenstein and Zhukovsky!* And those of the Southern Army, of the 'fourteenth,'* you understand," (and here Vassily Ivanovich pursed his lips significantly) "I knew them all inside out. Well, it didn't concern me; know your lancet, that's enough! But your grandfather was a highly esteemed man, a real soldier."

"Admit it, he was a real blockhead," Bazarov said lazily.

"Oh, Yevgeny, how can you talk that way! For mercy's sake . . . Of course, General Kirsanov was not one of those who . . ."

"Well, let him be," Bazarov interrupted. "When I was driving up here, I was delighted to see your birch grove; it's grown splendidly."

Vassily Ivanovich revived. "And look what a garden I have now. I planted every shrub myself. There are fruit trees, berry bushes and all sorts of medicinal herbs. No matter how clever you may be, young gentlemen, just the same, old Paracelsus* spoke the Lord's truth: *in herbis, verbis et lapidibus* . . .* Of course, you know, I've stopped practising, but a couple of times a week I have occasion to relive my youth. They come for advice—you can't throw them out. It just happens that poor people come for help. And there isn't any doctor here at all. Imagine, one of the neighbors here, a retired major, gives treatments too. I asked about him, whether he'd studied medicine. I was told: 'No, he hasn't studied; he does it more out of philanthropy.' . . . Ha-ha! Out of philanthropy! Eh? What a thing! Ha-ha! Ha-ha!"

"Fedka! Fill me a pipe!" Bazarov said harshly.

"And then there's another doctor here, who arrives to see a patient," Vassily Ivanovich continued in a sort of despair, "when the patient is already *ad patres;*the servant won't let the doctor in and says: 'Now it's no longer necessary.' The doctor hadn't expected that, gets confused, and asks: 'Well, did your master hiccup before dying?' 'He hiccupped, sir.' 'And hiccupped a great deal?' 'A great deal.' 'Well then—that's fine,'—and back home he goes. Ha-ha-ha!"

Only the old man laughed; Arkady managed a smile; Bazarov merely stretched. The conversation went on in this fashion for about an hour; Arkady had time to visit his room, which turned out to be the dressing room for the bath, but was very pleasant and clean. Finally Tanyusha came in to announce that dinner was ready.

Vassily Ivanovich was the first to get up. "Come, gentlemen! Be kind enough to forgive me if I bored you. Perchance the hostess will give you more satisfaction than I."

The dinner, although prepared hurriedly, turned out to be very good, and even abundant, but the wine had, so to speak, gone awry—almost black sherry, bought by Timofeich in town from a merchant friend, it tasted of something like copper or resin. The flies were a nuisance too. Usually the houseboy chased them away with a big leafy branch, but this time Vassily Ivanovich had sent him away for fear of censure on the part of the young generation. Arina Vlassevna had had time to change into her finery: she had put on a high mobcap with silk ribbons and a sky-blue printed shawl. She started crying again as soon as she saw her Yenusha, but her husband did not have to reprove her: she wiped her tears herself as quickly as possible to prevent their falling on her shawl. Only the young people ate; their hosts had had dinner a long time ago. They were served by Fedka, obviously overburdened by boots he was not accustomed to, and assisted by a one-eyed woman with a masculine face named Anfisushka, who fulfilled the duties of housekeeper, poultry maid and laundress. Throughout the entire dinner, Vassily Ivanovich walked up and down the room and, with a completely happy, even blissful face, elaborated on the grave fears aroused in him by Napoleon's policies, and the complexity of the Italian question. Arina Vlassevna did not notice Arkady and made no effort to entertain him; her tiny fist propping up her round face, whose kindly expression was enhanced by her plump cherry-colored lips and the moles on her cheeks and above her eyebrows, she never lifted her eyes from her son and sighed incessantly; she was dying to know how long he would stay, but she didn't dare ask him. "What if he says for two days," she thought, and her heart sank.

After the main course, Bazarov's father disappeared for a moment and returned with an uncorked, half-empty bottle of champagne. "There," he exclaimed, "even though we live in the wilds, we have the wherewithal to make merry on festive occasions." He poured three goblets and a wine glass, proposed the health of the "inestimable" guests, downed his goblet in one swallow, military-fashion, and made Arina Vlassevna empty her glass to the last drop. When it was time for the preserves, Arkady, who could not bear anything sweet, nevertheless felt it his duty to taste four different, freshly made varieties, especially since Bazarov flatly refused and immediately lit up a cigar. Then tea with cream, buns and butter appeared on the scene; afterwards, Vassily Ivanovich led everyone into the garden to enjoy the beauty of the evening. As they passed a little bench, he whispered to Arkady, "I love to philosophize on this bench while watching the setting sun: it befits a recluse. And there, a little farther on, I've planted several of the trees beloved by Horace."

"What kind of trees?" Bazarov asked, overhearing.

"Acacias—of course."

Bazarov began yawning.

"I suppose it's time the travelers were in the arms of Morpheus," his father remarked.

"That is, it's time to sleep!" Bazarov rejoined. "That's sound judgment. It's time, exactly."

Saying good night to his mother, he kissed her on the forehead while she, embracing him, furtively made the sign of the cross three times behind his back. Vassily Ivanovich escorted Arkady to his room and wished him "as favorable a repose as I savored at your happy age." And in fact, Arkady slept very well in his dressing room; there was an odor of mint in it, and two crickets rivaled each other chirping lullingly behind the stove. Vassily

Ivanovich went from Arkady to his study where, curling up at his son's feet on the couch, he prepared to have a chat with him; however, Bazarov immediately sent him away, saying that he wanted to sleep, although he lay awake until morning. Eyes wide open, he stared into the darkness with rancor: childhood memories had no power over him, and he was, moreover, unable to rid himself of recent bitter emotions.

Arina Vlassevna first prayed to her heart's content, then had a long, long chat with Anfisushka who, standing in front of her mistress as though transfixed and staring at her with her single eye, divulged all her observations and fancies about Yevgeny Vassilievich in a mysterious whisper. Joy, wine and cigar smoke had set the old woman's head spinning; her husband tried to start a conversation with her and threw up his hands.

Arina Vlassevna was a true Russian lady of the olden days; she should have lived two hundred years before in the days of old Moscow. She was very devout and sentimental; she believed in every possible kind of omen, in fortune-telling, charms and dreams; she believed in the prophesies of imbeciles, in hobgoblins and werewolves, in encounters with evil spirits, in bewitchment, in folk medicine, in blessing salt on Holy Thursday, in the imminent end of the world; she believed that if the candles brought home from church the eve of Easter do not go out, the buckwheat crop will be plentiful; and that the mushroom stops growing if seen by a human eye; she believed that the devil likes to be near water, and that every Jew has a bloody mark on his chest; she was afraid of mice, snakes, frogs, sparrows, leeches, thunder, cold, water, drafts, horses, goats, red-headed people and black cats, and considered crickets and dogs unclean; she would not eat veal or pigeons or crayfish or cheese or asparagus or Jerusalem artichokes or hare or watermelons, because a cut-open watermelon reminded her of the head of John the Baptist; she was unable to mention oysters without a shudder; she loved to eat—and fasted rigidly; she slept ten hours out of twenty-four—and did not even lie down if Vassily Ivanovich so much as had a headache; she had not read a single book except for *Aleksis, or the*

Cottages in the Forest; she wrote one, or at the most two letters a year, but knew her business in housekeeping, drying and preserving foods, although she did not touch anything with her own hands, and was generally reluctant to bestir herself.

Arina Vlassevna was very kind and, in her way, not stupid at all. She knew that in the world there were lords who were supposed to command, and simple people who were supposed to serve—and therefore she had no aversion to servility or obeisances; she treated her inferiors kindly and gently, never let a single beggar go away empty-handed, and never spoke ill of anyone, although she gossiped now and then. She was very nice-looking in her youth, played the clavichord and could manage a little French; but in the course of the long peregrinations with her husband, whom she had married against her will, she had swollen and had forgotten both music and French. She loved and feared her son beyond words. She left the running of the estate to Vassily Ivanovich—and did not concern herself with any part of it: whenever the old man began to talk about imminent reforms and his plans, she would fan herself with a handkerchief and raise her eyebrows higher and higher with fear. She was timorous, continually expected some sort of enormous misfortune, and burst into tears whenever she remembered something sad. . . . Such women are disappearing now. God knows whether one should rejoice over that!

xxi

On arising, Arkady opened the window—the first object to meet his eyes was Vassily Ivanovich. Wearing an oriental dressing gown tied with a handkerchief, the old man was digging energetically in the vegetable garden.

Noticing his young guest, he leaned on his spade and cried, "A very good day to you! How did you manage to sleep?"

"Splendidly," Arkady answered.

"While I'm here, as you see, like Cincinnatus,* breaking ground for a crop of late turnips. The time has come now—but, thank God for it!—when each person has to procure his subsistence with his own hands; it's no use relying on others; one has to labor one's self. Thus it turns out that Jean-Jacques Rousseau was right. Half an hour ago, sir, you would have seen me in a completely different situation. For a woman who was complaining about oppression, as they say—we say dysentery, I—how can I put it—I poured out a dose of opium; then for another woman, I pulled out a tooth. I offered that one ether . . . but she wouldn't agree. All this I do *gratis—anamateur.** However, it's nothing new to me; I'm just a plebian, *homo novus**—not one of those patricians, like my spouse. But wouldn't you like to come over here in the shade, to breathe some morning freshness before breakfast?"

Arkady went out to join him.

"It's good to welcome you again!" said Vassily Ivanovich, touching his hand in a military salute to the soiled skull cap covering his head. "You, I know, are used to luxury, to pleasures; but the greats of this world don't disdain spending a short time under a cottage roof."

"Good heavens," Arkady cried out, "what kind of great of this world am I? And I'm not used to luxury."

"Allow me, allow me," Vassily Ivanovich said with a polite smirk. "I'm practically abandoned to the archives now, but I have also been around in the world—I can tell birds by their flight. I'm also a psychologist in my own way, and a physiognomist. If I hadn't that gift, the chances are that I would have been lost long ago; a little man like me would have been eradicated. I tell you, compliments aside, I'm sincerely delighted by the friendship I've observed between you and my son. I've just seen him: according to his usual custom, which you're probably familiar with, he jumped up very early and went for a walk around the neighborhood. Allow me to be curious—have you known Yevgeny long?"

"Since this winter."

"So. And allow me to ask you this—but hadn't we better sit down?—allow me to ask you, as a father, in complete sincerity: what is your opinion of my Yevgeny?"

"Your son—is one of the most remarkable people I've ever met," Arkady answered with animation.

Vassily Ivanovich's eyes suddenly lighted up and his cheeks flushed slightly. The spade dropped out of his hand.

"Then you assume—" he began.

"I am certain," Arkady interrupted, "that a great future awaits your son, that he will bring honor to your name. I became convinced of that at our first meeting."

"How—how was that?" Vassily Ivanovich barely uttered the words. His broad lips parted in an enraptured smile which remained fixed.

"You want to know how we met?"

"Yes . . . and all . . ."

Arkady began talking and telling about Bazarov with even greater ardor, greater enthusiasm than he had the evening he danced the mazurka with Odintsova.

Vassily Ivanovich listened to him, listened, blew his nose, twisted his handkerchief with both hands, coughed, rumpled his hair—and finally, unable to restrain himself, embraced Arkady and kissed him on the shoulder.

"You've made me completely happy," he said, beaming; "I should tell you that I—idolize my son; I won't even talk about my old woman: you know—a mother! But I don't dare show my feelings in front of him because he doesn't like it. He hates any effusiveness. Many people even condemn him for having such a harsh nature and see in it a sign of pride or insensitivity; but men like him can't be measured by the usual yardstick, can they? Look here, for example; another in his place would have been a constant drain on his parents. Would you believe it? Since he was born, he's never taken an extra kopeck from us, by God!"

"He's an unselfish, honest person," Arkady remarked.

"Especially unselfish. While I, Arkady Nikolaich, not only idolize him, I'm proud of him, and my sole ambition is that in time the following words will appear in his biography: 'The son of a simple army doctor who, however, was able to recognize his worth early and never begrudged anything for his education . . .'" The old man's voice broke.

Arkady pressed his hand.

"What do you think?" Vassily Ivanovich asked after a short silence. "He won't reach the renown you predict for him in a medical career, will he?"

"Of course not in medicine, although he will be one of the foremost scholars in that field as well."

"Then in what, Arkady Nikolaich?"

"It's hard to say now, but he will be famous."

"He will be famous!" the old man repeated and became lost in thought.

"Arina Vlassevna sent me to tell you tea is served," Anfisushka said, passing by with an enormous bowl of ripe raspberries.

Vassily Ivanovich gave a start. "Will the cream for the raspberries be cold?"

"Yes, sir."

"Cold, mind you! Don't stand on ceremony, Arkady Nikolaich, take some more. Why isn't Yevgeny here?"

"I'm here," Bazarov's voice was heard from Arkady's room.

Vassily Ivanovich turned around quickly.

"Aha! You wanted to visit your friend, but you were too late, *amice*, and we've already had a long chat together. Now it's time for breakfast; Mother's calling. By the way, I must have a talk with you."

"What about?"

"There's a peasant here who's suffering from icteric—"

"That is, jaundice?"

"Yes, chronic and very stubborn icteric. I prescribed knapweed and St. John's wort for him, ordered him to eat carrots, and gave him soda; but these are all *palliative* remedies—something more effective is needed. Even though you laugh at medicine, I'm still sure you can give me useful advice. But we'll talk about this later. Now let's go have tea."

Vassily Ivanovich jumped up from the bench vivaciously and began singing from *Robert le Diable*:*

"The law, the law, the law we set ourselves is
  To live for ha—for ha—for happiness!"

"Remarkable vitality!" Bazarov remarked, moving away from the window.

It was midday. The sun burned from behind a thin screen of unending white clouds. Everything was still. In the village, only roosters called to each other, their irritable cries arousing in everyone who heard them a strange sensation of drowsiness and monotony; somewhere high up in the trees, the incessant piping of the young sparrow hawk's plaintive call rang out. Arkady and Bazarov lay in the shade of a small haystack on a bed they had made with two armfuls of crackling but still green and fragrant grass.

"That aspen tree," Bazarov began, "reminds me of my childhood. It grows on the edge of the pit where the bricks were dug, and in those days I believed that pit and the aspen possessed a special talisman—I was never bored near them. I didn't understand then that I was never bored because I was a child. But now I'm grown up, the talisman doesn't work."

"How much time did you spend here in all?" asked Arkady.

"About two years in a row; then we went on the road. We led a tramp's life; traipsed around cities most of the time."

"And has this house been here a long time?"

"A long time. It was built by my grandfather, my mother's father."

"Who was your grandfather?"

"The devil knows. A major of some sort. He served with Suvorov and was always telling about the march over the Alps. Lies, probably."

"That's why there's a portrait of Suvorov* hanging in

your parlor. I like little houses like yours, old and warm; they have a kind of special odor, too."

"A smell of lamp oil and sweet clover," Bazarov said, yawning. "But what flies those nice little houses have . . . Ugh!"

"Tell me," Arkady began after a brief silence, "weren't they strict with you as a child?"

"You can see what my parents are like—not severe people."

"Do you love them, Yevgeny?"

"I love them, Arkady."

"They love you so much."

Bazarov fell silent.

"Do you know what I'm thinking about?" he said at last, throwing his hands behind his back.

"I don't know. What?"

"I'm thinking: my parents have a good life! At sixty my father is bustling around, talking about 'palliative' remedies, doctoring people, being big-hearted with the peasants—he's on a spree, in other words. It's pleasant for Mother, too—her day is so crammed with all kinds of tasks, with oh's and ah's, that she never has time to come to; while I . . ."

"While you?"

"While I'm thinking: here I lie in a haystack. . . . The infinitesimal place I take up is so tiny compared to the rest of space where I'm not, and which has nothing to do with me; and the portion of time given me to live is so negligible next to the eternity in which I haven't existed and won't—while in this atom, this decimal point, the blood courses, the brain works, and wants something also. . . . What an outrage! What nonsense!"

"Let me point out to you that what you're saying applies to everyone in general—"

"You're right," Bazarov interrupted. "I meant to say that they, that is, my parents, are busy and aren't worrying about their own insignificance; they're not conscious of the stench . . . while I—I feel only boredom and anger."

"Anger? Why anger?"

"Why? What do you mean, why? Have you forgotten?"

"I remember everything, but just the same I don't accept your having the right to be angry. You're unhappy, I grant you, but—"

"Indeed! I see, Arkady Nikolayevich, that you understand love the same way all modern young people do: 'Cluck, cluck, cluck,' you call to the little hen, but as soon as the hen comes close, you take to your heels! I'm not one of those. But enough of that. What can't be helped, shouldn't be talked about." He turned over on his side. "Aha! There's a brave ant dragging a half-dead fly. Go on, drag it, brother! Ignore its resistance; use your privilege as an insect not to feel pity, unlike us self-destroyers!"

"You've no right to say that, Yevgeny! When did you destroy yourself?"

Bazarov raised his head. "That's the only thing I pride myself on. I haven't destroyed myself; therefore a mere woman isn't going to destroy me. Amen! It's finished! You won't hear another word about it from me."

The friends lay in silence for some time.

"Yes," Bazarov began, "man's a strange being. If one looks from a distance at the dull life 'fathers' live here, it seems that there couldn't be anything better. You eat, drink, and know you're behaving in the most reasonable way possible. But boredom prevails. One wants to deal with people if only to curse them; but, anyhow, to deal with them."

"One should arrange one's life so that every moment of it is significant," Arkady said thoughtfully.

"Really! The significant is agreeable even when it happens by mistake, but one can become reconciled to the insignificant. But there's rubbish, rubbish—that's what's unfortunate!"

"Rubbish doesn't exist for a man if he simply refuses to recognize it."

"Hmmm . . . what you said is an *inverse commonplace*."

"What? What did you call it?"

"Here's what: if you say, for example, that civilization is beneficial, that's a commonplace; while if you say civilization is harmful, that's an inverse commonplace.

It sounds more elegant, but in reality it's exactly the same thing."

"But where's the truth, on which side?"

"Where? I answer you like an echo: where?"

"You're in a melancholy mood today, Yevgeny."

"Really? I must be soft-headed from the sun, and one should never eat that many raspberries."

"In that case, a nap wouldn't hurt," Arkady remarked.

"All right; only don't look at me. Everyone's face looks stupid when he's asleep."

"But aren't you indifferent to what people think of you?"

"I don't know what to tell you. A real man shouldn't worry about that; a real man is one there's no use thinking about, who has to be obeyed or hated."

"Strange! I don't hate anyone," Arkady said after a moment's thought.

"And I so many. You're a tender soul, soft; how could you hate! You're timid, you don't expect much of yourself—"

"And you," Arkady interrupted, "do you expect much of yourself? Do you have a high opinion of yourself?"

Bazarov fell silent.

"When I meet a man who doesn't give way to me," he said with deliberation, "then I'll change my opinion of myself. Hate! Here, for example, in passing the hut of our village elder, Filip, today, you said—it's so nice, so clean—look, you said, Russia will have attained perfection when the lowest peasant has such a place to live, and each of us must contribute to that. . . . While I hated that lowest peasant, Filip or Sidor, for whom I'm supposed to turn myself inside out, and who won't even thank me—and furthermore, what do I need his thanks for? So he'll be living in a clean hut, while I'll have burs growing out of me, then what?"

"Enough, Yevgeny. Listening to you today, one is forced to agree with those who accuse us of a lack of principles."

"You talk like your uncle. Principles don't exist in general—you still haven't grasped that!—but there are instincts. Everything depends on them."

"How so?"

"Like this. Take me, for example: I have a negative disposition—I find it pleasant to negate, my brain is built that way—and that's that! Why does chemistry appeal to me? Why do you like apples?—also by instinct. It's all the same. People will never penetrate deeper than that. Not everyone will tell you that, nor will I tell you that next time."

"What? And honesty is—instinct?"

"Definitely!"

"Yevgeny!" Arkady began in a plaintive voice.

"Well? What? Don't you like it?" Bazarov interrupted. "No, brother! Once you've decided to make a clean sweep —include the ground you're standing on, too! . . . But we've philosophized enough. 'Nature breathes the silence of sleep,' as Pushkin said."

"He never said anything of the sort," Arkady rejoined.

"Well, if he never said it, as a poet he could have and should have. By the way, he must have been in military service."

"Pushkin was never a soldier."

"Heavens, in every line he has: To battle, to battle! For the honor of Russia!"

"What fairy tales you think up! That's outright slander!"

"Slander? What's the difference! What a word he thought up to frighten me. No matter what slander is heaped on a man, he actually deserves twenty times worse."

"We'd do better to sleep," Arkady said with vexation.

"With the greatest pleasure," answered Bazarov.

But neither one slept. An almost hostile feeling enveloped the hearts of both young people. Five minutes later they opened their eyes and exchanged glances in silence.

"Look," Arkady said suddenly, "a dry maple leaf fell off and is dropping to the ground; its movement is exactly like the flight of a butterfly. Isn't it strange? The most mournful and dead—resembles the most gay and lively."

"Oh, Arkady Nikolaich, my friend!" Bazarov cried. "I've one request: don't talk pretty."

"I talk as I can . . . and anyway, that's despotism. A thought came into my head; why not express it?"

"True; and why can't I express my own thoughts too? I find pretty talk—indecent."

"What's decent then? Swearing?"

"Oh-oh! I see you really intend to follow your uncle's footsteps. How that idiot would rejoice if he could hear you."

"What did you call Pavel Petrovich?"

"I called him, appropriately—an idiot."

"But that's intolerable!" Arkady exclaimed.

"Aha! Family feeling spoke up," Bazarov said calmly. "I've noticed that it persists very stubbornly in people. A man can be ready to forsake everything, to give up every prejudice; but to confess that, for example, his brother who steals another's handkerchief is a thief—that's beyond his strength. And, in fact, could *my* brother, *mine*—not be a genius . . . is it possible?"

"It was a simple feeling of justice which spoke up in me and not family feeling at all," Arkady objected vehemently. "But as you don't understand that feeling, as you don't have that instinct, you can't judge it."

"In other words: Arkady Kirsanov is too exalted for my understanding—I bow and hold my tongue."

"Enough, please, Yevgeny; we'll finally quarrel."

"Ah, Arkady! Do me a favor, let's have a good quarrel for once—to the last ditch, to the finish."

"Look, this way, I predict, we'll end by—"

"Fighting?" Bazarov interrupted. "What then? Here on the hay, in such an idyllic setting, far from the world and human eyes—why not? But you'll be no match for me. I'll seize you by the throat . . ."

Bazarov spread his long, hard fingers. Arkady turned around and prepared to defend himself as though in fun. But his friend's face looked so ominous to him, and he saw such an unplayful menace in Bazarov's crooked grin and flaring eyes, that he felt an involuntary fear.

"Aha! That's where you wandered to," the voice of

Vassily Ivanovich broke in at that moment, and the old army doctor stood before the young people, arrayed in a homemade linen jacket with a straw hat, also homemade, on his head. "I've been looking and looking for you. But you chose an excellent spot and are indulging in a wonderful pastime. To lie on 'earth,' to look at 'heaven' . . . You know—there's a rather special meaning in that."

"I look at heaven only when I feel like sneezing," Bazarov grumbled, and turning to Arkady, added in an undertone, "Too bad he interrupted."

"Come, that's enough," Arkady whispered, squeezing his friend's hand furtively. "But no friendship will survive such clashes for long."

"I look at you, my young conversationalists," Vassily Ivanovich was saying in the meantime, nodding his head and leaning with crossed arms on a rather curiously twisted walking stick of his own devising with the figure of a Turk in place of a cane-head, "I look and I can't help admiring. You have so much strength, youth in full flower, abilities, talents! Simply—Castor and Pollux!*

"There he goes—he's off into mythology," said Bazarov. "We can see right away that in his time he was strong in Latin! As I remember, you won a silver medal for composition, eh?"

"The Dioscuri, Dioscuri!"* Vassily Ivanovich reiterated.

"Anyway, that's enough, Father; no flattery."

"It's permissible once in a lifetime," the old man muttered. "However, I didn't seek you out, gentlemen, to pay you compliments; but to . . . In the first place, I wanted to warn you, Yevgeny. You're an intelligent man, you know people, and you know women, and therefore you'll forgive. . . . Your mother wanted to hold a Te Deum for your arrival. Don't think I'm asking you to assist at this Te Deum: it's already over, but Father Aleksei—"

"The preacher?"

"Well, yes, the priest; he'll . . . eat with us. I hadn't expected this and even advised against it . . . but it

somehow turned out that way . . . he misunderstood
me. Well, and Arina Vlassevna . . . Furthermore, he's a
very good and sensible man."

"He won't eat up my portion of dinner, will he?"
Bazarov asked.

Vassily Ivanovich laughed. "Heavens; what you won't
say!"

"But I don't ask for anything more. I'm ready to sit
at the table with any man."

Vassily Ivanovich straightened his hat. "I was sure in
advance," he said, "that you were above all prejudices.
Look at me—I'm an old man, in my sixty-second year,
and I don't have any." (Vassily Ivanovich didn't dare
confess that he himself had wanted the Te Deum—he
was no less devout than his wife.) "Anyway, Father
Aleksei would like very much to meet you. You'll like
him; you'll see. He's not averse to playing cards and
even—but this is between us—smokes a pipe."

"So? Then we'll sit down to whist after supper and
I'll beat him."

"Heh-heh-heh, we'll see! That remains to be seen!"

"What? Are you reliving your youth?" Bazarov said
with special emphasis.

Vassily Ivanovich's bronzed cheeks flushed uneasily.

"For shame, Yevgeny. . . . What happened is past.
Well, but I'm prepared to confess in front of *him* that
I had that passion in my youth—indeed; and how I paid
for it! But how hot it is. Let me sit down with you. I'm
not interrupting, am I?"

"Not a bit," Arkady answered.

Vassily Ivanovich let himself down, groaning, onto the
hay.

"Your present bed, my lords," he began, "reminds me
of my military, bivouacing life, of field-dressing stations,
also somewhere near a haystack like this, and we thanked
God for that." He sighed. "I went through a lot, a lot
in my day. For example, if you permit, I'll tell you a
curious episode about the plague in Bessarabia."

"For which you received the Vladimir Cross?" Bazarov
interrupted. "We know, we know. . . . By the way, why
aren't you wearing it?"

"I told you, didn't I, that I don't respect conventions," Vassily Ivanovich muttered (he had just had the red ribbon ripped off his frock coat the day before), and began recounting the episode of the plague. "But look, he fell asleep," he suddenly whispered to Arkady while pointing to Bazarov and winking good-naturedly. "Yevgeny! Get up!" he added aloud. "Let's go have dinner."

Father Aleksei, a stately, corpulent man with thick, carefully combed hair and an embroidered sash over his violet silk cassock, seemed to be very clever and resourceful. He quickly took the initiative in pressing Bazarov's and Arkady's hands, as though he understood that they were not in need of his blessing, and his behavior was unconstrained in general. He was not false to himself nor did he offend others; at the appropriate times, he made fun of seminary Latin and stood up for the prelate; he finished two glasses of wine, but refused a third; he accepted a cigar from Arkady, but did not light it, saying he would take it home. The only thing about him which was not altogether pleasant was that he was constantly raising his hand slowly and carefully to catch flies on his face, and in doing so, sometimes squashed them. He sat down at the card table with a moderate expression of pleasure, and finished by winning two rubles and fifty kopecks from Bazarov in paper money, as no one in Arina Vlassevna's house had any notion of reckoning in silver.

She sat near her son as always (she did not play cards), propping her cheek on her little fist as always, and getting up only to order some new delicacy served. She was afraid to caress Bazarov and he did not encourage her, did not invite her caresses; furthermore, Vassily Ivanovich had advised her not to "disturb" him much. "Young people don't like it," he urged her (there is no need to describe that day's dinner; Timofeich had galloped in person that morning at dawn to fetch some kind of special Circassian meat; the village elder went in the opposite direction after blennyfish, perch and crayfish; for the mushrooms alone, the peasant women received forty-two copper kopecks); but Arina Vlassevna's eyes, constantly turned towards Bazarov, did not express devotion and tenderness alone; they showed sorrow mixed with curiosity and fear, and a kind of resigned reproach.

However, Bazarov was far from analyzing exactly what his mother's eyes expressed; he rarely addressed her, and then only with a brief question. Once he requested her hand "for luck"; she laid her soft little hand gently on his hard broad palm.

"And so," she asked after a short wait, "didn't it help?"

"It went worse than ever," he answered with a careless smile.

"He's playing for high stakes," Father Aleksei observed regretfully and stroked his handsome beard.

"Napoleon's rule, Father, Napoleon's," Vassily Ivanovich put in as he led with his ace.

"It led him to the Isle of St. Helena," declared Father Aleksei as he trumped the ace.

"Don't you want some currant water, Yenushschka?" Arina Vlassevna asked.

Bazarov just shrugged his shoulders.

"No," he said to Arkady the following day, "I'm leaving tomorrow. I'm bored; I'd like to work and it's impossible here. I'll go back to your place in the country; anyway, I left all my equipment there. At least one can shut one's self up at your house. But here Father assures me, 'My study is at your disposal—no one will disturb you'; while he himself is always at my heels. And it doesn't seem right, somehow, to shut him out; or Mother either. I hear her sighing on the other side of the wall, but if you go to her—there's nothing to say to her."

"She'll be very sad," Arkady said, "and so will he."

"I'll come back to them again."

"When?"

"Well, on the way to St. Petersburg."

"I'm particularly sorry for your mother."

"Why so? Has she won you over with berries?"

Arkady averted his eyes.

"You don't know your mother, Yevgeny. She's not just an excellent woman; she's very intelligent, really. This morning she talked to me for half an hour, and so sensibly, interestingly."

"Indeed; did she go on about me?"

"The conversation wasn't only about you."

"It's possible; you're an onlooker. If a woman can keep up a half hour's conversation, that's already a good sign. Just the same, I'm leaving."

"It'll be difficult for you to tell them the news. They're always discussing what we'll be doing two weeks from now."

"Difficult. The devil got into me today and I teased Father: he recently ordered one of his peasants flogged —and he did well; yes, yes, don't look at me with such horror—he did very well because the man's the world's worst thief and drunkard; only Father had never expected I would, so to speak, become informed. He was very embarrassed and now I have to make him sad to boot. . . . It's nothing! He'll live to grow old."

Bazarov said, "It's nothing!"—but a whole day went by before he made up his mind to inform Vassily Ivanovich of his intentions. Finally, as he was saying good night to his father in the study, he added with a drawn-out yawn:

"Yes . . . I almost forgot to tell you . . . Send our horses to Fedot's for a relay tomorrow."

Vassily Ivanovich was dumfounded.

"You mean Mr. Kirsanov is leaving us?"

"Yes; and I'm leaving with him."

Vassily Ivanovich felt the ground fall from under him.

"You're leaving?"

"Yes—I have to. Arrange for the horses, please."

"Very well . . ." the old man stammered. "Send for a relay . . . very well . . . only . . . only . . . How can it be?"

"I have to go to his place for a short while. Then I'll come back here again."

"Yes! For a short while . . . Very well." Vassily Ivanovich drew out a handkerchief and, blowing his nose, bowed almost to the ground. "Well? That . . . Everything will be done. I had been thinking you'd stay—a bit longer. Three days—that's, that's, after three years, rather little, rather little, Yevgeny!"

"But I'm telling you I'll come back soon. It's essential."

"Essential . . . Well? Duty comes first. . . . Send for the horses, eh? Very well. Of course, Arina and I hadn't expected this. Here she asked the neighbor for flowers, she wanted to embellish your room." (Vassily Ivanovich did not even mention that every morning at dawn, standing with bare feet in slippers, he consulted with Timofeich and, dealing out one torn paper bill after the other with trembling fingers, charged him with various purchases, particularly comestibles and red wine, which the young people appeared to be very fond of.) "The main thing is freedom; that's my rule . . . one must not hinder . . . not . . ."

He suddenly fell silent and went towards the door.

"We'll see each other soon, Father, really."

But Vassily Ivanovich just waved his hand without turning around and went out. Returning to the bedroom, he found his wife already in bed, and began to pray in a whisper in order not to wake her. Nevertheless she awoke.

"Is that you, Vassily Ivanovich?" she asked.

"It's I, little Mother!"

"You came from Yenusha's? You know, I'm afraid it may not be comfortable for him sleeping on the couch. I had Anfisushka put your field-mattress and the new pillows out for him; I would have given him our featherbed, but I seem to remember he doesn't like to sleep on a soft bed."

"It doesn't matter, little Mother, don't worry. He's fine. . . . Father, forgive us our sins," he continued his prayer in a low voice. Vassily Ivanovich was sorry for his old wife; he did not want to tell her that night what sorrow awaited her.

Bazarov and Arkady left the following day. From morning on, the whole house was saddened; dishes fell out of Anfisushka's hands; even Fedka was puzzled and ended up taking off his boots. Vassily Ivanovich was more fidgety than ever. He was obviously summoning all his courage; he spoke in a loud voice and stamped his feet, but his face sagged, and his glances continually slid past his son. Arina Vlassevna cried quietly; she would have completely lost her wits and been unable to contain herself, if early that morning her husband had not spent two whole hours prevailing upon her. When Bazarov, after reiterated promises to return in no case later than a month, finally broke out of the embraces restraining him and sat in the buggy; when the horses stirred, the harness bell began to jingle, the wheels to turn—when there was no point in looking after them, and the dust had settled, and Timofeich, all bent and tottering, trudged slowly back to his little room; when the old couple were left alone in front of their house, which also seemed suddenly shriveled and decrepit— Vassily Ivanovich, after waving his handkerchief bravely on the steps for several minutes more, sank down on a chair and dropped his head on his chest. "He abandoned, abandoned us," he faltered, "abandoned; he got bored with us. Alone like a finger now, alone!" he repeated several times and each time lifted his hand, extending a solitary index finger. Then Arina Vlassevna drew near him and leaning her gray head against his gray head said, "What can you do, Vassya! Our son—is a slice cut off from us. He's like a hawk: had a whim— flew in, had a whim—flew away; while you and I sit in a row like mushrooms in a tree-hollow and never budge. I alone remain unchanged for you forever, as you for me."

Vassily Ivanovich lifted his hands from his face and embraced his wife, his companion, more fervently than he ever had in his youth. She had comforted him in his sorrow.

xxii

Our friends traveled to Fedot's in silence, with only rare exchanges of inconsequential remarks. Bazarov was not entirely satisfied with himself. Arkady was dissatisfied with him. In addition, he felt in his heart that irrational dejection which only very young people know. The coachman harnessed fresh horses, climbed up on the coach box, and asked: "Right or left?"

Arkady started. The right-hand road led to town, and from there home; the left-hand road led to Odintsova's.

He glanced at Bazarov.

"Yevgeny," he asked, "left?"

Bazarov turned his back.

"What kind of foolishness is that?" he muttered.

"I know it's foolish," Arkady answered. "But where's the harm in it? It's not our first time, is it?"

Bazarov pulled his cap down over his forehead.

"You decide," he said at last.

"Go left," Arkady cried.

The buggy rolled in the direction of Nikolskoye. But, having committed themselves to *foolishness*, the friends were more stubbornly silent than ever and even looked angry.

By the way the major-domo met them on the steps of Odintsova's house, the friends could tell that they had acted unwisely in yielding to a sudden whim. They obviously were not expected. They sat a rather long time in the parlor with somewhat foolish expressions. Finally Odintsova came out to them. She greeted them with her usual politeness, but was surprised at their quick return and, as far as could be judged from the apathy of her movements and speech, was not overly delighted by it. They hastened to announce that they had just dropped in on the way, and in three or four hours would head on farther, to town. She confined herself to a mild exclamation, asked Arkady to give her respects to his father, and sent for her aunt. The princess appeared looking sleepy, which made the expression on her wrinkled face still more malevolent. Katya was indisposed; she did not emerge from her room. Arkady suddenly realized that he wanted to see Katya at least as much as he did Odintsova herself. Four hours went by in insignificant chatter about this and that; Odintsova listened and spoke without a smile. Only when they were saying good-by did her former friendliness seem to stir within her.

"I've had a fit of melancholy," she said, "but don't pay any attention to that and come again—both of you —in a little while."

Both Bazarov and Arkady answered her with a silent bow, got in the carriage, and without stopping anywhere, went home to Marino, where they arrived safely the evening of the following day. Throughout the whole journey, neither one so much as mentioned Odintsova's name; Bazarov, in particular, hardly opened his mouth and looked off to the side all the time, away from the road, with a sort of obdurate intensity.

At Marino everyone was overjoyed to see them. Nikolai let out a shout, swung his legs, and bounced up from the couch when Fenechka ran to him with sparkling eyes to announce the arrival of the "young masters." Even Pavel experienced a certain pleasant agitation and smiled indulgently as he shook the hands of the returned travelers. Then came questions, comments: Arkady did most of the talking, particularly during supper, which lasted long after midnight. Nikolai ordered up several bottles of porter which had just been sent from Moscow, and he himself indulged until his cheeks became raspberry-red and he had a continual sort of half-childish, half-nervous chuckle. The general animation spread to the servants as well. Dunyasha ran back and forth as if possessed, slamming doors right and left, while Piotr was still trying to play a Cossack waltz on a guitar after two o'clock in the morning. The chords sounded plaintive and agreeable in the motionless air, but with the exception of a short opening flourish, nothing came of the learned valet's efforts: nature had denied him musical talent as it had all others.

Life at Marino had not been going too well, and poor Nikolai was in bad straits. Difficulties on the farm developed every day—depressing, senseless difficulties. The troubles with the hired laborers were becoming unbearable. Some demanded immediate payment or raises; others left, taking their advance wages; the horses fell

sick; the equipment was destroyed as quickly as if by
fire; tasks were executed negligently; the threshing machine ordered from Moscow turned out to be worthless
because of its weight; another one was ruined on the
first try; half the cattle shed burned down because one
of the house servants, a blind old woman, went to fumi-
gate her own cow with a torch in windy weather—it is
true that the old woman maintained that the entire misfortune came from the master's taking it into his head
to introduce unheard-of cheeses and milk products. The
overseer suddenly turned lazy and even began to get fat,
as every Russian does when he happens on a soft berth.
On seeing Nikolai in the distance, he would demonstrate
his zeal by throwing a chip of wood at a pig running
past or threatening a half-naked urchin, but, on the other
hand, he did more sleeping than anything else. The
peasants who had been put on the tenant system failed
to meet their payments and stole wood; almost every
night the watchmen discovered the peasants' horses on
the "farm's" meadows and sometimes seized them after a
skirmish. Nikolai was about to establish a fine for dam-
age to the crops caused by cattle grazing on his fields,
but the matter usually ended with the horses being returned to their owners after spending a day or two on
the master's fodder.

To top it all, the peasants began quarreling among
themselves; brothers were demanding the subdivisions of
their land; their wives were unable to get along in one
house. The squabble would suddenly come to a boil, all
the peasants would suddenly rise as if on command and
assemble on the run in front of the office; often drunk
and battered, they used to climb up to the master and
demand justice and redress; a tumult of voices would
arise, women's wailing shrieks mixed with male cursing.
It would then be necessary to separate the hostile sides
and to shout one's self hoarse with the foreknowledge
that arriving at a just decision was in any case impossible.

There were not enough hands for the harvest: a neighboring freeholder of the most honorable appearance con-
tracted to furnish reapers at a commission of two rubles

per field, then practised the most unscrupulous kind of swindle; his own peasant women asked unheard-of wages, while the grain fell off the stalk without their making any progress in the reaping, and at the same time the Guardian's Council* was threatening and demanding immediate and full payment of its percentage.

"I'm at the end of my strength!" Nikolai exclaimed with despair more than once. "I can't chastise them myself; my principles won't permit sending for the militia, yet nothing can be done without the fear of punishment!"

"*Du calme, du calme,*" Pavel would remark at this, while he himself mumbled, frowned and tugged on his mustaches.

Bazarov kept himself aloof from these "wrangles"; moreover, it did not behoove him, as a guest, to meddle in others' affairs. The day after his arrival at Marino, he busied himself with his frogs, infusoria and chemical formulas, and was constantly occupied with them. Arkady, on the other hand, felt it his duty, if not to help his father, at least to give the appearance of being ready to help him. He listened to him patiently and once offered some advice, not to have it followed, but rather to demonstrate his participation. He had no adverse reaction to administrative affairs, and even found satisfaction in pondering over agricultural matters, but different thoughts were evolving in his head at that time. Arkady —to his own amazement—thought about Nikolskoye constantly; he would have just shrugged his shoulders if someone had told him earlier that he could become bored under the same roof with Bazarov, and particularly under that one—his parental roof; but he was indeed bored, and longed to leave. He resorted to walking until exhausted, but that was of no help. Once, talking to his father, Arkady learned that Nikolai had some rather interesting letters written to his late wife at some time by Odintsova's mother. Arkady kept after his father until he got the letters, for which Nikolai was forced to rummage in two dozen trunks and boxes. Once he had come into possession of these half-rotted papers, Arkady seemed calmer, as though he had just

glimpsed clearly in front of him the aim he had to reach.
" 'Both of you,' she added herself," he whispered incessantly. "I'll go, I'll go, the devil with it!" But he remembered the last visit, the cold reception and that past awkwardness, and timidity overcame him.

The "here goes" spirit of youth, a secret desire to test
his luck, to try his strength on his own without any
support whatsoever—these won out in the end. It had
not been ten days since his return to Marino when, under
the pretext of studying the organization of Sunday
schools, he galloped back to town and thence to Nikolskoye. Continually urging his coachman on, he rushed
there like a young officer going to combat: he had fear
in him, and gaiety, and impatience was choking him.
"The main thing is—not to think," he kept repeating to
himself. He happened to get a spirited coachman, who
stopped in front of every tavern to ask, "A snort?" or:
"How about a snort?"—but once he had *snorted*, he did
not spare the horses.

Now at last the high roof of the familiar house appeared. "What am I doing?" suddenly flashed through
Arkady's mind. "But there's no turning back!" The three
horses raced along in unison; the coachman whooped
and whistled. Now the little bridge was already rattling
under the hoofs and wheels, now the alley of clipped firs
was rushing towards them. . . . A pink feminine dress
flashed in the dark greenery, a young face glanced from
under the light fringe of a parasol—he recognized Katya
and she recognized him. Arkady ordered the coachman
to stop the galloping horses, sprang out of the carriage,
and went up to her. "It's you!" she said, slowly blushing.
"Come to my sister, she's there in the garden; she'll be
happy to see you."

Katya led Arkady into the garden. His meeting with
her struck him as a particularly good omen; he was
delighted with her as if she were a kindred soul. Everything worked out so well: no major-domo, no announce-
ment. At a turn in the path he caught sight of Odintsova.
She stood with her back towards him. Hearing footsteps,
she slowly turned around.

Arkady was on the verge of embarrassment again, but

the first words she pronounced calmed him at once. "Hello, Runaway!" she said in her even, friendly voice and came to meet him, smiling and squinting in the sun and wind. "Where did you find him, Katya?"

"I brought you something, Anna Sergeyevna," he began, "which you didn't expect at all—"

"You brought yourself; that's the best of all."

xxiii

After seeing Arkady off with mock regret and making it understood that he was not at all deceived about the real object of the trip, Bazarov went into complete isolation; he was overcome by a fever of work. He no longer quarreled with Pavel, particularly since the latter assumed an even more excessively aristocratic air in his presence and expressed his opinions more by sounds than words. On one occasion only, Pavel was about to enter into a controversy with the nihilist over the then fashionable question of the rights of Baltic nobles, but he sud denly stopped, saying with cold civility: "However, we can't understand each other; at least I haven't the honor of understanding you."

"Naturally!" Bazarov exclaimed. "A man is capable of understanding everything—how ether waves undulate, and what's happening on the sun; but how another man can blow his nose differently from the way he himself does—that he's incapable of understanding."

"Is that supposed to be witty?" Pavel queried as he moved away.

On the other hand, he sometimes asked permission to witness Bazarov's experiments, and once even put his perfumed face, washed with excellent fragrant soap, close to the microscope to watch a transparent infusoria gulp down a green particle and masticate it eagerly and thoroughly with a form of very agile clappers located in its throat. Nikolai visited Bazarov much more often than his brother did; he would have come every day to "study," as he put it, if difficulties in running the estate had not distracted his attention. He did not disturb the young naturalist; he sat in a corner of the room and watched attentively, now and then allowing himself a discreet question. During dinner and supper, he tried to direct the conversation to physics, geology or chemistry, as all other topics, even agriculture, to say nothing of politics, could lead, if not to clashes, at least to mutual displeasure.

Nikolai suspected that his brother's hatred for Bazarov had not diminished in the least. An unimportant incident, among many others, supported his suspicion. Cholera had broken out here and there in the vicinity and even "uprooted" two people from Marino itself. One night Pavel had a fairly severe attack. He was in torment until morning, but did not call on Bazarov's art for assistance. On seeing Bazarov the next morning and being asked why he had not sent for him, Pavel, still very pale, but nevertheless carefully combed and shaved, answered, "But if I recall, you yourself said you didn't believe in medicine?" So the days passed. Bazarov worked sullenly and stubbornly. But meanwhile, there was someone in Nikolai's house with whom one couldn't say he found consolation, but with whom he enjoyed talking—it was Fenechka.

He usually met her early in the morning in the garden or the yard; he never visited her in her room and she came to his door only once, to ask him—should she bathe Mitya or not? She not only trusted him, not only was not afraid of him—in his presence she behaved more freely and easily than in the presence of Nikolai himself. It is difficult to say why this was: perhaps because she unconsciously felt in Bazarov the absence of anything aristocratic, or anything superior of that sort, which both attracts and frightens. In her eyes he was both an excellent doctor and a simple man. She used to fuss over her child, uninhibited by his presence, and once, when she had a sudden dizziness and headache, accepted a spoonful of medicine from his hand. In the presence of Nikolai she seemed to avoid Bazarov, not out of slyness, but out of some sort of feeling of seemliness. Pavel she feared more than ever; some time ago he had begun to watch her, and used to appear unexpectedly as though he had sprung up out of the earth behind her back in his English suit, with his immobile, vigilant face and his hands in his pockets. "Like a dose of cold water on you," Fenechka complained to Dunyasha, while the latter sighed in answer and thought about the other "unfeeling" man. Bazarov, without suspecting it, had become the *cruel tyrant* of her soul.

Fenechka liked Bazarov, and was liked by him as well. Even his face changed when he talked to her: it took on an open expression, almost kindly, and his usual carelessness was infused with a kind of playful attentiveness. Fenechka grew prettier every day. There are times in the lives of young women when they suddenly begin to bud and flower like summer roses; such a time had come for Fenechka. Everything contributed to it, even the July heat which hung over those days. Dressed in a delicate white dress, she herself seemed whiter and more delicate. She did not tan, and the heat from which she could not shield herself, and which flushed her cheeks and ears lightly and instilled a gentle indolence through her whole body, was reflected in a drowsy languor in her pretty eyes. She was almost incapable of working; her hands just seemed to slide into her lap. She could barely walk, and sighed and complained all the time with comic helplessness.

"You should bathe more often," Nikolai used to say to her. He had built a big bath shielded by a linen cover in the only pond which hadn't completely dried up yet.

"Oh, Nikolai Petrovich! Before you get to the pond—you die; and when you come back—you die. There's no shade at all in the garden."

"That's true, there's no shade," Nikolai would answer, rubbing his forehead.

One day, returning from a walk at seven o'clock in the morning, Bazarov found Fenechka in the lilac arbor, which was still thick and green, although its blossoms had dropped long ago. She was sitting on the bench, a white kerchief tossed over her head as usual; beside her lay a mass of red and white roses, still damp with dew.

"Ah! Yevgeny Vassilich!" she said. To look at him, she raised a corner of her kerchief a bit, and in doing so bared her arm to the elbow.

"What are you doing here?" said Bazarov, sitting down next to her. "Making a bouquet?"

"Yes; for the table, for breakfast. Nikolai Petrovich likes it."

"But it's a long way to breakfast. What a pile of flowers!"

"I picked them now before it gets hot and one can't go out. You can only breathe now. I've got so weak from this heat. I'm even afraid maybe I'm getting sick?"

"What kind of nonsense is that! Let me feel your pulse." Bazarov took her hand, felt the steadily pulsing vein, and did not even start counting the beats. "You'll live a hundred years," he said, releasing her hand.

"Ah, God forbid!" she exclaimed.

"Why? Don't you want to live a long time?"

"Yes, but a hundred years! We had an old woman who was eighty-five—and what a martyr she was by then! Black, deaf, hunchbacked, coughed all the time; she was just a burden to herself. What kind of a life is that!"

"So it's better to be young?"

"Of course, what else?"

"But in what way is it better? Tell me!"

"What do you mean, what way? Just take me now, I'm young, I can do everything—and I go, and I come, and I bring, and I don't have to ask anyone for anything. What's better than that?"

"But take me—it's just the same to me whether I'm young or old."

"How can you say that—just the same? It's impossible, what you're saying."

"Well, you judge yourself, Fedosya Nikolayevna; what good is my youth to me? I live alone, a poor fellow . . ."

"That always depends on you."

"It isn't up to me at all! If only someone would take pity on me."

Fenechka looked at Bazarov out of the corner of her eye, but said nothing.

"What kind of book do you have there?" she asked after a brief pause.

"This one? It's a learned book; deep."

"But do you study all the time? And you don't get bored? It seems to me you already know everything."

"Obviously not everything. You try reading a little."

"But I won't understand anything in there. Is it Russian?" Fenechka asked, taking the heavily bound volume in both hands. "What a thick one!"

"It's Russian."

"Just the same, I won't understand anything."

"I didn't really suggest it for you to understand. I wanted to watch you, to see how you read. When you read, the tip of your little nose moves very prettily."

Fenechka, who was about to begin deciphering in a low voice an article she had opened to, entitled "About Creosotes," started to laugh and threw the book aside—it slid from the bench onto the ground.

"I like it when you laugh, too," Bazarov said.

"Enough!"

"I like it when you talk. It's like a little brook gurgling."

Fenechka turned her head away.

"How funny you are!" she said, sorting over the flowers with her fingers. "Why do you listen to me, anyway? You've had conversations with such clever ladies."

"Alas, Fedosya Nikolayevna!—believe me: all the clever ladies in the world aren't worth your little finger."

"What a fib you've told again," Fenechka whispered, and folded her hands.

Bazarov lifted the book from the ground.

"This is a medical book; why did you throw it away?"

"Medical?" Fenechka repeated, and turned towards him. "But do you know what? Since you gave me those little drops, remember—how well Mitya sleeps! I simply can't imagine how I can thank you; you're really so kind."

"But, actually, one should pay the doctor," Bazarov remarked with a grin. "As you yourself know, doctors are greedy people."

Fenechka looked up at Bazarov with eyes which looked even darker in contrast to the white reflection falling across her forehead. She did not know whether he was joking or not.

"If you wish, we'll be glad . . . It will be necessary to ask Nikolai Petrovich—"

"You think that I want money, then?" Bazarov interrupted her. "No, I don't need money from you."

"What then?" Fenechka asked.

"What?" repeated Bazarov. "Guess."

"I'm no fortune-teller!"

"Then I'll tell you; I need—one of those roses."

Fenechka laughed again, even clapping her hands, Bazarov's wish seemed so comical to her. She laughed and at the same time felt flattered. Bazarov looked at her intently.

"As you wish, as you wish," she said at last, and bending over the bench, started sorting the roses. "What would you like, a red or a white one?"

"Red, and not too big."

She straightened up.

"Here, take it," she said, but instantly jerked back her outstretched arm and, biting her lips, looked towards the entrance of the arbor, then pricked up her ears.

"What's that?" Bazarov asked. "Nikolai Petrovich?"

"No . . . He went to the fields. . . . Anyway, I'm not afraid of him—but Pavel Petrovich—I felt . . ."

"What?"

"I felt he was walking around. No . . . there's no one. Take it." Fenechka gave Bazarov the rose.

"What makes you afraid of Pavel Petrovich?"

"He frightens me all the time. That is—he doesn't talk, but looks so strange. And anyway, you don't like him. You remember, you used to quarrel with him all the time. I don't even know what your quarrel is about, but I can see that you twist him around like this and like that."

Fenechka demonstrated with her hands how, in her opinion, Bazarov twisted Pavel Petrovich around.

Bazarov smiled.

"And if he started to get the better of me," he asked, "would you stand up for me?"

"How could you need me to stand up for you? No, he's no match for you."

"You think so? But I know the hand which, if it wished, could fell me with a finger."

"What hand is that?"

"But don't you know, really? See how wonderful the rose you gave me smells."

Fenechka bent her little neck and brought her face close to the flower. . . . The kerchief slid from her head onto her shoulders; a soft mass of dark, shiny, slightly disheveled hair appeared.

"Wait, I want to smell it with you," Bazarov said, and leaning down, kissed her parted lips firmly.

She started, pushed against his chest with both hands, but pushed feebly, and he was able to renew and prolong his kiss.

A dry cough was heard behind the lilacs. Fenechka instantly moved away to the other end of the bench. Pavel appeared, bowed slightly, and after saying with rather sardonic sadness, "You're here," went away. Fenechka immediately gathered up her flowers and went straight out of the arbor. "It was sinful of you, Yevgeny Vassilich," she whispered as she left. There was a genuine reproach in her whisper.

Bazarov remembered another scene of not long ago and felt shame, annoyance and self-contempt. But he quickly tossed his head, ironically congratulated himself "on a formal entrance into libertinism," and went towards his room.

Meanwhile, Pavel went out of the garden and, walking slowly, wandered up to the woods. He stayed there a fairly long time; when he returned for breakfast, Nikolai anxiously asked him if he was well, his face had grown so somber.

"You know I sometimes suffer from liver trouble," Pavel answered him calmly.

xxiv

Two hours later he knocked on Bazarov's door.

"I must apologize for interrupting you in your scientific activities," he began, sitting down on a chair near the window and resting both arms on a handsome cane with an ivory head (he usually did not carry a cane); "but I am obliged to ask you to spare me five minutes of your time—no more."

"All my time is at your disposal," answered Basarov, who had felt a shadow pass over his face the moment Pavel crossed the threshold.

"Five minutes are enough for me. I came to put one question to you."

"A question? What about?"

"Be so kind as to hear me through. At the beginning of your stay in my brother's house, when I had not yet denied myself the pleasure of conversing with you, I had the opportunity of hearing your opinions on many subjects; but so far as I remember, the conversation never touched, either between us or in my presence, on individual combat, on dueling in general. May I have your opinion on this subject?"

Bazarov, who had half risen to meet Pavel, sat down on the edge of his chair and folded his arms.

"This is my opinion," he said: "from the theoretical point of view a duel—is an absurdity; from the practical point of view, however—it's another matter."

"That is, you mean, if I understood you, that regardless of your theoretical outlook on a duel, in practice you would not allow yourself to be insulted without demanding satisfaction?"

"You have fully grasped my thought."

"Very good, sir. I'm very pleased to hear that from you. Your words relieve my uncertainty—"

"Indecision, you mean."

"It's all the same, sir; I express myself in a way which will be understood; I'm—I'm not a bookworm. Your words save me from a certain regrettable necessity. I've resolved to fight with you."

Bazarov stared with amazement. "With me?"

"Absolutely. With you."

"But for heaven's sake, what for?"

"I could explain the reason to you," Pavel began. "However, I prefer to keep silent about it. To my taste, you're superfluous here; I can't stand you, I despise you, and if that's not enough for you . . ."

Pavel's eyes began to flash . . . Bazarov's also took fire.

"Very good, sir," Bazarov said. "Further explanations are not necessary. You have taken it into your head to test your quixotic spirit on me. I could refuse you this pleasure, but let that pass!"

"I'm deeply indebted to you," Pavel answered, "and I can now anticipate that you will accept my challenge without forcing me to resort to violent measures."

"In other words, to speak without metaphors, to that stick?" Bazarov observed coolly. "That is absolutely right. It is not at all necesary for you to insult me. It is not even completely safe. You can remain a gentleman. I accept your challenge in gentlemanly fashion also."

"Excellent," Pavel said, placing his cane in a corner. "Now we will have a few words about the conditions of our duel; but I should like to know first whether you consider it necessary to resort to the formality of a slight dispute to serve as the pretext for my challenge?"

"No, it's better without formalities."

"I think so myself. I also consider it out of place to go into the real reason for our antagonism. We can't stand each other. What more could one want?"

"What more could one want?" Bazarov repeated ironically.

"As far as the conditions for the duel are concerned, as we won't have seconds—for where would we get them?"

"Indeed, where would we get them?"

"Therefore I have the honor of offering you the following suggestion: to fight early tomorrow, let us say at six o'clock, behind the grove, with pistols; at ten paces—"

"Ten paces? All right; we hate each other enough at that distance."

"It could be eight," Pavel remarked.

"It could, why not!"

"Two shots; and to cover all eventualities, each shall put a note in his pocket making himself responsible for his own end."

"Now there I don't quite agree," Bazarov said. "It sounds a little like a French novel; somewhat implausible."

"Perhaps. However, you do agree that it would be unpleasant to incur suspicion of murder?"

"I agree. But there is a way to avoid such an unfortunate aspersion. We will have no seconds, but there can be a witness."

"Who, exactly, if I may ask?"

"Why, Piotr."

"Which Piotr?"

"Your brother's valet. He's a man who stands at the peak of contemporary civilization, and he will fulfill his role with all the *comilfo** such circumstances demand."

"I believe you're joking, my dear sir."

"Not in the least. After you've thought over my suggestion, you'll be convinced that it is full of common sense and simplicity. You can't hide a light under a bushel, and I'll take it on myself to prepare Piotr properly and to bring him to the field of combat."

"You've still joking," Pavel pronounced, rising from his chair. "But after the gratifying readiness you've shown, I haven't the right to make further claims on you. . . . Then it's all arranged. . . . By the way, I don't suppose you have any pistols?"

"Why would I have pistols, Pavel Petrovich? I'm not a soldier."

"In that case, I offer you mine. You can rest assured that it has been five full years since I've shot them."

"That's heart-warming news."

Pavel picked up his cane.

"And now, my dear sir, it only remains for me to

thank you and to return you to your activities. My compliments."

"Till the pleasure of our next encounter, my dear sir," Bazarov said, accompanying his guest to the door.

Pavel left. Bazarov stood in front of the door and suddenly exclaimed, "Damn it all! How grand and how foolish! What a comedy we played! Like trained dogs dancing on their hind legs. But refusing was out of the question; after all, he might have hit me, and then . . ." (Bazarov turned pale at the thought alone; all his pride rose in one wave.) "Then I would have had to strangle him like a kitten."

He turned back to his microscope, but his heart beat faster and the calm essential to scientific observations had disappeared. "He saw us today," he thought, "but could he possibly be going to such lengths on his brother's behalf? What's the importance of a kiss? There's something else to it. Bah! But couldn't he be in love himself? Of course he's in love; it's clear as day. What a mess, really! . . . It's vile," he decided at last, "vile no matter how you look at it. First I'll have to stick my neck out, and then leave no matter what happens; and there's Arkady—and that ladybug, Nikolai Petrovich. Vile, vile!"

The day passed in rather singular quietness and drowsiness. Fenechka was not to be seen; she sat in her room like a little mouse in its hole. Nikolai looked preoccupied. He had been informed that ergot had appeared in the wheat crop on which he had particularly counted. Pavel quelled everyone, even Prokofich, with his icy politeness. Bazarov started a letter to his father, then tore it up and threw it under the table. "If I die," he thought, "they'll hear; but I won't die. No, I'll be scraping around the earth for a long time yet." He gave Piotr orders to come to him the following day just after dawn for an important matter; Piotr presumed Bazarov wanted to take him along to St. Petersburg. Bazarov went to bed late and was tormented all night by confused dreams. . . . Odintsova whirled in front of him; she was his mother; behind her walked a kitten with black whiskers, and the kitten was Fenechka, while Pavel Petrovich

appeared before him in the guise of a big forest with
which he had to fight just the same. Piotr woke him at
four o'clock; Bazarov dressed and set off with him at
once.

It was a pleasant, fresh morning; small, many-hued
clouds flocked across the pale clear azure; fine dew, scattered on the leaves and grass, shone like silver on the
cobwebs; the damp, dark earth still bore the rosy trace
of dawn; the songs of larks showered from every corner
of the sky. Bazarov reached the grove, sat down in the
shade on its outskirts, and only then divulged to Piotr
what service he expected of him. The sophisticated
lackey was frightened to death; however, Bazarov calmed
him with the assurance that he would bear no responsibility whatsoever. "And furthermore," Bazarov added,
"think what an important role you have to play." Piotr
threw up his hands in despair, hung his head and, green
with fear, propped himself against a birch tree.

The road from Marino, which curved around the
grove, was covered with a light dust, undisturbed by
foot or wheel since the day before. Bazarov involuntarily
watched the road, plucked and chewed blades of grass,
and kept repeating over and over to himself, "What
foolishness!" The chill of the morning made him shiver
a couple of times. Piotr looked at him dolefully, but
Bazarov just smiled back: he was not afraid.

Horses' hoofs were heard tramping on the road. A
peasant came into sight from behind the trees, driving
two hobbled horses in front of him. As he passed by, he
looked at Bazarov rather strangely without raising his
cap, an occurrence which obviously disturbed Piotr as a
bad omen. "There's one who got up early too," Bazarov
thought, "but at least for work; while we . . . ?"

"I believe the gentleman is coming, sir," Piotr whispered suddenly.

Bazarov raised his head and caught sight of Pavel.
Dressed in a light checked jacket and snow-white trousers,
he was walking briskly along the road; under his arm
he carried a small case wrapped in green cloth.

"Excuse me, I believe I have kept you waiting," he

said, bowing first to Bazarov, then to Piotr, whom he considered at that moment as something on the order of a second. "I didn't want to wake my valet."

"It doesn't matter, sir," Bazarov answered; "we ourselves just arrived."

"Ah! So much the better!" Pavel glanced around. "No one to be seen, no one to interfere. . . . We may proceed?"

"Let us proceed."

"I presume you don't require any new explanations?"

"I do not."

"Do you wish to load?" Pavel asked, taking the pistols out of the box.

"No; you load, and I will measure off the paces. My legs are longer," Bazarov added with a wry smile. "One, two, three . . ."

"Yevgeny Vassilich," Piotr stammered with difficulty (he was shaking as in a fever), "with your permission, I'll withdraw."

"Four . . . five . . . withdraw, brother, withdraw; you may even stand behind a tree and stop your ears, just don't close your eyes; but run to pick up whoever falls. Six . . . seven . . . eight . . ." Bazarov stopped. "Enough?" he said, turning to Pavel, "or should I count off two more?"

"As you like," the other replied, driving in the second bullet.

"Well, we'll add two more paces." Bazarov drew a line on the ground with the toe of his boot. "There's the barrier. By the way, how many paces shall we take back from the barrier? That's also an important question. There was no discussion of it yesterday."

"Ten, I suppose," Pavel answered, handing Bazarov both pistols. "Be so kind as to choose."

"I will be so kind. But you must agree, Pavel Petrovich, that our duel is unusual to the point of absurdity. Just take a look at the physiognomy of our second."

"You like to joke all the time," Pavel answered. "I don't deny the strangeness of our duel, but I consider it my duty to warn you that I intend to fight in earnest. *A bon entendeur, salut!*"*

"Oh, I don't doubt that we've decided to exterminate each other, but why not laugh and unite *utile dulci*?* So it goes: you speak French to me and I speak Latin to you."

"I will fight in earnest," Pavel repeated and went towards his position. On his side, Bazarov counted off ten paces from the barrier and stopped.

"Are you ready?" asked Pavel.

"Quite."

"We may approach each other."

Bazarov moved slowly forward and Pavel, his left hand in his pocket, walked slowly towards him while gradually raising the muzzle of his pistol.

"He's aiming right at my nose," Bazarov thought, "and how carefully he aims, the bandit. I must say it's an unpleasant sensation. I shall look at his watch chain. . . ." Something whined sharply right next to Bazarov's ear, and at that same moment a shot rang out. "I heard it, therefore it's all right," had time to flash through his head. He took another step and without aiming, squeezed the trigger.

Pavel gave a slight start and clutched his thigh with his hand. A trickle of blood flowed down his white trousers.

Bazarov threw the pistol aside and approached his adversary.

"You are wounded?" he said.

"You were entitled to call me up to the barrier," Pavel replied. "This is a mere trifle. According to the agreement, each still has one shot."

"Come now, that's for another time," Bazarov answered, and caught hold of Pavel, who was beginning to turn pale. "Now I'm no longer a duelist but a doctor, and must take a look at your wound first of all. Piotr! Come here, Piotr! Where are you hiding?"

"This is all nonsense . . . I don't need anyone's help," Pavel said haltingly, "and . . . must . . . again . . ." He was about to tug on his whiskers, but his hand faltered, his eyes grew dim, and he lost consciousness.

"Now what! A fainting fit . . . Whatever for!" Bazarov exclaimed involuntarily as he laid Pavel down on the grass. "Let's see." He pulled out a handkerchief, wiped away the blood and felt around the wound. "The bone is intact," he muttered through his teeth; "the bullet went straight through, not deep; grazed one muscle, *vastus externus*. He'll be dancing around in three weeks! . . . But a fainting fit! Oh, those nervous people! That's a thin skin for you."

"Is he killed, sir?" Piotr's quavering voice hissed behind his back.

Bazarov looked around. "Fetch water quickly, brother, and he'll outlive both of us yet."

But the enlightened servant appeared not to understand his words and did not budge; Pavel slowly opened his eyes. "He's dying!" Piotr whispered and began crossing himself.

"You're right . . ." the wounded gentleman said with a forced smile; "what a stupid physiognomy!"

"But go and fetch the water, damn it!" Bazarov cried.

"No need . . . It was a momentary *vertige*. . . . Help me sit up. . . . There . . . This scratch just needs to be stopped with something and I'll get home on foot, or else a droshky can be sent for me. The duel, if you agree, is not to be resumed. You acted honorably—today, today—mind you."

"No point in recalling the past," Bazarov retorted, "while so far as the future is concerned, there's no use racking your mind over that either because I intend to slip off immediately. Here, let me bandage your leg now; your wound is not dangerous—just the same, it's best to stop the blood. But I must first bring this mortal back to life."

Bazarov shook Piotr by the collar and sent him for a droshky.

"See that you don't alarm my brother," Pavel said to him. "Don't take it into your head to notify him."

Piotr rushed off. While he was running for a droshky, the two adversaries sat on the ground in silence. Pavel tried not to look at Bazarov. He still did not want to make peace with him; he was ashamed of his vainglory, his failure, ashamed of the whole affair he had instigated, although he felt that it could not have ended in a more favorable way. "At least he won't be hanging around here," he reassured himself, "and that's something to be thankful for." The silence persisted, heavy and awkward. Both felt ill at ease. Each recognized that the other understood him. This consciousness is agreeable among friends, but totally disagreeable for enemies, particularly when it is impossible either to become reconciled or part company.

"I haven't bandaged your leg too tightly, have I?" Bazarov asked at last.

"No, it's all right, it's splendid," Pavel answered and added, after a short wait, "My brother can't be fooled; he'll have to be told that we quarreled over politics."

"Very good," Bazarov said. "You can say that I insulted all anglomaniacs."

"Splendid. What do you suppose that man is thinking about us now?" Pavel continued, pointing to the same peasant who had driven his hobbled horses past Bazarov a few minutes before the duel and, returning along the same road, "jumped to" and took off his hat at the sight of the "masters."

"Who knows!" Bazarov answered. "Most probably he isn't thinking anything. The Russian peasant—it's that same mysterious unknown Mrs. Radcliffe* used to elaborate on so extensively. Who can understand him? He doesn't understand himself."

"Ah! So that's what you think!" Pavel began, then suddenly exclaimed, "Look what your stupid Piotr has done now! There's my brother galloping here!"

Bazarov turned around and caught sight of Nikolai's pale face in the droshky. Nikolai jumped out before it had come to a stop and dashed up to his brother.

"What does this mean?" he said in an agitated voice. "Yevgeny Vassilich, for heaven's sake, what is this?"

"Nothing," answered Pavel. "They alarmed you for nothing. Mr. Bazarov and I had a little quarrel, and I paid a little for it."

"But how did it all happen, for the love of God?"

"What should I say? Mr. Bazarov spoke disrespectfully of Sir Robert Peel* I hasten to add that I alone am guilty

in all this, while Mr. Bazarov's conduct was above reproach. I challenged him."

"But good heavens, you're bleeding!"

"Did you think I had water in my veins? But this
blood-letting is even good for me. Isn't that right, doctor?
Help me sit in the droshky and don't let yourself be depressed. I'll be well tomorrow. There; splendid! Drive on,
coachman."

Nikolai followed the droshky; Bazarov was about to
stay behind. . . .

"I must ask you to take care of my brother," Nikolai
said to him, "until they fetch another physician from
town."

Bazarov bowed his head in silence.

An hour later, Pavel was already lying in bed with a
skillfully dressed leg. The whole household was in
alarm; Fenechka fainted. Nikolai was wringing his
hands, while Pavel, laughing and joking, particularly
with Bazarov, put on a delicate batiste shirt, a silk
smoking jacket and a fez, refused to allow the blinds to
be drawn, and complained amusingly about the necessity
of abtaining from food.

Towards night, however, he developed a fever and his
head began to throb. The doctor from town arrived.
(Nikolai had not listened to his brother's wishes—and,
moreover, Bazarov himself had urged the calling of another doctor. Bazarov had sat in his own room all day,
bilious and ill-tempered, paying only the briefest possible
visits to the patient; twice he happened to meet Fenechka, but she recoiled from him in terror.) The new
doctor recommended cooling drinks, but supported Bazarov's assertion that there was no foreseeable danger of
any kind. Nikolai told him his brother had wounded
himself through carelessness, to which the doctor replied, "Hmmm"—but on having twenty-five silver rubles
put in his palm, he said, "Indeed! That often happens,
to be sure."

No one in the house went to bed or even undressed.
Nikolai was constantly going in and out of his brother's
room on tiptoe; Pavel would doze a little, sigh softly,

say in French, *"Couchez-vous"*—and request something to drink. Nikolai once asked Fenechka to bring Pavel a glass of lemonade; Pavel looked at her fixedly and drank the glass down. Towards morning the fever increased somewhat and a slight delirium developed. At first Pavel uttered incoherent words; then he suddenly opened his eyes, and seeing his brother anxiously bending over his bed, said:

"But isn't it true, Nikolai, that Fenechka has something in common with Nelly?"

"With what Nelly, Pasha?"

"How can you ask that? With Princess R——! Particularly in the upper part of the face. *C'est de la même famille.*"*

Nikolai did not answer, but marveled at the vitality of dormant emotions in a man.

"It's come to the surface now," he thought.

"Ah, how I love that frivolous creature!" Pavel moaned, throwing his hands behind his head in despair. After a short pause he added, "I will not tolerate having some cad presume to touch . . ."

Nikolai simply sighed; he did not suspect to whom these words referred.

Bazarov came to see him the following day at eight o'clock. He had already had time to pack and to set free all his frogs, insects and birds.

"You came to say good-by to me?" Nikolai said, rising to meet him.

"Precisely, sir."

"I understand you and fully approve. My poor brother is, of course, guilty; and he is punished for it. He told me that he made it impossible for you to act otherwise. I believe there was no way for you to avoid that duel, which—which is to some extent explained by the permanent antagonism between your respective points of view alone." (Nikolai stumbled over his own words.) "My brother's—a man of the old stamp, hot-headed and obstinate. Thank God that it ended this way, at least. I have taken the necessary steps to avoid its becoming known."

"I'll leave you my address in case any scandal ensues," Bazarov remarked indifferently.

"I hope no scandal will ensue, Yevgeny Vassilich. I'm very sorry that your stay in my home had such—such an end. It's all the more distressing for me that Arkady—"

"I'll probably be seeing him," interrupted Bazarov, who was always made impatient by anything on the order of "explanations" and "declarations." "In case I don't, I beg you to give him my compliments, and please accept my regrets."

"And I beg—" Nikolai was answering with a bow. But Bazarov left without waiting for the end of his sentence.

When he heard Bazarov was leaving, Pavel asked to see him and shook his hand. Bazarov, however, remained cold as ice; he understood that Pavel wanted to be magnanimous. He was not able to say good-by to Fenechka; he just exchanged glances with her through the window. Her face seemed sad to him. "Well, she's lost!" he said to himself. "But, she'll pull out of it somehow!" On the other hand, Piotr carried on so that he cried on Bazarov's shoulder until the latter chilled him by asking if he had a waterfall in place of eyes; Dunyasha was forced to run off to the woods to hide her agitation.

The cause of all this grief climbed up in a horse-drawn cart, lit a cigar, and when at a bend two and a half miles down the road, the Kirsanov estate with its new manor house stood in his sight for the last time, he simply spat, and muttering "Damned feudalists!" wrapped his coat closer around him.

Pavel got better quickly, but was confined to bed for about a week. He endured his "captivity," as he called it, patiently enough, except that he fussed over his appearance a great deal and constantly ordered his room fumigated with eau de cologne. Nikolai read the papers to him; Fenechka waited on him as before, bringing bouillon, lemonade, soft-boiled eggs and tea, but a hidden terror came over her every time she entered his room. Pavel's unexpected action had frightened everyone in the house, but Fenechka most of all; only Prokofich was not disconcerted and explained that in his time gentlemen used to fight, "except only well-born people fought among themselves, while such rapscallions they'd have horsewhipped in the stables for their impudence."

Fenechka's conscience hardly bothered her at all, but the thought of the real reason for the dispute tormented her from time to time; and Pavel looked at her so strangely—in a way that made her feel his eyes on her even when she had her back turned towards him. She grew thinner from continual inner turmoil and, as usually happens, became even prettier.

Once—it was in the morning—Pavel was feeling well and moved from his bed to the couch; Nikolai, after inquiring about his health, went off to the threshing floor. Fenechka brought Pavel a cup of tea, put it on a little table, and was about to withdraw. Pavel detained her.

"Where are you hurrying, Fedosya Nikolayevna?" he began. "Do you have work to do?"

"No, sir . . . yes, sir . . . I have to pour out tea there."

"Dunyasha will do that without you; sit down a moment with a sick man. Incidentally, I must have a talk with you."

Fenechka silently sat down on the edge of an armchair.

"Listen," Pavel said, tugging his mustaches, "I wanted to ask you long ago; you seem rather afraid of me?"

"I, sir?"

"Yes, you. You never look at me; it's as though your conscience were not clear."

Fenechka blushed, but looked at Pavel. He seemed somewhat strange to her, and her heart fluttered slightly.

"Your conscience is clear, isn't it?" he asked her.

"Why shouldn't it be clear?" she whispered.

"How should I know! However, towards whom could you be guilty? Towards me? It's improbable. Towards anyone else here in the house? That's also unlikely. Perhaps towards my brother? But you love him, don't you?"

"I do."

"With all your soul, all your heart?"

"I love Nikolai Petrovich with all my heart."

"Truly? Look at me now, Fenechka" (it was the first

time he had addressed her that way). "You know—it's a great sin to lie!"

"I'm not lying, Pavel Petrovich. If I didn't love Nikolai Petrovich—why, then I wouldn't have any reason to live!"

"And you wouldn't trade him for anyone?"

"Who would I trade him for?"

"How should I know! What about that gentleman who just left here, for example?"

Fenechka stood up.

"God help me, Pavel Petrovich, why are you torturing me? What have I done to you? How can one talk like that?"

"Fenechka," Pavel said sadly, "but I saw . . ."

"What did you see, sir?"

"There—in the arbor."

Fenechka reddened to the tip of her ears and the roots of her hair.

"But how am I to blame for that?" she uttered with difficulty.

Pavel raised himself.

"You're not to blame? No? Not the least bit?"

"I love Nikolai Petrovich alone in the world and I'll love him for a century!" Fenechka said with sudden force, sobs rising in her throat; "while what you saw, and I'll say it on doomsday, is no fault of mine and wasn't, and it would be better for me to die right away if I can be suspected of such a thing towards my benefactor, Nikolai Petrovich . . ."

But there her voice failed her, and at that moment she felt Pavel seize and press her hand. She looked at him and stood as if petrified. He was even paler than before; his eyes were glowing, and most astonishing of all, a heavy, lone tear was rolling down his cheek.

"Fenechka!" he said in a strange whisper, "love, love my brother! He's such a kind, good man! Don't be untrue to him for anyone on earth, don't listen to anyone's fine speeches! Imagine, what can be more terrible than to love and not be loved! Never abandon my poor Nikolai!"

Fenechka was so startled that her tears dried and her

fear left her. But what did she feel when Pavel, Pavel Petrovich himself, pressed her hand to his lips and held it close without kissing it, sighing convulsively from time to time. . . .

"My God!" she thought. "Is he having a stroke?"

At that moment his whole broken life was surging within him.

The staircase creaked under brisk footsteps. He quickly pushed her away and threw his head back on the pillow. The door opened—and Nikolai appeared, jolly, fresh and ruddy. Mitya, as fresh and ruddy as his father, dressed only in a shirt, was bouncing in his father's arms and grasping at the big buttons of Nikolai's country jacket with bare little feet.

Fenechka literally threw herself at Nikolai, and encompassing both him and her son in her arms, nestled her head on his shoulder. Nikolai was surprised: Fenechka, timid and reserved, had never displayed her affection for him in the presence of anyone else.

"What's wrong with you?" he asked, and looking at his brother, handed Mitya over to her. "You don't feel worse?" he said, going up to Pavel.

Pavel thrust his face in a linen handkerchief. "No . . . really . . . I'm all right. . . . Actually, I'm much better."

"You shouldn't have moved to the couch so fast. Where are you going?" Nikolai added, turning to Fenechka; but she had already shut the door after her. "I was just bringing my treasure to show you; he's been missing his uncle. Why did she take him away? What's wrong with you, though? Did something happen between you here?"

"Brother!" Pavel said solemnly.

Nikolai started. He felt anxious, though he did not understand why himself.

"Brother," Pavel repeated, "give me your word that you will fulfill one request."

"What request? Tell me."

"It is very important. As I see it, your whole life's happiness depends on it. All this time I've been pondering over what I want to say to you now. . . . Brother, fulfill your duty, the duty of an honorable and generous man;

put an end to the temptation and the poor example you are setting—you, the best of men!"

"What do you mean, Pavel?"

"Marry Fenechka . . . she loves you; she's—the mother of your son."

Nikolai took a step back and threw up his hands. "You are saying that, Pavel? You, whom I've always considered the most inflexible opponent of such marriages! You're saying that! But didn't you know that it was solely out of respect for you that I hadn't fulfilled what you so justly call my duty!"

"You were wrong to respect me in that case," Pavel replied with a wan smile. "I'm beginning to think that Bazarov was right when he accused me of aristocraticism. No, my dear brother, we've given ourselves airs and pondered about the world enough: we're already old and subdued; it's time for us to put all frivolity aside. Just as you say, we must do our duty; and we shall get happiness into the bargain."

Nikolai rushed to embrace his brother.

"You've opened my eyes for good!" he exclaimed. "I haven't been constantly asserting that you're the kindest and most intelligent man in the world for nothing; but now I see that you're as wise as you are magnanimous."

"Gently, gently," Pavel interrupted him. "Don't hurt the leg of your wise brother who, at past fifty, went and fought a duel like an ensign. So, the matter is settled; Fenechka will be my—*belle-soeur*."

"My dear Pavel! But what will Arkady say?"

"Arkady? He'll be overjoyed, of course! His principles don't admit marriage, but then his feeling of equality will be satisfied. And actually, what do castes mean *au dix-neuvième siècle*?"

"Ah, Pavel, Pavel! Let me kiss you once more. Don't be afraid, I'll be careful."

The brothers embraced.

"What do you think, shouldn't you tell her your intentions now?" Pavel asked.

"Why hurry?" Nikolai countered. "Or did you discuss it with her?"

"Discuss it with her? *Quelle idée!*"

"Well, fine. First of all, get well; there's plenty of time for this. We must think it over thoroughly, consider . . ."

"But you have made up your mind, haven't you?"

"Of course I've made up my mind, and I thank you with all my heart. I'll leave you now, you need to rest; excitement is bad for you. . . . But we'll talk about it again. Go to sleep, my soul, and God give you health!"

"What is he thanking me for?" Pavel thought, once he was alone. "As if it hadn't been up to him! But as soon as he is married, I'll go somewhere far away, to Dresden or Florence, and live there till I croak."

Pavel moistened his forehead with eau de cologne and closed his eyes. Illuminated by the glaring daylight, his handsome, gaunt head lay on the white pillow like the head of a dead man—and he was, in effect, a dead man.

XXV

In the garden of Nikolskoye, Katya and Arkady were sitting on a turf bench in the shade of a tall ash; Fifi had settled on the ground near them, her long body twisted in that elegant curve hunters refer to as "a hare's resting position." Arkady and Katya were both silent; he held a half-opened book in his hands, while she picked left-over crumbs of white bread out of a little basket and threw them to a family of sparrows, which, with their habitual timorous impertinence, were hopping and chirping right at her feet. A faint breeze, stirring the leaves of the ash, made pale-gold specks of light swing slowly to and fro across the shady path and Fifi's tawny back. An unbroken shadow enveloped Arkady and Katya; from time to time, a bright stripe flashed in her hair. They were both silent, but the way they were silent, the way they sat side by side, revealed their trusting closeness: neither seemed to be conscious of the other, yet each was inwardly delighted at being close together. Their faces had changed, too, since we last saw them: Arkady looked calmer and Katya livelier, bolder.

"Don't you find," Arkady began, "that the ash is well-named in Russian? It sounds like the word for 'bright,' and there's no other tree which glimmers so lightly and brightly in the air."

Katya raised her eyes upwards and said, "Yes," while Arkady thought, "This one doesn't reproach me for expressing myself *prettily*."

"I don't like Heine when he's either mocking or crying," Katya said, looking at the book Arkady held in his hands. "I like him when he's pensive and sad."

"While I like him when he's mocking," Arkady remarked.

"Those are the remaining traces of your old satirical bent. . . ." ("Remaining traces!" thought Arkady. "If Bazarov heard that!") "Wait a bit, we'll transform you."

"Who'll transform me?"

"Who? My sister; Porfiry Platonovich, with whom you've stopped arguing; my aunt, whom you escorted to church day before yesterday."

"How could I have refused! And as far as Anna Sergeyevna is concerned, you remember, she herself agreed with Yevgeny about many things."

"My sister was under his influence then just as you were."

"As I was! Are you under the impression that I've freed myself from his influence?"

Katya remained silent.

"I know that you never liked him," Arkady continued.

"I can't judge him."

"Do you know, Katerina Sergeyevna, every time I hear that answer, I disbelieve it. There's no person alive who can't be judged by any one of us! That's just an evasion."

"Well, as I told you—it isn't that I don't like him, but I feel that he's alien to me, and I'm alien to him . . . yes, and you're alien to him."

"Why so?"

"How can I tell you? . . . He's a bird of prey, while you and I are tame."

"I'm tame too?"

Katya nodded her head.

Arkady scratched his ear.

"Look here, Katerina Sergeyevna: that's, after all, basically disparaging."

"Would you want to be a bird of prey?"

"No—but strong, energetic."

"That's not something one can wish for. Look at your friend; he doesn't want it, but it's in him."

"Hmm! And you think he had a great influence over Anna Sergeyevna?"

"Yes. But no one can keep the upper hand over her for long," Katya added in a low voice.

"Why do you think that?"

"She's very proud . . . that isn't what I mean . . . she values her independence very highly."

"Who doesn't value it?" Arkady asked, while "What good is it?" flashed through his mind. "What good is it?" flashed through Katya's too. Young people who are frequently and amicably close together constantly have the same thoughts occur to them.

Arkady smiled and moving a bit nearer Katya, said in a whisper, "Confess that you are a little afraid of *her*."

"Of whom?"

"*Her*," Arkady repeated meaningfully.

"And you?" Katya asked in turn.

"I too; notice, I said: *I, too*."

Katya shook her finger at him.

"That surprises me," she began; "my sister was never so well disposed towards you as right now; much more so than at your first visit."

"Indeed!"

"But haven't you noticed it? Doesn't it please you?"

Arkady became thoughtful.

"How could I have merited Anna Sergeyevna's good graces? It couldn't be because I brought her letters from your mother?"

"For that, and other reasons, which I won't tell."

"Why so?"

"I won't tell."

"Oh! I know: you're very stubborn."

"I'm stubborn."

"And observant."

Katya looked at Arkady from the corner of her eye.

"Perhaps. Does that make you angry? What are you thinking about?"

"I'm thinking about where you could have acquired that talent for observation which you really do have. You're so timid, so distrusting; you shy away from everyone . . ."

"I've lived alone a great deal; you begin to meditate in spite of yourself. But I don't shy away from everyone, do I?"

Arkady gave Katya a grateful glance.

"That's all very fine," he continued, "but people in your position, that is, with your means, rarely have that gift; as with the tsars, the truth has trouble reaching them."

"But you see I'm not rich."

Arkady was astonished and did not understand Katya at first. "Actually, the estate is all her sister's!" crossed his mind; he did not find this thought disagreeable.

"How well you said that!" he commented.

"What?"

"You said it well; simply, with neither shame nor pretence. Incidentally, I imagine there must be something special in the feeling of a person who knows and says that he's poor, something which is a kind of vanity in its own way."

"Because of my sister's kindness, I never experienced anything of that sort; I referred to my own means only because it happened to come up."

"True; but confess that you have a bit of that vanity I was just talking about."

"For example?"

"For example, you—forgive my question—you wouldn't marry a rich man?"

"If I loved him very much . . . No, I think even then I wouldn't marry him."

"Ah! There, you see!" Arkady exclaimed, then added

after a brief pause, "But why wouldn't you marry him?"

"Because even the songs tell the fate of the beggarly bride."

"Perhaps you want to dominate or . . ."

"Oh, no! What for? On the contrary, I'm ready to yield; it's just inequality which is difficult. While to keep one's self-respect and yield—that I understand; that's happiness. But a subordinate existence . . . No, enough of that."

"Enough of that," Arkady repeated after Katya. "Yes, yes," he continued, "it's not for nothing that you have the same blood as Anna Sergeyevna; you are just as independent as she; but you're more secretive. I'm certain you wouldn't ever dream of expressing your feeling first, no matter how strong and vital it was . . ."

"But how could it be otherwise?" asked Katya.

"You're just as intelligent; you have as much if not more character than she—"

"Don't compare me with my sister, please," Katya interrupted hastily. "It's too disadvantageous for me. You seem to have forgotten that my sister is both beautiful and witty, and—you in particular, Arkady Nikolaich, shouldn't say such things, and with such a serious face, too."

"What does that mean: 'you in particular'—and what leads you to conclude that I'm joking?"

"Of course you're joking."

"You think so? And what if I were convinced of what I say? If I find that I haven't even expressed myself strongly enough?"

"I don't understand you."

"Really? Now I see that I've overestimated your powers of observation."

"How so?"

Arkady turned aside without answering. Katya found a few more crumbs in the basket and began throwing them to the sparrows, but she swung her arms so vigorously that the birds flew off without touching the bread.

"Katerina Sergeyevna!" Arkady said suddenly. "It probably doesn't matter to you, but you should know that I wouldn't trade you—not only for your sister—but for anyone in the world."

He stood up and walked off quickly as if frightened by the words which had slipped out unguardedly.

Katya let both hands drop with the basket onto her lap, and with bowed head, gazed after Arkady for a long time. Little by little a crimson flush came over her cheeks, but her lips were unsmiling and her dark eyes expressed perplexity and another as yet nameless feeling.

"Are you alone?" Odintsova's voice rang out near her. "I thought you had gone to the garden with Arkady."

Katya turned slowly towards her sister. Odintsova, elegantly, even exquisitely dressed, was standing in the path and scratching Fifi's ear with the tip of her open parasol. Katya answered her slowly:

"I'm alone."

"I see that," the other answered with a laugh. "I suppose he has gone to his room?"

"Yes."

"You were reading together?"

"Yes."

Odintsova put her finger under Katya's chin and lifted up her face.

"You haven't quarreled, I hope?"

"No," Katya said, and gently took away her sister's hand.

"How solemnly you answer! I had hoped to find him here and invite him to go for a walk with me. He is always begging me to. Some shoes arrived from town for you; go try them on. I noticed yesterday that your old ones have completely worn out. You generally don't pay enough attention to that, though you have such attractive little feet! Your hands are nice too—a bit large, perhaps; you must display your little feet. But you're certainly no coquette."

Odintsova continued down the path, her beautiful dress rustling softly; Katya got up from the bench, and taking Heine with her, also left—but not to try on the shoes.

"Attractive little feet," she thought, slowly and lightly

climbing the sun-bleached, hot stone steps on the terrace; "attractive little feet, you say . . . Well, he will be
at those feet."

But a feeling of shame instantly came over her and
she ran swiftly upstairs.

Arkady went down the corridor towards his room; the
major-domo overtook him to announce that Mr. Bazarov
was waiting for him there.

"Yevgeny!" Arkady muttered almost fearfully. "Has he
been here long?"

"He just came this minute and gave orders not to be
announced to Anna Sergeyevna, but to be taken directly
to you."

"Could something have happened at home?" thought
Arkady, and hurriedly running up the stairs, he flung
the door open. Bazarov's expression immediately reassured him, although a more experienced eye would
probably have discerned signs of inner agitation in the
sunken but still energetic features of the unexpected
guest. With his dusty overcoat on his shoulders and his
cap on his head, he was sitting on the window sill; he
did not get up even when Arkady threw himself on his
neck with noisy exclamations.

"What a surprise! What brought you!" Arkady repeated over and over, bustling around the room like a
man who both imagines himself delighted and is anxious
to show that he is. "Well, is everything all right at home,
everyone well, I suppose?"

"Everything is all right at your house, but not everyone is well," Bazarov said. "Don't be such a chatterbox,
order me some *kvass*,* sit down, and listen to what I'll
tell you in a few, but I hope rather forceful words."

Arkady kept still while Bazarov told him about his
duel with Pavel. Arkady was very surprised and even
distressed, but saw no need to show it; he simply asked
if his uncle's wound was really not dangerous, and on
receiving the answer that it was most interesting—but
not in a medical sense—gave a forced smile, although at
heart he felt anxious and somehow ashamed. Bazarov
seemed to understand.

"Yes, brother," he said, "that's what it means to live

with feudalists. You turn into a feudalist yourself and end up taking part in knightly tournaments. Well, sir, I set off for Father's," Bazarov concluded, "and on the way I turned off here . . . if I didn't consider a useless lie foolishness, I'd say I came to tell you all this. No, I turned off here—the devil knows why. You see, it's sometimes useful for a man to take himself by the top of his head and pluck himself out like a radish out of the ground; that's what I managed to do the other day. . . . But I wanted to look once more at what I had parted from; at the ground where I once sat."

"I hope those words don't refer to me," Arkady said with feeling; "I hope you are not thinking of parting *with me*."

Bazarov looked at him fixedly, almost piercingly.

"And would that distress you so? It appears to me that *you* have already parted with me. You look so bright and fresh—things must be going well between you and Anna Sergeyevna."

"What things?"

"Well, you came here from town on her account, didn't you, fledgling? By the way, how are the Sunday schools coming along there? You're in love with her, aren't you? Or have you finally reached the stage of reticence?"

"Yevgeny, you know I was always frank with you. I can assure you, I vow to you, that you are wrong."

"Hmm! A new word," Bazarov remarked in a low voice. "But you don't have to get all excited over it, because it makes no difference to me. A romantic would say: I feel that our paths are beginning to divide, but I simply say that we have grown tired of each other."

"Yevgeny . . ."

"My friend, it's not a tragedy; what else won't one tire of in this world! But now, I think, we should say good-by, shouldn't we? Since I've been here, I feel sullied, just as if I had been pouring over Gogol's letters to the governor of Kaluga's wife. By the way, I didn't order the horses unharnessed."

"Heavens, that's impossible!"

"And why?"

"I'm not talking about myself now; but that would be

the height of discourtesy towards Anna Sergeyevna, who undoubtedly wants to see you."

"Well, there you're wrong."

"On the contrary, I am certain that I'm right," Arkady retorted. "And why are you pretending? If it comes to that, didn't you yourself come here on her account?"

"That, perhaps, is true, but you're mistaken all the same."

But Arkady was right. Odintsova wanted to see Bazarov and sent word through the major-domo for him to come to her. Bazarov changed before he went: it turned out that he had packed his new suit where he could easily put his hands on it.

Odintsova received him, not in that room in which he had unexpectedly revealed his love to her, but in the parlor. She extended the tips of her fingers to him affably, but her face revealed an involuntary tenseness.

"Anna Sergeyevna," Bazarov hastened to say, "I must first reassure you. Before you stands a mortal who has long ago come to his senses and hopes that others, too, have forgotten his foolishness. I am going away for a long time and you will agree that, although I am not a tender soul, it would be unpleasant for me to carry with me the thought that you remember me with disgust."

Odintsova sighed deeply like someone who has just ascended a high peak, and her face lighted up with a smile. She again stretched out her hand to Bazarov and returned his handclasp.

"Let him who recalls the past lose an eye," she said, "particularly since, to be honest, I was guilty then, if not of coquetry, then of something else. In a word: let us be friends as before. That was a dream, wasn't it? And who remembers dreams?"

"Who remembers them? And then love . . . is just an imaginary feeling."

"Really? I'm delighted to hear that."

So spoke Odintsova, and so spoke Bazarov; they both thought they were telling the truth. Was it the truth, the whole truth? They themselves did not know, and the author knows even less. But their conversation continued as though they fully believed each other.

Odintsova asked Bazrov, among other things, what he had been doing at the Kirsanovs'. He almost started to tell her about his duel with Pável, but restrained himself at the thought that she might think he was bragging, and answered her that he had spent the whole time working.

"While I," said Odintsova, "was depressed at first, God knows why; I was even getting ready to go abroad, imagine! . . . Then that passed; your friend Arkady Nikolayevich arrived, and I fell back into my rut, my true role."

"What role, if I may ask?"

"The role of aunt, tutor, mother, whatever you want to call it. By the way, you know, I didn't understand your close friendship with Arkady Nikolayevich very well before; I found him fairly insignificant. But now I've gotten to know him better and I've become convinced he's intelligent. And the main thing is that he's young, young—not like you and me, Yevgeny Vassilich."

"Is he still just as timid in your presence?" asked Bazarov.

"But was he . . ." Odintsova began, then added after a moment's thought, "Now he's grown more confident; he talks to me. He avoided me before. On the other hand, I didn't seek his company. He is more Katya's friend."

Bazarov felt annoyed. "It's impossible for women not to be sly!" he thought. "You say he avoided you," he pronounced with a cold smile. "But it probably didn't remain a secret to you that he was in love with you?"

"What? He too?" Odintsova asked inadvertently.

"He too," Bazarov repeated with a humble bow. "Is it possible you didn't know it and I'm announcing the news?"

"You are mistaken, Yevgeny Vassilich."

"I don't think so. But perhaps I shouldn't have brought it up," Bazarov replied, adding to himself, "and don't you be sly in the future."

"Why not bring it up? But I believe you are attaching too much importance to a fleeting impression. I am beginning to suspect you are inclined to exaggerate."

"We had better not talk about that, Anna Sergeyevna."

"Why not?" she said, but she herself led the conversa-

tion down another path. She still felt uneasy with
Bazarov although she had told him and had assured herself that all was forgotten. In the simplest exchanges
with him, even in joking with him, she felt her heart
constrict slightly with fear. In the same way, people on a
ship at sea talk and laugh no more and no less carelessly
than on dry land; but let there be the slightest halt, let
the slightest sign of something out of the ordinary appear, and a special, worried expression immediately
comes over everyone's face, evidence of the constant consciousness of constant danger.

Odintsova's talk with Bazarov did not last long. She
became lost in her own thoughts, made absent-minded
replies, and finally suggested they go into the drawing
room, where they found the princess and Katya. "But
where is Arkady Nikolaich?" the hostess asked, and learning that he had not put in an appearnace for over an
hour, she sent for him. He was not quickly found: he
had climbed into the thickest part of the garden where
he was sitting, his chin propped on his folded arms, ab-
sorbed in thoughts. They were deep and important,
those thoughts, but not sad. He knew that Odintsova was
alone with Bazarov, and he did not feel jealous as he
used to; on the contrary, his face gradually grew brighter;
he seemed to be wondering about something, and re-
joicing, and reaching a decision.

xxvi

The late Odintsov had not liked innovations, but had
tolerated "a certain play of inspirational taste," as a result of which he had had a structure on the order of a
Greek portico built out of Russian brick in his garden
between the greenhouse and the pond. Along the blind

back wall of this portico or gallery, there were six niches for statues which Odintsov was planning to import from abroad. These statues were to depict: Solitude, Silence, Meditation, Melancholy, Modesty and Sensitivity. One of them, the goddess Silence, with her finger held to her lips, arrived and was put in place, but her nose was broken by some of the houseboys on the day of her installation. Although the local mason undertook to make her a nose "twice as good as the old one," Odintsov ordered her removed and she found herself in a corner of the threshing shed, where she stood for many long years, arousing the superstitious fear of the peasant women. The front of the portico had been overgrown by thick bushes long ago; only the capitals of the columns appeared above the dense greenery.

The interior of the portico was cool, even at midday. Odintsova had disliked visiting this place ever since she had seen a snake in it, but Katya often came to sit on the big stone bench set under one of the niches. Surrounded by freshness and shade, she would read, work, or yield to that feeling of complete serenity which is probably known to everyone, and the delight of which consists of a hardly conscious, mute preception of the broad current of life, endlessly flowing around us and inside ourselves.

The day after Bazarov's arrival, Katya was sitting on her favorite bench and Arkady was again sitting next to her. He had begged her to go to the "portico" with him.

There was still about an hour until dinner; the dewy morning was already turning into a hot day. Arkady's face had the same expression as yesterday; Katya looked preoccupied. Her sister had called her into her study immediately following breakfast, and after a preliminary caress (which always alarmed Katya a little), advised her to be careful of her conduct with Arkady and in particular to avoid going off alone with him, as this seemed to have attracted the attention of her aunt and the entire household. In addition, even the evening before, Odintsova had been in low spirits, and Katya felt uneasy as if she were in some way to blame. In giving in to Arkady's request, she told herself that this was the last time.

"Katerina Sergeyevna," he said with a kind of timid familiarity, "since I have had the happiness of living under the same roof with you, I have talked about many things with you, but there is one thing which is very important to me—a matter which I haven't yet broached. You remarked yesterday that I've been transformed here," he added, catching and avoiding Katya's questioning look. "I have actually changed in many ways, and you know this better than anyone else—you, to whom I am basically indebted for this change."

"I? . . . To me? . . ." said Katya.

"I am no longer the arrogant boy I was when I came here," Arkady continued; "I haven't turned twenty-three for nothing; I want to be useful, as ever; I want to devote all my strength to the truth. But I no longer look for my ideals where I looked for them before; they are . . . much closer to me. Up to now, I hadn't understood myself, I set myself tasks which weren't within my strength. . . . My eyes were opened not long ago, thanks to a feeling . . . I am not expressing myself quite clearly, but I hope you will understand me. . . ."

Katya made no reply, but stopped looking at Arkady.

"I suppose," he began again in a somewhat more agitated voice, while a finch unconcernedly warbled his song in the leaves of the birch above; "I suppose that it is the obligation of every honest man to be completely frank with those . . . with those people who . . . in a word, with people close to him, and therefore I . . . I intend . . ."

But there Arkady's eloquence failed him; he became confused, hesitated, and was forced to be silent for a moment. Katya still did not raise her eyes. She seemed not to understand what he was leading up to, and was waiting.

"I foresee that I shall surprise you," Arkady resumed when he had recovered himself, "the more so as this feeling is related in some way . . . some way, mind you—to you. Yesterday, I recall, you accused me of a lack of seriousness," Arkady continued with the appearance of a man who has wandered into a swamp, feels that he is sinking deeper and deeper with each step, and still hurries forward in the hope of getting across as quickly as possible; "this reproach is often directed . . . falls . . . on young people, even when they stop deserving it; and if I had more self-confidence . . ." (But give me a little help, help me!—Arkady was thinking with despair but, as before, Katya did not turn her head.) "If I could hope . . ."

"If I could be convinced of what you say," Odintsova's clear voice was heard to say at that moment.

Arkady immediately fell silent, while Katya turned pale. Right next to the bushes which screened the portico ran a little path. Odintsova was walking along it accompanied by Bazarov. Katya and Arkady could not see them, but heard each word, every rustle, even their breathing. Bazarov and Odintsova took a few steps and, as if on purpose, stopped directly in front of the portico.

"You see," Odintsova continued, "you and I made a mistake; we are neither of us still in our first youth, particularly I; we have lived, grown tired; we are both—why pretend?—intelligent; at first we interested one another, our curiosity was aroused . . . and then—"

"And then I became uninteresting," Bazarov interrupted.

"You know that was not the reason for our misunderstanding. But whatever it was, we didn't need one another, that's the main thing; we had too much—how can one say it—the same nature. We didn't understand that at first. On the other hand, Arkady . . ."

"Do you need him?" Bazarov asked.

"Enough, Yevgeny Vassilich. You say he is not indifferent to me, and I myself always felt that he liked me. I know I'm old enough to be his aunt, but I won't hide from you that I have begun to think about him more often. That youthful, fresh feeling has a kind of charm—"

"The word fascination is used more in such cases," Bazarov put in, the mounting of rancor audible in his calm but wooden voice. "Arkady was being rather secretive about something with me yesterday and talked about neither you nor your sister. That's a serious symptom."

"He is just like a brother with Katya," Odintsova said, "and I like that in him, although perhaps I shouldn't have allowed them to be so close."

"Is that the sister speaking in you?" Bazarov said with a drawl.

"Of course. . . . But why are we standing? Let's go. What a strange conversation we are having, aren't we? I could never have anticipated that I would talk that way with you. You know, I am afraid of you—and at the same time I trust you because you are essentially very kind."

"In the first place, I am not at all kind; and in the second place, I'm no longer important to you and you tell me I am kind. . . . It's just like putting a wreath of flowers on the head of a corpse."

"Yevgeny Vassilich, we are not able to . . ." Odintsova's voice began; but a breeze arose, rustled the leaves, and carried away her words.

"But you are free," Bazarov stated after a short silence. Nothing more could be distinguished; the steps went away . . . everything was still.

Arkady turned towards Katya. She was in the very same position except that her head had dropped even lower.

"Katerina Sergeyevna," he said, twisting his hands, his voice trembling; "I love you forever and irrevocably, and I love no one but you. I wanted to say that to you, to know what you think, and to ask for your hand, because I, too, am not rich and I feel I am ready for all the sacrifices. . . . You have no answer? You don't believe me? You think that I am talking irresponsibly? But think of these last days! Haven't you been convinced long ago that everything else—understand me—everything, everything else has disappeared without a trace long ago? Look at me, say one word to me. . . . I love . . . I love you . . . believe me!"

Katya looked at Arkady with a clear, serious look and, after reflecting a long time, barely smiling, said:

"Yes."

Arkady jumped up from the bench.

"Yes! You said yes, Katerina Sergeyevna! What does

that word mean? That is, that I love you, that you believe me . . . Or—or—I don't dare continue. . . ."

"Yes," Katya repeated, and this time he understood her. He seized both her large handsome hands and, breathless with joy, pressed them to his heart. He could barely stand on his feet and just repeated over and over, "Katya, Katya . . ." while she innocently started to cry, gently laughing at herself through her tears. Whoever has not seen such tears in the eyes of a loved one, has not experienced to what degree, overcome by gratitude and remorse, a man can be happy on earth.

The next day, early in the morning, Odintsova summoned Bazarov to her study and with a forced laugh handed him a folded sheet of writing paper. This was a letter from Arkady; in it he asked for her sister's hand.

Bazarov scanned the letter quickly and made an effort to control himself in order not to show the spiteful feeling which instantly flared up in him.

"So," he commented, "and I believe it was only yesterday that you thought he loved Katerina Sergeyevna with a brotherly love. What do you intend to do now?"

"What do *you* advise?" Odintsova asked, still laughing.

"Well, I suppose," Bazarov answered, also with a laugh, although he was not at all amused and did not feel like laughing any more than she, "I suppose that the thing to do is to give the young people your blessing. The match is a good one in every respect; Kirsanov has a passable fortune, he's the only son, and his father is a good-natured chap who won't oppose him."

Odintsova wandered around the room, her face alternately flushing and paling.

"You think so?" she said. "Well? I don't see any obstacles. I'm pleased for Katya—and for Arkady Nikolaich. Of course, I'll wait for the father's answer. I'll send Arkady off for the reply himself. And so it turns out that I was right yesterday when I told you that you and I are already old. How could I have failed to notice anything? That surprises me!"

Odintsova laughed again, then suddenly looked away.

"Today's youth has become terribly sly," Bazarov remarked, also laughing. "Good-by," he said after a brief silence. "I wish you the most agreeable ending to this affair, but I will rejoice from afar."

Odintsova quickly turned towards him.

"You mean you're leaving? Why don't you stay *now*? Stay . . . it's entertaining to talk to you. It's like walking on the edge of a precipice. At first one's timid, and then one gets courage from somewhere. Stay."

"Thank you for the invitation, Anna Sergeyevna, and for the flattering opinion of my conversational talents. But I find that I have already been mixing too long in a world alien to me. Flying fish can remain in the air for a certain time, but they soon have to flop down in the water; allow me to drop into my own element too."

Odintsova looked at Bazarov. A bitter grin twisted his pale face. "This man loved me!" she thought—and felt pity for him and extended her hand to him in sympathy.

But he also understood her.

"No!" he said, taking a step back. "I am a poor man, but I haven't accepted charity to this day. Farewell, and the best of everything to you."

"I am convinced that we are not seeing each other for the last time," Odintsova said with an involuntary movement.

"Anything can happen in this world!" Bazarov answered with a bow and left.

"So you decided you'd weave yourself a nest?" he said to Arkady that same day while squatting on the floor to pack his trunk. "Well? It's a good idea. But you didn't have to be so crafty. I expected a completely different tack from you. Or perhaps this took you by surprise too?"

"It wasn't exactly what I expected when I left you," Arkady answered, "but why are you being crafty yourself and saying, 'It's a good thing,' as if I weren't aware of your opinion on marriage?"

"Ah, my good friend!" Bazarov said; "the things you say! You see what I'm doing: there was an empty space left in the trunk which I'm filling with hay; that's how it is in our life's baggage; no matter what we stuff it with, it's better than having an empty space. Don't be offended, please: after all, you probably remember what my opinion always was about Katerina Sergeyevna. Many a lady is reputed to be intelligent just because she sighs intelligently; but yours will hold her own, yes, and hold her own so well that she'll take you in hand too—well, that's as it should be."

He banged the lid shut and got up from the floor. "And now I'll repeat to you in parting—because there's no point in deceiving ourselves: we are parting forever, and you feel this yourself—you have acted wisely. You weren't made for our bitter, harsh, lonely life. You have neither boldness nor hatred, although you have youthful courage and youthful passion; that isn't enough for our work. Your kind, you gentlemen, can't go beyond noble resignation or noble indignation, and that amounts to nothing. For one thing, you're not fighters, although you picture yourselves as heroes—while we want to fight. Well! Our dust will scratch out your eyes, our filth will soil you, and you haven't come near reaching our stature; you admire yourselves unconsciously, you enjoy criticizing yourselves, but we're fed up with that—give us other people! We need others to crush! You're a good fellow, but you're a soft little liberal aristocrat—*eh vollatoo,** as my parent would say."

"You are saying good-by to me forever, Yevgeny," Arkady said sadly, "and you have nothing else to say to me?"

Bazarov scratched the back of his head.

"I do, Arkady; I do have other things to say, but I'm not going to say them because that's romanticism—that's syrup. But marry as soon as possible; and furnish your nest, and make as many children as possible. They'll be intelligent simply by being born at the right time, unlike you and me. Aha! I see the horses are ready. It's time! I have taken leave of everyone. . . . Well, then? Shall we embrace?"

Arkady threw himself on the neck of his former mentor and friend, and tears seemed to gush from his eyes.

"That's what it means to be young!" Bazarov said calmly. "But I'm counting on Katerina Sergeyevna. You'll see how quickly she'll console you!"

"Farewell, brother!" he said to Arkady when he had already climbed into the wagon, and pointing to a pair of jackdaws sitting side by side on the roof of the stable, added: "There you are! Study them!"

"What does that mean?" asked Arkady.

"What? Are you so weak in natural history, or have you forgotten that the jackdaw is the most respected family bird? An example for you! . . . Farewell, *signor!*"

The cart lurched and rolled away.

Bazarov had been right In talking to Katya that evening, Arkady completely forgot his friend. He had already begun to give in to Katya, and she was conscious of this and not surprised. He was to go to Marino to see his father the following day. Odintsova did not want to interfere with the young people, and it was only for the sake of propriety that she avoided leaving them alone together too long. She good-naturedly kept the princess at a distance from them (the news of the forthcoming marriage had reduced the spinster to tearful rage). At first Odintsova was afraid that the sight of their happiness might be a little depressing for her, but it turned out to be just the opposite: this sight not only failed to oppress her, it occupied her, and in the end, made her more affectionate. She was both pleased and saddened by this. "It's clear Bazarov is right," she thought; "curiosity, curiosity alone, and love of tranquillity, and egoism . . ."

"Children!" she said aloud, "is it true that love's an imaginary feeling?"

But neither Katya nor Arkady even understood her. They shunned her; the inadvertently overheard conversation was ever-present in their minds. However, Odintsova reassured them before long, and it was not difficult for her: she had found reassurance herself.

xxvii

The old Bazarovs' delight at their son's arrival was enhanced by its unexpectedness. Arina Vlassevna was in such a state of agitation and bustled around the house so, that Vassily Ivanovich compared her to a "little partridge": the docked tail of her short blouse actually made her somewhat birdlike. He himself just cackled and chewed the amber stem of his pipe in the corner of his mouth; from time to time he would put his hands to his neck and turn his head from side to side as if testing whether it was well screwed on; then he would suddenly chuckle soundlessly, his wide mouth gaping.

"I've come to you for six whole weeks, old man," Bazarov said to him; "I want to work, so please, don't you bother me."

"You'll forget my features, that's how much I'll bother you!" Vassily Ivanovich answered.

He kept his promise. Installing his son in his study as before, he did everything but hide from him and kept his wife from any superfluous demonstrations of affection. "Little Mother," he told her, "the first time Yevgeny came, we were a bit of a bother to him; now we must be wiser." Arina Vlassevna followed her husband's advice, but found little comfort in it; she saw her son only at meals and was too afraid to engage him in conversation. "Yenushenka!" she used to say, but before he had time to look up, she would be fingering the tassels of her handbag and stammering: "It's nothing, it's nothing, I just said that"—and would then go to Vassily Ivanovich, and leaning on her hand, say to him, "How can one find out, dear, what Yenusha wants for dinner today, sour cabbage soup or borsht?" "Well, why didn't you ask him yourself?" "But I'll be bothering him!"

However, Bazarov soon stopped shutting himself in: the fever of work suddenly dropped and was replaced by melancholy boredom and gloomy restlessness. A strange weariness was noticeable in all his movements; even his gait, his firm, forcefully bold gait, was changing. He stopped walking in solitude and began to seek company; he drank tea in the parlor, wandered in the vegetable garden with Vassily Ivanovich and smoked with him in silence; he even inquired about Father Aleksei once.

Bazarov's father was pleased by this change at first, but his pleasure was short-lived. "Yenusha distresses me," he quietly complained to his wife; "he's not exactly displeased or angry, that would be nothing; he's hurt, he's sad—that's what's terrible. He's always silent; if he'd only take it out on us; he's getting thin, his color is so poor." "Oh Lord, Lord!" the old woman whispered. "I would put an amulet around his neck, but of course he won't allow it." Several times Vassily Ivanovich tried to question Bazarov as cautiously as possible about his work, about his health, about Arkady . . . But Bazarov answered him unwillingly and offhandedly. Once during a conversation, noticing that his father was rather stealthily leading up to something, Bazarov said to him with vexation: "Why are you always going around me as if on tiptoe? This behavior is even worse than before." "Come, come, come, I meant nothing!" poor Vassily Ivanovich answered hastily.

His political allusions were also without result. On one occasion he started to talk about the imminent freeing of the serfs, about progress, in the hopes of arousing a sympathetic response in his son, but the latter said indifferently: "Yesterday I was walking along the fence and heard the local peasant boys, instead of singing some old folk song, bawling a cabaret tune about 'the right time coming, the heart feeling love' . . . There's progress for you."

Bazarov sometimes went to the village and, bantering as usual, would enter into conversation with one of the peasants. "Well," Bazarov would say to him, "tell me your views on life, brother: they say all the strength and future of Russia is in you, a new epoch of history will spring from you—you will give us both a real language and laws." The peasant would either answer nothing or utter something on the following order: "Well, we perhaps . . . and anyway, because, I mean . . . what is put up to us—for example, we have—" "Will you explain to me what your *mir* is?" Bazarov would interrupt him. "And is it the same *mir* which stands on three fishes?"*

"It's the earth that's standing on three fishes, master," the peasant would explain soothingly, with a patriarchally good-natured sweetness; "against ours, that is, our *mir*, it's known, there's the gentlemen's will; therefore you are our fathers. And the more strict the master is, the better off the peasant."

One day when he heard such talk, Bazarov contemptuously shrugged his shoulders and turned away, while the peasant went slowly homewards.

"What was all the talk about?" another peasant of middle age and surly visage called to him from a distance, having witnessed his conversation with Bazarov from the doorway of his hut. "About unpaid debts, eh?"

"Debts, my foot, brother!" answered the first peasant, and in his voice there was no longer any trace of the patriarchal sweetness; on the contrary, a sort of cold coarseness was audible. "He was just babbling; his tongue was itching. Of course—a master; how could he understand anything?"

"Understand, bosh!" the other peasant answered, and shoving back their caps and tightening their belts, they set about discussing their affairs and needs. Alas, Bazarov, who had shrugged his shoulders with such contempt— Bazarov, who knew how to talk to the peasants (as he had boasted in his quarrel with Pavel)—that same self-confident Bazarov did not have the slightest suspicion that in their eyes he was nevertheless something on the order of a simple buffoon.

However, he found himself an occupation at last. One day Vassily Ivanovich was dressing the wounded leg of a peasant in Bazarov's presence, but the old man's hands trembled and he was unable to cope with the bandages;

his son helped him, and from that time on began to participate in his practice. However, Bazarov continued to make fun of the remedies he himself recommended, and of his father, who always immediately adopted them. But Bazarov's jeering did not disturb Vassily Ivanovich in the least; it was even a comfort to him. Holding his soiled dressing gown across his stomach with two fingers and smoking his pipe, he listened to Bazarov with pleasure, and the more malice there was in his sallies, the more good-naturedly his gratified father laughed, displaying every single one of his black teeth. He even repeated those sometimes pointless or nonsensical sallies. For example, during the course of several days, he kept repeating without rhyme or reason: "Well, that was a tenth-rate deed!" just because his son used this expression on learning he had gone to matins. "Thank God! He's stopped moping!" he whispered to his wife. "How he tore into me today, my!"

In addition, the thought of having such an assistant transported him with enthusiasm, filled him with pride. "Yes, yes," he said to a peasant woman wearing a man's overcoat and native headdress while handing her a vial of Goulard water or a jar of henbane salve, "you should thank God every minute, my good woman, that I have my son with me; now you're treated according to the most scientific and newest methods, do you understand that? Even the Emperor of the French, Napoleon, doesn't have a better physician." But the woman, who had come to complain that "it was rising in little shooting pains" (the meaning of these words she herself was unable to explain), merely bowed and reached in her bosom where she had put four eggs wrapped in the end of a towel.

Bazarov once even pulled out a tooth for a traveling cloth peddler, and although this tooth was average in every respect, Vassily Ivanovich nevertheless kept it as a rarity, and showed it to Father Aleksei, repeating over and over:

"Look at that root! What strength Yevgeny has! The merchant just shot up in the air . . . I think even an oak would have flown right out!

"Remarkable!" Father Aleksei said at last, not knowing what to answer or how to get away from the ecstatic old man.

One day a peasant from a neighboring village brought his brother, ill with typhus, to Vassily Ivanovich. Lying flat on a bundle of straw, the miserable wretch was dying; dark spots covered his body and he had long ago lost consciousness. Vassily Ivanovich expressed his regret that no one had thought of turning to medical aid earlier, and explained that there was no saving him. In fact, the peasant did not reach home with his brother; he died there in the cart.

Three days later Bazarov came into his father's room and asked if he had a caustic stone.

"Yes; what do you want it for?"

"I need it . . . to cauterize a cut."

"For whom?"

"Myself."

"What do you mean, yourself! What for? What kind of a cut? Where is it?"

"There, on my finger. I went to the village today, you know—the one from which they brought the peasant with typhus. For some reason they were getting ready to dissect him, and I had had no practice of that sort in a long time."

"Well?"

"Well, so I asked the district doctor's permission; well, and I cut myself."

Vassily Ivanovich suddenly turned very pale, and without a word, rushed to his study from which he immediately returned with a piece of caustic stone in his hand. Bazarov wanted to take it and leave.

"For the love of God," said Vassily Ivanovich, "let me do it myself."

Bazarov smiled at him.

"What a glutton for practice you are!"

"Don't joke, please. Show me your finger. The cut isn't big. Does it hurt?"

"Press harder, don't be afraid."

Vassily Ivanovich stopped.

"What do you think, Yevgeny, wouldn't it be better for us to cauterize it with an iron?"

"That would have had to be done earlier; now, actually, the caustic stone is of no use either. If I've caught it, it's too late now."

"How . . . too late . . ." Vassily Ivanovich could barely utter the words.

"Of course! Four hours and more have gone by since then!"

Vassily Ivanovich burned the cut a little more.

"But didn't the district doctor have a caustic stone?"

"None."

"How could that be, my God! A doctor—and he doesn't have such an essential thing!"

"You should have seen his lancets," Bazarov said and went out.

Until nightfall and throughout the entire next day, Vassily Ivanovich seized every possible pretext to go into his son's room; although he not only refrained from mentioning the cut, but even made an effort to talk about the most far-removed subjects, he still looked his son in the eyes so fixedly and watched him so anxiously, that Bazarov finally lost patience and threatened to leave. Vassily Ivanovich promised his son not to worry, particularly since Arina Vlassevna, from whom he had of course hidden everything, was beginning to ply him with questions as to why he didn't sleep and what was happening to him. He held himself in check for two whole days, although the appearance of his son, whom he kept watching furtively, was not very reassuring to him. But at dinner on the third day, he was no longer able to stand it. Bazarov was sitting with downcast eyes and was not touching a single dish.

"Why aren't you eating, Yevgency?" he asked, assuming his most carefree expression. "The food's very good, I find."

"I don't feel like it, so I'm not eating."

"You have no appetite? And your head?" he added in a timid voice. "Does it ache?"

"It aches. Why shouldn't it?"

Arina Vlassevna sat erect and became wary.

"Don't get angry, please, Yevgeny," Vassily Ivanovich continued, "but won't you let me feel your pulse?"

Bazarov stood up. "I can tell you without feeling it that I have a fever."

"And you've had chills?"

"And I've had chills. I'm going to lie down; and send me some lime tea. I must have caught cold."

"Yes, that's it, I heard you coughing last night," said Arina Vlassevna.

"I caught cold," Bazarov repeated and went away.

Arina Vlassevna busied herself making tea from lime flowers; Vassily Ivanovich went into the adjoining room and clutched his hair in silence.

Bazarov did not get up again that day, and spent the entire night in a heavy, half-conscious slumber. Around one in the morning, he opened his eyes with effort, saw the pale face of his father above him in the lamp-light, and ordered him to leave; his father obeyed, but immediately returned on tiptoe and, half-hidden behind the cupboard doors, stood staring intently at his son. Arina Vlassevna did not go to bed either; leaving the door of the study open a crack, she came near time and again to hear "how Yenusha is breathing," and to look at Vassily Ivanovich. She could see only his motionless, stooped back, but even that soothed her a little. In the morning, Bazarov tried to get up; his head spun, his nose began to bleed; he lay down again. Vassily Ivanovich attended to his needs silently; Arina Vlassevna came in to him and asked how he felt. He answered, "Better" —and turned towards the wall. Vassily Ivanovich waved his wife away; she bit her lip to keep back her tears and went out. Everything in the house suddenly turned dark; every face grew long, a strange silence fell. A squalling rooster was taken from the barnyard to the village where he loudly protested this incomprehensible treatment.

Bazarov continued to lie huddled against the wall. Vassily Ivanovich tried to ask him various questions, but they tired Bazarov, and the old man sat benumbed in his armchair, from time to time cracking his fingers. Occasionally he went into the garden for a few minutes where he stood like a statue, dumfounded with utter bewilderment (the expression of bewilderment never left his face); trying to avoid his wife's questions, he would return again to his son. At last she seized him by the hand and feverishly, almost threateningly, asked: "But what's wrong with him?" At that he shook himself and made an effort to smile at her in answer: but to his horror, instead of smiling, he somehow blurted out a laugh. He had sent word for the doctor at dawn; he considered it necessary to forewarn his son about this to avoid angering him.

Bazarov suddenly turned around on the couch, looked fixedly and blankly at his father and asked for something to drink.

Vassily Ivanovich gave him water and in passing felt his forehead. It was burning.

"Old man," Bazarov began in a hoarse, slow voice, "I'm in a bad way. I've caught it and in a few days you will be burying me."

Vassily Ivanovich staggered as if something had struck his legs.

"Yevgeny!" he stammered, "what are you saying! . . . God help you! You just caught a cold—"

"Enough," Bazarov interrupted him slowly. "A physician is not allowed to talk like that. You yourself know all the symptoms of infection."

"Where are the symptoms . . . of infection, Yevgeny? . . . for the love of heaven! . . ."

"And what's that?" Bazarov said, raising his shirt sleeve to show his father the ominous spots which were beginning to appear.

Vassily Ivanovich shuddered and turned cold with fear.

"Suppose," he said at last, "suppose . . . if . . . even if there should be something like . . . an infection . . ."

"Pyemia," prompted his son.

"Well, yes . . . like . . . an epidemic . . ."

"*Pyemia,*" Bazarov repeated harshly and distinctly. "Or have you already forgotten your textbooks?"

"Well, yes, yes, as you wish. . . . But in any case we will cure you!"

"That's humbug. But it's beside the point. I hadn't expected I'd die so soon; this is, to tell the truth, a very unpleasant turn. You and Mother should both take advantage of your religious strength now; here's an occasion for you to put it to the test." He drank a little more water. "But I want to ask you one thing . . . while I still have my head under control. Tomorrow or the day after, my brain, you know, will tender its resignation. Even now I'm not quite sure that I'm expressing myself clearly. While I was lying here, I kept imagining that there were red dogs running around me and you were setting them at me as at a woodcock. It was as if I were drunk. Do you understand me all right?"

"Heavens, Yevgeny, you are talking entirely correctly."

"So much the better; you told me you sent for the doctor . . . you comforted yourself by that . . . comfort me too: send a messenger—"

"To Arkady Nikolayevich," the old man interrupted.

"Who is Arkady Nikolayevich?" Bazarov said as if reflecting. "Ah, yes! That fledgling! No, don't bother him; he's turned into a jackdaw now. Don't be startled, that is not delirium, yet. But send a messenger to Odintsova, Anna Sergeyevna, the landowner over there—you know?" (Vassily Ivanovich nodded his head.) "Yevgeny, that is, Bazarov, sends his compliments and word that he is dying. You will do that?"

"I will. . . . Only could it possibly be true that you are dying, you, Yevgeny? . . . Judge for yourself! What justice will there be after this?"

"I don't know about that; but just send the messenger."

"I'll send him this minute, and I'll write the letter myself."

"No, why do that; have the messenger say that I send my respects; nothing more is necessary. And now back to my dogs. It's strange! I want to fix my mind on death and nothing comes of it. I see a kind of blot . . . and nothing more."

He turned painfully back towards the wall while Vassily Ivanovich left the study and reaching his wife's bedroom with difficulty, almost fell onto his knees in front of the saints' images.

"Pray, Arina, pray!" he moaned. "Our son is dying."

The doctor, the same district doctor who had been unable to produce a caustic stone, arrived, and after examining the patient, advised continuing the watch-and-wait method, and said a few words on the possibility of recovery.

"But have you ever happened to see people in my condition *not* go to the Elysian fields?" Bazarov asked, and suddenly seizing the leg of a heavy table next to the bed, shook it and shoved it out of place.

"Strength, the strength," he said, "is still all there, but one must die! . . . An old man at least has had time to estrange himself from life, while I . . . But, really, who can negate death? It negates you, and that's that! Who's crying there?" he added after a short pause. "Mother? Poor soul! Whom will she feed her marvelous borsch to now? And you are sniffling too, I believe, Vassily Ivanovich? Well, if Christianity doesn't help you, be a philosopher, a stoic, eh! You used to boast you were a philosopher, didn't you?"

"I'm no philosopher!" sobbed Vassily Ivanovich and tears rolled down his cheeks.

Bazarov became worse hour by hour; the illness took a swift course, as it usually does in surgical poisoning. He still remained conscious and understood what was said to him; he still resisted. "I don't want to be delirious," he whispered, clenching his fists, "what nonsense!" And the next moment he was saying, "Now what is eight minus ten?"

Vassily Ivanovich went about like a madman, proposing first one remedy then another, and doing nothing in the end other than cover his son's legs. "Wrapping in cold sheets . . . emetic . . . mustard plaster on the stomach . . . bleeding," he muttered tensely. The doctor, whom he had begged to stay, kept agreeing with him, fed the patient lemonade, and made constant requests on his own behalf for a pipe or something "strengthening and warming," that is, vodka. Arina Vlassevna sat on a low stool near the door and left only from time to time to pray; a few days before, a hand mirror had slipped out of her hand and shattered, and she had always considered this a very bad omen; even Anfisushka could say nothing to her. Timofeich had set off for Odintsova's.

Bazarov had a bad night—an intense fever tormented him. Towards morning he was better. He asked Arina Vlassevna to comb his hair, kissed her hand, and drank a swallow or two of tea. Vassily Ivanovich revived a little.

"Thank God!" he kept repeating. "The crisis is starting . . . the crisis is over."

"Just think!" said Bazarov. "What a word can mean! He found it, said: 'crisis'—and feels comforted. It's astonishing how a man still believes in a word. They tell him, for example, that he's a fool and don't beat him, and he is pained; they call him a wise man and don't give him money—he is gratified."

This little speech, which reminded Vassily Ivanovich of Bazarov's former "sallies," transported the old man.

"Bravo! Well said, well said!" he exclaimed, pretending to clap his hands.

Bazarov smiled sadly at him.

"Then in your opinion," he said, "is the crisis over or starting?"

"You're better, that's what I see, that's what makes me happy," Vassily Ivanovich answered.

"Well, fine; it never hurts to be happy. But about her, you remember? You sent someone?"

"I sent someone, of course."

The change for the better was not long-lasting. The attacks of the disease recurred. Vassily Ivanovich sat beside Bazarov. A particular thought seemed to be tormenting the old man. He got ready to speak several times—and could not.

"Yevgeny!" he said at last, "my son, my dear, sweet son!"

This unaccustomed tenderness had an effect on Bazarov. He turned his head a little, and obviously trying to work free from the crushing weight of his torpor, said:

"What, my father?"

"Yevgeny," Vassily Ivanovich continued and dropped onto his knees in front of Bazarov, although the latter did not open his eyes and could not see him, "Yevgeny, you are better now: God granting, you will recover; but take advantage of this time, comfort your mother, do your duty as a Christian! It's awful for me to say this to you; but more awful yet . . . it's forever, Yevgeny . . . think, what . . ."

The old man's voice broke, while a strange expression crossed his son's face, although he continued to lie with closed eyes.

"I won't refuse, if that can comfort you," he uttered at last, "but I think there's no need to hurry into anything. You yourself say I'm better."

"Better, Yevgeny, better, but who knows, all that is God's will, and having done the duty—"

"No, I'll wait," Bazarov interrupted. "I agree with you that the crisis has come. And if you and I should be wrong, what then!—they give the Sacrament to the unconscious too, you know."

"I beg you, Yevgeny . . ."

"I'll wait. But now I want to sleep. Don't bother me." And he let his head drop back.

The old man got up, sat down in the armchair and, chin in hands, began biting his fingers. . . .

The rattling of a light carriage on springs, that rattling which is so clearly distinguishable in the remote country, suddenly struck his ear. Closer, closer the light wheels rolled; now the snorting of the horses was already audible. . . . Vassily Ivanovich jumped up and rushed to the window. Turning into the courtyard of his little house was a two-seated carriage harnessed with four horses. Without thinking over what it might mean, on the impulse of a kind of senseless joy, he ran out onto the steps. A liveried lackey was opening the doors of the carriage; a lady with a black veil, in a black cloak, emerged from it.

"I am Odintsova," she said. "Is Yevgeny Vassilich alive? Are you his father? I brought a doctor with me."

"Benefactress!" Vassily Ivanovich exclaimed, and seizing her hand, feverishly pressed it to his lips while the doctor brought by Odintsova, a small man with glasses and German features, climbed leisurely out of the carriage. "Still alive, my Yevgeny is alive and now he will be saved! Wife! Wife! . . . An angel came to us from heaven. . . ."

"What is it, good heavens!" stammered the old woman who, running out of the parlor in complete bewilderment, fell at Odintsova's feet right there in the entrance and began to kiss the hem of her dress like a mad woman.

"What are you doing! What are you doing!" Odintsova repeated over and over, but Arina Vlassevna paid no attention to her and Vassily Ivanovich continued to say, "Angel, angel!"

"Wo ist der Kranke? Where is the patient?" the doctor said at last, not without a certain exasperation.

Bazarov's father came to his senses. "Here, here, please follow me, *wertester Gerr Kollega,"** he added, recalling the words from the far past.

"Eh!" the German said and smiled acidly.

Vassily Ivanovich led him into his study.

"It's Anna Sergeyevna Odintsova's doctor," he said, bending close to his son's ear, "and she herself is here."

Bazarov suddenly opened his eyes. "What did you say?"

"I am saying that Anna Sergeyevna Odintsova is here and brought you her physician."

Bazarov glanced around the room. "She's here . . . I want to see her."

"You'll see her, Yevgeny; but first we must have a talk with the physician. I'll tell him the whole history of the illness inasmuch as Sidor Sidorich has left" (so the district doctor was called), "and we'll have a little consultation."

Bazarov looked at the German. "Well, talk as quickly as possible, but not in Latin; I understand what *jam moritur** means."

"Der Herr scheint des Deutschen mächtig zu sein . . ."*

began the new foster-son of Asclepius* addressing Vassily Ivanovich.

"*Ih . . . gabe . . .* You had better speak Russian," said the old man.

"Ah ha! *So dot's it, dot's how it ees. . . . Pliss . . .*"

And the consultation began.

A half hour later Odintsova came into the study with Vassily Ivanovich. The doctor had had time to whisper to her that there was no hope of the patient's recovery.

She glanced at Bazarov . . . and was so struck by the inflamed yet deathly pale face with its dim eyes turned towards her, that she stopped in the doorway. She felt afraid with a rather cold and oppressive fear; the thought that she would not have felt that if she had really loved him instantaneously flashed through her mind.

"Thank you," he said, starting to speak with an effort; "I wasn't expecting this. It's a good deed. Well, we have seen each other once again, as you promised."

"Anna Sergeyevna was good enough—" Vassily Ivanovich began.

"Father, leave us—Anna Sergeyevna, you will permit that? I think now . . ."

He indicated with a nod his prostrate, powerless body. His father went out.

"Well, thank you," Bazarov repeated. "This is regal. They say the tsars also visit the dying."

"Yevgeny Vassilich, I hope . . ."

"Ah, Anna Sergeyevna, let us speak the truth. It's over with me. I've fallen under the wheel. And it turns out that there was no point in thinking about the future. Death is an old joke, but new to everyone. Up to now I've no fear . . . but come unconsciousness and *pffft!*" (He weakly waved his hand.) "Well, what can I say to you? . . . I loved you! That didn't make sense even before, much less now. Love—is a form, and my own form is already decomposing. Better for me to say how lovely you are! And there you stand now, so beautiful . . ."

Odintsova involuntarily shuddered.

"It's nothing, don't worry . . . sit down there . . . don't come near me: my illness is contagious."

Odintsova swiftly crossed the room and sat down in an armchair near the couch on which Bazarov was lying.

"Noble one!" he whispered. "Oh, how close, and how young, fresh, pure . . . in this foul room! . . . Well, farewell. Live long, that's the best thing, and make use of the time while it lasts. You see what an outrageous spectacle it is: the worm half-squashed but still wiggling. And of course I also thought: I'll take on many tasks, I won't die, why should I! There is an objective, and I'm a giant! But now the giant's sole objective—is how to die decently, although no one cares about it. . . . All the same, I won't turn tail."

Bazarov fell silent and began feeling for his glass with his hand. Odintsova helped him drink without removing her glove, and holding her breath in fear.

"You will forget me," he began again; "a corpse is no companion for the living. Father will tell you, of course: look what a man Russia is losing. . . . That's rubbish; but don't disillusion the old man. Whatever comforts the children—you know. And be kind to Mother. You couldn't find people like them in your great world if you searched for them with a lantern in broad daylight. . . . I'm needed by Russia . . . no, it's obvious I'm not needed. But who is needed? The cobbler is needed, the tailor is needed, the butcher . . . sells meat . . . the butcher . . . Wait, I am confused. . . . There is a forest here . . ."

Bazarov put his hand to his forehead.

Odintsova bent over him.

"Yevgeny Vassilich, I'm here . . ."

He at once took his hand away and raised himself.

"Farewell," he said with sudden strength, and his eyes lighted with a last light. "Farewell . . . Wait . . . I didn't kiss you then . . . Blow on the dying lamp and let it go out. . . ."

Odintsova put her lips to his forehead.

"Enough!" he said, and sank back on the pillow. "Now . . . darkness . . ."

Odintsova quietly left.

"Well?" Vassily Ivanovich asked her in a whisper.

"He fell asleep," she answered almost inaudibly.

Bazarov was doomed not to awaken. Towards evening he fell into total unconsciousness, and the next day he died. Father Aleksei performed the final rites over him. When he was given extreme unction, when the holy oil touched his chest, one of his eyes opened, and it seemed as if at the sight of the priest in his vestments, the smoking censers, the taper in front of the image—something like a shudder of horror was momentarily reflected on his livid face. When, finally, he breathed his last and a general wailing arose in the house, a sudden rage took hold of Vassily Ivanovich. "I said I'd start grumbling," he cried in a hoarse voice with a burning, racked face, shaking his fist in the air as if threatening someone, "and I will grumble, I will grumble!" But Arina Vlassevna, all in tears, clung to his neck, and they fell to the ground together. "Just like that," as Anfisushka recounted later in the servants' room, "side by side and hanging their little heads like ewe lambs at midday . . ."

But the heat of midday passes, and evening and night fall, and with them the return to a quiet refuge where sleep is sweet to the toilworn and weary. . . .

xxviii

Eight months passed. It was a white winter with the cruel stillness of cloudless frosts, heavy crackling snow, rosy hoarfrost on the trees, pale emerald sky, caps of smoke over the chimneys, puffs of steam escaping from momentarily opened doors, the fresh stinging faces of people and the bustling trot of the chilled horses. A January day was already drawing to an end; the evening cold was tightening its grip on the motionless air, and the blood-red sunset was swiftly dying. Lights were beginning to appear in the windows of the house at Marino; Prokofich, in a black frock coat and white gloves, was setting seven places at the table with particular ceremony. A week ago two weddings had taken place in the small parish church; quietly and almost without witnesses, Arkady married Katya and Nikolai married Fenechka. On this day, Nikolai was giving a farewell dinner for his brother, who was going to Moscow on business. Odintsova had gone there herself immediately following the wedding, after giving the young people lavish gifts.

Promptly at three o'clock everyone gathered at the table. Mitya was seated there too; he now had a nurse in a brocaded headband. Pavel sat between Katya and Fenechka; the "husbands" were placed next to their wives. Our friends had undergone a change of late; the women seemed to have become prettier, the men handsomer. Although Pavel had grown thinner, this only seemed to enhance the elegance and air of *"grand seigneur"* of his expressive features. Fenechka had been transformed too. In a new silk dress with a wide velvet headdress on her hair and a gold chain around her neck, she sat in respectful immobility—respectful towards herself, towards those around her—and she smiled as if wanting to say, "You will forgive me . . . I am not to blame." And she was not the only one—all the others were also smiling and looking apologetic. It was a little awkward for everyone, a little sad, and in reality very pleasant. Everyone served everyone else with comical attentiveness as if they had agreed to act out some kind of naive comedy. Katya was the calmest of all; she looked trustingly around her, and it could be seen that Nikolai had already become very fond of her. Before dinner was over, he got up, and raising his glass, turned to Pavel.

"You are leaving us . . . you are leaving us, dear brother," he began, "of course, not for long; but just the same, I can't help expressing to you what I . . . we . . . how I . . . how we . . . There's the misfortune! We don't know how to make speeches! Arkady, you speak."

"No, Papasha, I'm not prepared."

"And I'm well prepared, I suppose! Simply, brother, allow me to embrace you, to wish you the best of everything and a quick return to us."

Pavel embraced everyone including, of course, Mitya; he also kissed Fenechka's hand, which she still had not learned to offer properly, and draining his glass, refilled for the second time, he said with a deep sigh, "Be happy, my friends! *Farewell!*" This final farewell in English passed unnoticed, but everyone was moved.

"To the memory of Bazarov," Katya whispered in her husband's ear and clinked glasses with him. In answer, Arkady squeezed her hand tightly, but decided not to propose this toast aloud.

This would seem to be the end. But perhaps one of the readers wishes to know what each of the characters presented by us is doing now, at this moment. We are ready to satisfy him.

Odintsova was married not long ago, though out of conviction, not love, to one of the future men of action of Russia, a very intelligent man, a lawyer with a strong practical sense, a firm will and a remarkable gift for words—a man still young, kind, and cold as ice. They live together in great harmony and will live, perhaps, to attain happiness—perhaps, love. Princess Kh—— died, forgotten on the very day of her death. The Kirsanovs, father and son, have settled at Marino. The affairs are beginning to straighten out. Arkady has turned into a zealous proprietor and the "farm" is already producing a fairly important income. Nikolai has fallen into the position of arbiter in his commune for problems arising from the recent abolition of serfdom; he works at it with all his strength, travels continually around his district and delivers long speeches (he clings to the opinion that it is necessary to explain everything to the peasants, that is, to reduce them to quiescence by frequent repetition of the very same words). And to tell the truth, he still does not fully satisfy either the educated aristocrats who speak with chic or with melancholy about the "mahnci-pation" (pronouncing *ahn* through their noses), or the uneducated aristocrats who unceremoniously curse "this

muncipation." He is too mild to suit either of them.
Katerina Sergeyevna has given birth to a son, Kolya, and
Mitya is already running about briskly and chattering
volubly. After her husband and Mitya, there is no one
Fenechka (now called Fedosya Nikolayevna) adores as
much as Katya, and when she sits down at the piano,
Fenechka is happy to stay at her side the whole day. A
word about Piotr in passing. He has grown completely
stiff with stupidity and importance and pronounces all
"e's" as "u's", but he, too, has gotten married, and received a sizeable dowry with his bride, the daughter of
the town vegetable farmer, who had refused two good
suitors just because they had no watches; Piotr not only
had a watch—he wore patent-leather shoes.

On the Brühl Terrace in Dresden, between two and
four o'clock, the most fashionable time for strolling,
you may meet a man of about fifty, already completely
gray and apparently suffering from gout, but still handsome, elegantly dressed, and bearing that particular
stamp which a man acquires only by prolonged contact
with the highest circles of society. This is Pavel Petrovich. He left Moscow to go abroad to recover his health
and settled down in Dresden, where he consorts more
and more with the English and with Russians traveling
abroad. With the English he behaves simply, almost
modestly, but not without dignity; they find him a bit
boring, but respect him as a "perfect gentleman." He is
more relaxed with the Russians, gives free rein to his
acid wit and makes fun of himself and of them; but he
does so very pleasantly, indifferently and decorously. He
adheres to Slavophilism: it is well known that in high
circles this is considered *très distingué*. He reads nothing
Russian, but on his desk he has a silver ashtray in the
form of a primitive peasant sandal. He is much sought
after by our tourists. Matvei Ilyich Kolyazin, finding
himself in "temporary exile," paid a stately visit to him
on his way to a watering place in Bohemia. The natives,
whom Pavel very seldom sees, almost worship him. No
one can get invitations to the court concerts, the theater,
etc. as quickly and easily as *der Herr Baron von Kirsanoff*.
He does everything correctly, still creates a bit of a stir

(he has not been a social lion for nothing), but living is hard for him—harder than he himself suspects. . . . One has only to glance at him in the Russian church and see him leaning against the wall a little to the side, falling into thought and remaining motionless for a long time, bitterly compressing his lips, then suddenly coming to and beginning to cross himself almost imperceptibly . . .

Kukshina has wandered abroad too. She is now in Heidelberg and is no longer studying natural science, but architecture, in which, she claims, she has discovered new principles. As before, she associates mostly with students, particularly the young Russian physicists and chemists with which Heidelberg is filled and who, at first amazing the naive German professors with their sound views on things, in the course of time amaze those same professors by their complete inactivity and absolute laziness.

With two or three such chemists (unable to distinguish oxygen from nitrogen, but full of scorn and self-esteem) and with the great Yelisevich himself, Sitnikov, preparing to become great too, roams around St. Petersburg and claims to be continuing the "work" of Bazarov. It is said that someone gave him a beating recently, but Sitnikov did not remain in his debt long; in a short, obscure article crowded into an obscure magazine, he hinted that the person who beat him was a coward. He calls this irony. His father makes his life wretched as before, while his wife considers him a simpleton—and a man of letters.

There is a small village cemetery in one of the remote corners of Russia. Like almost all our cemeteries, it is a pitiful sight. The ditches around it became overgrown long ago; the gray wooden crosses have dropped and are rotting under their once-painted shelters; the stone slabs are all displaced, as if someone were pushing them from below; two or three denuded trees give barely any scanty shade; sheep wander freely among the graves. But there is one grave which is undisturbed by man and untrampled by beast; only birds perch on it and sing at daybreak; an iron fence encloses it; two young fir trees are planted at either end; Yevgeny Bazarov is buried in this grave.

It is often visited by two now very old people from the little village near by—a man with his wife. Leaning on one another they come, walking with heavy steps; they go up to the fence, fall on their knees, and kneeling, cry endlessly and bitterly, and look endlessly and intensely at the mute stone under which lies their son. Exchanging a few brief words, brushing some dust off the stone, straightening a twig of the fir tree, they start to pray again and are unable to leave this place in which they seem nearer to their son, to memories of him. . . . But can their prayers, their tears be fruitless? Can love, holy, dedicated love not be all-powerful? Oh no! However passionate, sinful and rebellious the heart hidden in that grave may be, the flowers growing on it look at us undisturbed with their innocent eyes; they do not speak to us of eternal peace alone, of that supreme peace of the "impassive universe"; they also speak of eternal reconciliation and eternal life.

NOTES

8. *Il est libre, en effet*: As a matter of fact, he's free.

13. *s'est dégourdi*: is more on his toes.

20. *Vous avez changé tout cela*: You have changed all that.

24. von Liebig: Baron Justus von Liebig (1803-1873), German chemist.

31. *Mais je puis vous donner de l'argent*: But I can give you money.

34. *Streltsy*: two-volume historical novel by the popular Russian 19th century author, Konstantin Masalsky. The title is the name given to the elite troops formed by Ivan the Terrible in the 16th century and outlawed for mutiny by Peter the Great in the 17th.

43. *Stoff und Kraft*: correctly titled *Kraft und Stoff (Force and Matter)*, this book, written by the German philosopher and physician Ludwig Büchner in 1855, aroused such active opposition because of its materialist views that Büchner was forced to resign from his post at the University of Tübingen.

46. *bien public*: public welfare.

50. *un barbouilleur*: a dauber, a dabbler in painting or writing.

page

52. *vieilli*: old-fashioned.

58. *L'énergie est la première qualité d'un homme d'état*: Energy is the primary quality of a statesman.

    Guizot: François Pierre Guillaume Guizot (1787-1874), French statesman and historian.

    Condillac: Etienne Bonnot de Condillac (1715-1780), French philosopher.

    Madame Swetchine: Madame Anne Sophie Soymonoff Swetchine (1782-1857), Russian author who had a literary salon, first in Russia, then in Paris.

59. *Il a fait son temps*: it has had its day.

60. Slavophile: term used in Russia to designate those believing Russia should build her future on Slavic origins alone and refrain from adopting Western material and cultural developments.

65. Bunsen: R. W. Bunsen (1811-1899), German chemist; inventor of a gas burner.

66. *Domostroi*: *The Homebuilder*, a book written by Father Sylvester in the 16th century giving the autocratic views of that time on the organization of family life and the household.

67. *De l'Amour*: correctly titled *L'Amour* (*Love*); written in 1859 by Jules Michelet, French historian and writer.

68. *en vrai chevalier français*: like a true French knight.

69. "*Si j'aurais*" instead of "*si j'avais*": "If I should have" instead of "if I had."

76. *Optime*: perfect.

78. *granzhanr* (*grand genre*): grand style.

111. *omfay* (*homme fait*): a grown man.

page

112. Hufeland: Christoph Wilhelm Hufeland (1762-1836), the most celebrated practical physician of his time in Germany.

    Suum cuique: to each his own.

114. Rademacher and Schönlein: doctors well known during the first half of the 19th century; Schönlein (1793-1864) was a specialist in therapy and pathology.

    voila tout: That's all.

115. Wittgenstein and Zhukovsky: Prince Louis de Wittgenstein, Russian field marshal, and Vasil Andreevich Zhukovsky, Russian poet; both fought in the campaign against Napoleon.

    the fourteenth: a reference to an aristocratic plot against the state known as the conspiracy of 14 December, 1825.

    Paracelsus: Philippus Aureolus Paracelsus (1493-1541); Swiss alchemist and physician.

    In herbis, verbis et lapidibus: in grasses, words and stones.

    ad patres: gathered to his fathers.

20. Cincinnatus: Lucius Quinctius Cincinnatus, born about 519 B.C., an early military and political hero of Rome who, after routing an enemy army in one day, chose to return to his farm rather than accept the dictatorship of Rome.

    anamateur (en amateur): as an amateur.

    homo novus: a new species of man.

123. *Robert le Diable*: opera by Meyerbeer written in 1831.

    Suvorov: Count Alexander Suvorov (1729-1800), famous Russian field marshal under Catherine the Great.

129. Castor and Pollux: twin sons of Zeus in Greek mythology.

    Dioscuri: another name for Castor and Pollux.

139. Guardian's Council: local governing unit.

150. *Comilfo (comme il faut)*: capacity for doing the proper thing at the proper time.

153. *A bon entendeur, salut!*: Take heed!

154. *utile dulci*: business with pleasure.

156. Mrs. Radcliffe: English novelist (1768-1823).

    Sir Robert Peel: English statesman and prime minister (1788-1850).

158. *C'est de la même famille*: It's of the same stock.

170. *kvass*: A thin, sour, fermented beverage made from barley or rye.

181. *Eh vollatoo (et voilà tout)*: and that's all.

185. *mir*: the Russian word *mir* stands for both the village commune and the world, which, according to legend, was supported by three fishes.

195. *Wertester Gerr Kollega (würdigster Herr Kollege)*: most worthy colleague.

    jam moritur: he is already dying.

    Der Herr scheint des Deutschen mächtig zu sein: The gentleman seems to have a good grasp of German.

196. Asclepius: Greek god of medicine; reputed to be the son of Apollo.

    Ih gabe (Ich habe): I have.

AMERICAN CLASSICS

★★★★★★★★★★★★★★

Bantam Classics bring you the best of American literature at affordable prices. These time-tested favorites bring American history to life. Capturing the American spirit, they appeal to all ages. And, with their beautifully designed covers, these are books you will read and cherish.

Titles by Mark Twain:

Titles by Mark Twain:

☐ 21001	THE ADVENTURES OF TOM SAWYER	$1.50
☐ 21079	THE ADVENTURES OF HUCKLEBERRY FINN	$1.75
☐ 21091	A CONNECTICUT YANKEE IN KING ARTHUR'S COURT	$1.75
☐ 21081	LIFE ON THE MISSISSIPPI	$1.75
☐ 21004	PUDD'NHEAD WILSON	$1.50
☐ 21005	THE CALL OF THE WILD/WHITE FANG Jack London	$1.75
☐ 21054	THE LAST OF THE MOHICANS James Fenimore Cooper	$1.95
☐ 21007	MOBY DICK Herman Melville	$1.95
☐ 21011	RED BADGE OF COURAGE Stephen Crane	$1.50
☐ 21009	SCARLET LETTER Nathaniel Hawthorne	$1.50
☐ 21055	UNCLE TOM'S CABIN Harriet Beecher Stowe	$2.25
☐ 21012	WALDEN AND OTHER WRITINGS Thoreau	$1.75
☐ 21094	BILLY BUDD Herman Melville	$1.95
☐ 21087	DR. JEKYLL and MR. HYDE Robert Louis Stevenson	$1.95
☐ 21099	TREASURE ISLAND Robert Louis Stevenson	$1.75

Buy them at your local bookstore or use this handy coupon for ordering:

Bantim Books, Inc., Dept. CL2, 414 East Golf Road, Des Plaines, Ill. 60016

Please send me the books I have checked above. I am enclosing $_____ (please add $1.00 to cover postage and handling). Send check or money order— no cash or C.O.D.'s please.

Mr/Mrs/Miss_____

Address_____

City_____ State/Zip_____

CL2—6/82

Please allow four to six weeks for delivery. This offer expires 12/82.

GREAT BOOKS FROM GREAT BRITAIN

The English literary heroes and heroines you've adored are now available from Bantam Classics in specially low-priced editions. These beautifully designed books feature the characters of Jane Eyre, Sydney Carton from *A Tale of Two Cities* and Pip from *Great Expectations*. All these Bantam Classics bring you the best in English Literature at affordable prices.

- ☐ 21019 **EMMA** Jane Austen $1.75
- ☐ 21051 **DAVID COPPERFIELD** Charles Dickens $2.50
- ☐ 21015 **GREAT EXPECTATIONS** Charles Dickens $1.95
- ☐ 21017 **A TALE OF TWO CITIES** Charles Dickens $1.50
- ☐ 21088 **HEART OF DARKNESS** and **THE SECRET SHARER** Joseph Conrad $1.75
- ☐ 21027 **LORD JIM** Joseph Conrad $1.95
- ☐ 21020 **JANE EYRE** Charlotte Bronte $1.75
- ☐ 21059 **THE TURN OF THE SCREW AND OTHER SHORT FICTION** Henry James $1.95

Titles by Thomas Hardy:

- ☐ 21023 **JUDE THE OBSCURE** $1.75
- ☐ 21024 **THE MAYOR OF CASTERBRIDGE** $1.95
- ☐ 21080 **THE RETURN OF THE NATIVE** $1.95
- ☐ 21061 **TESS OF THE D'URBERVILLES** $2.25

- ☐ 21021 **WUTHERING HEIGHTS** Emily Bronte $1.75

Buy them at your local bookstore or use this handy coupon for ordering:

Bantam Books, Inc., Dept. CL3, 414 East Golf Road, Des Plaines, Ill. 60016

Please send me the books I have checked above. I am enclosing $________ (please add $1.00 to cover postage and handling). Send check or money order —no cash or C.O.D.'s please.

Mr/Mrs/Miss____________________

Address____________________

City______________State/Zip____________

CL3—6/82

Please allow four to six weeks for delivery. This offer expires 12/82.